D0955214

The GRAVE'S
a FINE *and* PRIVATE PLACE

"As those of us with Flavia-mania know from previous books, the plucky adolescent is terrifically entertaining— the world's foremost brainiac/chemist/sleuth/busybody/ smarty-pants. Nobody can touch her in that category."
—*The Seattle Times*

"Provides all her fans with their Flavia fix . . . The Flavia de Luce books fall into that somewhat rare category for me. I delight in the witticisms and language and the fla- vor and color of the well-developed characters, wanting to read slowly, savoring every word, but then there is the mystery to be solved, so I find myself rushing to the end. Only one solution I can come up with: Read them again . . . and again."
—Fredericksburg *Free Lance–Star*

"[Bradley] lets Flavia be her hilarious, inimical best, and perfectly captures village life in 1950s Britain. Historical fiction and mystery readers alike are sure to rejoice at getting to spend another afternoon in Flavia's agreeable world."
—*Shelf Awareness*

"Bradley's style of writing is quick-witted, fact-laden and extremely fun to read. . . . A wonderful series for most ages."
—*Killer Nashville*

THRICE *the* BRINDED CAT HATH MEW'D

"Bradley's heroine is one of the most delightful, and one of the sharpest, sleuths to come along in a long, long time."

—*Alfred Hitchcock Mystery Magazine*

"The preteen version of Miss Marple . . . In addition to the meticulous investigations, what makes these novels, including this eighth in the series, so enjoyable is the personality of the primary character who, while being a murder investigator savant, is also an emotionally vulnerable little girl. It is a very unusual combination . . . and it works."

—*Mystery Scene*

"Mystery fans seeking novels of wit, an immersive English countryside setting, and rich characterizations will be rewarded with this newest entry in the award-winning series."

—*Library Journal* (starred review)

"A Flavia de Luce mystery is a bitter, dark, and thoroughly scrumptious treat. . . . Highly recommended; don't miss this!"

—Historical Novel Society

"Bradley's preteen heroine comes through in the end with a series of deductions so clever she wants to hug herself. So will you."

—*Kirkus Reviews*

As CHIMNEY SWEEPERS COME to DUST

#1 Pick for LibraryReads
#1 *Maclean's* bestseller
#3 *New York Times* bestseller
#6 Indie bestseller
#7 *Publishers Weekly* bestseller

"Eleven-year-old Flavia de Luce, perhaps contemporary crime fiction's most original character—to say she is Pippi Longstocking with a Ph.D. in chemistry (speciality: poisons) barely begins to describe her—is finally coming home."

—*Maclean's*

"Plot twists come faster than Canadian snowfall. . . . Bradley's sense of observation is as keen as gung-ho scientist Flavia's. . . . The results so far are seven sparkling Flavia de Luce mysteries."

—LibraryReads

"Even after all these years, Flavia de Luce is still the world's greatest adolescent British chemist/busybody/sleuth."

—*The Seattle Times*

The DEAD in THEIR VAULTED ARCHES

"Bradley's latest Flavia de Luce novel reaches a new level of perfection. . . . These are astounding, magical books not to be missed."

—*RT Book Reviews* (Top Pick)

"It's hard to resist either the genre's pre-eminent preteen sleuth or the hushed revelations about her family."

—*Kirkus Reviews*

"Excellent . . . Flavia retains her droll wit. . . . The solution to the murder is typically neat, and the conclusion sets up future books nicely."

—*Publishers Weekly* (starred review)

"Young chemist and aspiring detective Flavia de Luce [uses] her knowledge of poisons, and her indefatigable spirit, to solve a dastardly crime in the English countryside while learning new clues about her mother's disappearance."

—National Public Radio

SPEAKING *from* AMONG *the* BONES

"The precocious and irrepressible Flavia continues to delight. Portraying an eleven-year-old as a plausible sleuth and expert in poisons is no mean feat, but Bradley makes it look easy."

—*Publishers Weekly* (starred review)

"Bradley's Flavia cozies, set in the English countryside, have been a hit from the start, and this fifth in the series continues to charm and entertain."

—*Booklist*

"An excellent reminder that crime fiction can sparkle with wit, crackle with spirit and verge on the surreal . . . Flavia, once more, entertains and delights as she exposes the inner workings of her investigative mind to the reader."

—*National Post* (Canada)

I AM HALF-SICK *of* SHADOWS

"Every Flavia de Luce novel is a reason to celebrate, but Christmas with Flavia is a holiday wish come true for her fans."

—*USA Today* (four stars)

"This is a classic country house mystery in the tradition of Agatha Christie, and Poirot himself would approve of Flavia's skills in snooping and deduction. Flavia is everything a reader wants in a detective—she's smart, logical, intrepid and curious. . . . This is a refreshingly engaging read."

—*RT Book Reviews*

"This is a delightful read through and through. We find in Flavia an incorrigible and wholly lovable detective; from her chemical experiments in her sanctum sanctorum to her outrage at the idiocy of the adult world, she is unequaled. Charming as a stand-alone novel and a guaranteed smash with series followers."

—*Library Journal* (starred review)

A RED HERRING *Without* MUSTARD

"Bradley's third book about tween sleuth Flavia de Luce will make readers forget Nancy Drew."

—*People*

"Think preteen Nancy Drew, only savvier and a lot richer, and you have Flavia de Luce. . . . Don't be fooled by Flavia's age or the 1950s setting: *A Red Herring* isn't a dainty tea-and-crumpets sort of mystery. It's shot through with real grit."

—*Entertainment Weekly*

"Delightful . . . The book's forthright and eerily mature narrator is a treasure."

—*The Seattle Times*

"Bradley's characters, wonderful dialogue and plot twists are a most winning combination."

—*USA Today*

The WEED That STRINGS the HANGMAN'S BAG

"Flavia is incisive, cutting and hilarious . . . one of the most remarkable creations in recent literature."

—*USA Today*

"Bradley takes everything you expect and subverts it, delivering a smart, irreverent, unsappy mystery."

—*Entertainment Weekly*

"The real delight here is her droll voice and the eccentric cast. . . . Utterly beguiling."

—*People* (four stars)

"Endlessly entertaining . . . The author deftly evokes the period, but Flavia's sparkling narration is the mystery's chief delight. Comic and irreverent, this entry is sure to build further momentum for the series."

—*Publishers Weekly* (starred review)

The SWEETNESS *at the* BOTTOM *of the* PIE

THE MOST AWARD-WINNING BOOK OF ANY YEAR!

WINNER:
Macavity Award for Best First Mystery Novel
Barry Award for Best First Novel
Agatha Award for Best First Novel
Dilys Award
Arthur Ellis Award for Best Novel
Spotted Owl Award for Best Novel
CWA Debut Dagger Award

"Impressive as a sleuth and enchanting as a mad scientist . . . Flavia is most endearing as a little girl who has learned how to amuse herself in a big lonely house."
—Marilyn Stasio, *The New York Times Book Review*

"Sophisticated, series-launching . . . It's a rare pleasure to follow Flavia as she investigates her limited but boundless-feeling world."
—*Entertainment Weekly* (A-)

"A delightful new sleuth. A combination of Eloise and Sherlock Holmes . . . fearless, cheeky, wildly precocious."
—*The Boston Globe*

BY ALAN BRADLEY

Flavia de Luce Novels

The Sweetness at the Bottom of the Pie

The Weed That Strings the Hangman's Bag

A Red Herring Without Mustard

I Am Half-Sick of Shadows

Speaking from Among the Bones

The Dead in Their Vaulted Arches

As Chimney Sweepers Come to Dust

Thrice the Brinded Cat Hath Mew'd

The Grave's a Fine and Private Place

The Golden Tresses of the Dead

Flavia de Luce Stories

The Curious Case of the Copper Corpse

The **GOLDEN TRESSES**
of the **DEAD**

BANTAM BOOKS
NEW YORK

The GOLDEN TRESSES

of the DEAD

A Flavia de Luce Novel

ALAN BRADLEY

◆ ◆ ◆

2019 Bantam Books Trade Paperback Edition

Published in the United States by Bantam Books, an imprint of Random House, a division of Penguin Random House LLC, New York.

BANTAM BOOKS and the HOUSE colophon are registered trademarks of Penguin Random House LLC.

Originally published in hardcover in the United States by Delacorte Press, an imprint of Random House, a division of Penguin Random House LLC, in 2019.

LIBRARY OF CONGRESS CATALOGING-IN-PUBLICATION DATA
Names: Bradley, C. Alan, author.
Title: The golden tresses of the dead : a Flavia de Luce novel / Alan Bradley.
Description: First edition. | New York : Delacorte Press, [2019] | Series: Flavia de Luce ; 10
Identifiers: LCCN 2018039374| ISBN 9780345540034 (trade paperback) | ISBN 9780345540041 (ebook)
Subjects: | BISAC: FICTION / Mystery & Detective / General. | FICTION / Thrillers. | FICTION / Historical. | GSAFD: Mystery fiction.
Classification: LCC PR9199.4.B7324 G65 2019 | DDC 813/.6--dc23
LC record available at https://lccn.loc.gov/2018039374

Printed in the United States of America on acid-free paper

randomhousebooks.com

2 4 6 8 9 7 5 3 1

Book design by Diane Hobbing

For Shirley with love: first, last, and always

Thus is his cheek the map of days outworn,
When beauty lived and died as flowers do now,
Before these bastard signs of fair were born,
Or durst inhabit on a living brow;
Before the golden tresses of the dead,
The right of sepulchres, were shorn away,
To live a second life on second head;
Ere beauty's dead fleece made another gay:
In him those holy antique hours are seen,
Without all ornament, itself and true,
Making no summer of another's green,
Robbing no old to dress his beauty new;
    And him as for a map doth Nature store,
    To show false Art what beauty was of yore.

—William Shakespeare, "Sonnet 68"

The GOLDEN TRESSES
of the DEAD

ONE

I'D LIKE TO REMARK at the outset that I'm a girl with better than an average brain. Just as some people are given the gift of a singular and often quite remarkable talent—such as Violet Cornish's uncanny ability to break wind to the tune of "Joy to the World"—I myself, in much the same way, have been blessed with the power of logical thinking. As Violet could easily confirm, it's something you're born with, and then improve by much practice.

The many occasions upon which I had been consulted by the constabulary had sharpened my already considerable detection skills to the point where I had little choice but to turn professional. And so I had set up with Dogger, my late father's valet, gardener, and all-round sounding board, a small agency to which we gave the name—to signal respectability—Arthur W. Dogger & Associates.

Little did we know that our very first case would be so close to home.

But I'm getting ahead of myself. Let me begin at the beginning.

My sister Ophelia's wedding was spoiled only slightly by someone calling out coarsely, as the bride floated in modest beauty up the aisle of the ancient church, "Hubba hubba, ding-ding, twenty years in Sing Sing!" The culprit was Carl Pendracka, one of Feely's former suitors. It was his Cincinnati accent that gave him away.

We all of us pretended we hadn't heard, except my odious, moon-faced cousin, Undine, who let out one of her long, wet, horrible, slobbering snickers, such as might have been made by a herd of cannibal cows.

More troubling, though, was when, just a few moments later—at the precise moment the vicar addressed the congregation: "If any man can show any just cause, why they may not lawfully be joined together, let him now speak, or else hereafter forever hold his peace"—one of the carved and painted angels, from its place high among the roof beams, cried out suddenly, in the zany voice of a certain cinema cartoon character, "I do! I do! Call the police!"

It was Undine, of course, who, bored by lack of attention, decided to practice her ventriloquism—which she had been studying for some time from a sixpenny book.

Aside from that—except for the human remains—it was a beautiful occasion.

Preparations had begun far in advance. First there had been the cake.

"The weddin' cake must be laid down 'least six months before the nup-chools," Mrs. Mullet had said, waving a batter-coated wooden spoon at me in the kitchen. "Else the marriage'll be poisoned."

The mention of poison captured my undivided attention.

"What kind of poison?" I asked.

"The worst kind. The poison of leavin' things to be done on the spurt of the moment. Just look at that Lucy Havers, as was, and then talk to me about darin' the devil. Left it till the day before 'er weddin' to 'ave 'er cake baked at that Bunne Shoppe in 'Inley, if you can credit it, an' look what happened to 'er!"

I raised my eyebrows in a "What happened to her?" signal.

"'Er 'usband—one o' them Simmonses, 'e was—run off with a tart from the Bunne Shoppe the day after they got 'ome from their 'oneymoon in 'Astings."

"If it were me, I'd have run off with an apple pie," I said, pretending I didn't understand her meaning, a tactic I am increasingly forced to employ in order to protect my alleged innocence.

Mrs. Mullet smiled at my modesty. "Like I said, a weddin' fruitcake must be laid down six months ahead o' time and left to sleep in the larder till required," she said, returning to her theme. Mrs. Mullet could be uncommonly informative when allowed to lecture uninterrupted, and I pulled up a chair to listen.

"Like layin' the keel of a battleship," she went on. "You mustn't leave it till the enemy's in sight."

"Who's the enemy?" I asked. "The groom?"

Mrs. Mullet laid a forefinger alongside her nose in the ancient sign of secrecy. "That's for every woman to find out for 'erself," she said, tapping the finger and causing her nose to give off an alarming hollow knocking sound. She lowered her voice. "And till she does, she needs all the spells she can get to keep away the Old Ones."

The Old Ones? This was becoming truly interesting. First poisons, and now malevolent supernatural spirits. And it wasn't yet ten o'clock in the morning!

Mrs. Mullet was now scraping the batter out of the bowl and into a large cake pan.

"Here, let me help you," I said, reaching for the oven door.

"Not yet," Mrs. Mullet said, surprisingly short-tempered. "First things first. Grab an 'andful o' them sticks and toss 'em on top of the fire.

"In the basket there," she added, pointing with the spoon, as if I hadn't seen them.

A wicker basket beside the cooker was half filled with a tangle of twigs and branches. "Run a bit of water in the sink," she said. "We wants 'em good an' damp."

I did as I was told.

"To make steam?" I asked, wondering how the steam was going to find its way from the firebox to the oven chamber.

"Somethin' like that," Mrs. Mullet said, as I opened

the firebox and threw the wet wood on top of the fire. "An' somethin' else besides."

Again, the finger beside the nose.

"Protection," I guessed. "Against the enemy?"

"That's right, dear," Mrs. Mullet said. "'Azel and 'aw-thorn. I gathered 'em with my own 'ands in Gibbet Wood. Now, one more thing an' we're ready to pop in the cake."

She pulled a sprig of needled leaves from the pocket of her apron. "Rosemary!" I exclaimed. I recognized it from the kitchen garden.

"That's right, dear," Mrs. Mullet said again, as the warm spicy odor of the herb filled the kitchen. "To re-mind Miss Ophelia of 'er 'ome, and all them as 'ave ever loved 'er. Rosemary in the oven for the cake and rose-mary in 'er bouquet. It also 'elps keep off the 'obgoblins."

"I thought rosemary was for funerals," I said.

I remembered that because Daffy was always quoting Shakespeare.

"An' so it is, dear. Funerals and weddin's both. That's why it's such an 'andy 'erb to 'ave round the 'ouse. Which is why we grows it in the kitchen garden. If we wants it for weddin's we soaks it in scented water and braids it into the bride's veil and bouquet. For funerals, we wets it with rainwater an' tosses it into the open grave on top of the coffin.

"We also tucks a bit of it into the shroud," she added. "If we 'ave one, of course, which most of us doesn't nowa-days, what with it bein' charged as an extra expense by the undertakers."

"And the hazel sticks?" I asked.

"Guarantees descendants," she said, her face suddenly serious.

Poor Feely, I thought. Alone upstairs at this very moment, innocently picking her pimples in a sterling silver hand mirror without the faintest idea that the cook was in the kitchen, already fiddling with her future. It almost made me feel sorry for my sister.

"Now don't ask me no more pesky questions," Mrs. Mullet said. "I've got four more layers to bake an' dinner to get started for you lot."

"What about the hawthorn?" I asked, even though I already knew the answer. It is believed by some—but not by me—that the haws, or berries, and the flowers of the hawthorn preserve in their smell the stench of the Great Plague of London, whereas I, with my scientific mind, know perfectly well that both haws and flowers of the tree contain a substantial quantity of trimethylamine, which is the chemical compound responsible for the smell of putrefaction.

"Never you mind," Mrs. Mullet said. "Ask me no questions and I shall tell you no lies."

It was her standard response to any question whose expected answer had to do with the birds and the bees.

"Thanks, Mrs. M," I said cheerfully. "It's just as I suspected."

And I skipped out of the kitchen before she could fling a piece of pastry at me.

Anyway, as I was saying, the wedding was . . . well . . . interesting.

Although it was autumn, St. Tancred's was decked with exotic flowers: early narcissi, show pinks, and snapdragons, all flown in for the occasion from the Isles of Scilly by Feely's godfather, Bunny Spirling, a dear old friend of our late father. Feely had asked Bunny to give her away.

"If only it were for keeps," I had remarked when she told me the news.

"Silence, you suppurating cyst!" Feely had shot back. "What makes you think it won't be? You may never ever see me again."

"Oh, you'll be back," I told her. "There are two things in life that can be counted upon to return: a married sister and the smell of drains. Quite frankly, I'd prefer the drains."

I shot Dieter a sidelong wink to let him know I bore him no hard feelings. You can't punish a basically decent chap simply for marrying the resident witch.

But to get back to the wedding . . .

There had been a last-minute panic when it was discovered, ten minutes before the scheduled time, that Dieter's best man had still not arrived.

"He'll turn up," Dieter said. "Reggie is an honorable man."

"Like Brutus?" Daffy had blurted. Daffy sometimes has the habit of putting her mouth in gear before engaging her brain.

Reggie Mould was the British pilot who had shot Dieter down and was, therefore, the cause of Dieter's remaining in England after the war. They had since become fast friends and shared, like all pilots, that mystic brother-hood of the air.

Dieter took Daffy and me aside. "You mustn't be surprised when you meet Reggie. He's a member of the Guinea Pig Club."

We both of us looked at Dieter blankly.

"After he bagged me, Reggie himself went down into the Channel in flames. He was very badly burned. He spent ages in Queen Victoria Hospital. You have probably read about it."

We shook our heads.

"Dr. McIndoe worked miracles with skin grafts. . . ."

A shadow crossed his face.

"But still . . ." he added, trailing off into some silent memory of his own.

"Don't stare," I said, grasping his meaning immediately.

Dieter's face lit up in a glorious grin. "Exactly," he said. "Look. Here he comes now."

An ancient green MG with a blatting exhaust was looming at the lych-gate, and a young man extracted himself gingerly from the low-slung cockpit.

He came slowly toward us through the churchyard.

"Tallyho!" he shouted as soon as he spotted Dieter.

"*Horrido!*" Dieter replied.

Saint Horridus, I recalled Dieter telling me, was the patron saint of hunters and fighter pilots.

The two men hugged and slapped each other on the back—carefully, I noticed, in Dieter's case.

"I thought I'd put paid to you the first time I had you in

my sights." Reggie laughed. "Now I'm back to jolly well finish off the job properly."

Dieter laughed graciously, as he had learned to do since meeting my sister. "I'd like to introduce to you my sisters-in-law," he said.

I was grateful that he hadn't said "future."

Even though I had been forewarned, as Reggie turned, the air went out of me.

His face was a ghastly blank: a grotesque mask of dry and fragile sheeting, as if someone had coated his skin with papier-mâché and painted it white and then red. His mouth was a round black hole.

Only the eyes were alive, sparkling mischievous fire at me from their raggedly deep dark sockets.

"Charmed," Reggie croaked. His voice was that of a man who had breathed flames. "You're the Shakespeare authority," he said, offering Daffy a handshake.

"Well, not actually," she began as Reggie turned to me.

"And you're the poisonous one, Flavia. We must have a chat before I leave."

Then, assuming a hissing, bloodcurdling, snakelike voice, he added: "I have dark designs on several of my lesser enemies."

He needed to say no more. He had won my heart.

"Wizard!" I said, with a grin like the blazing sun, and trotting out the only bit of RAF slang I could remember at the moment.

Dieter then introduced Reggie to Aunt Felicity, who, offering him a cigarette, launched into a questionable RAF joke, which rather shocked me, but which I realized was meant to set Reggie instantly at ease, and to make the two of them forever comrades-in-arms.

Dieter's parents had flown over from Germany to attend the wedding. Although his father was a publisher and his mother an archaeologist, they stood off to one side at the church door, not forgotten, but too exotic, perhaps, to be casually chatted up by the villagers of Bishop's Lacey.

I wandered over for a few words, having learned earlier that both spoke excellent English. Complimenting their son's fine singing voice seemed an appropriate and welcoming way to open the conversation.

"Dieter must have learned to sing at twenty thousand feet," I said.

They looked at me blankly.

"From the angels," I explained, and they both laughed heartily.

"We thought we had lost him to England," Dieter's mother confessed, "but it is comforting to know that someone has already found him."

I wasn't quite sure that I understood completely, but we all three of us beamed at one another like fellow magistrates.

"Your English weather is quite like our own in autumn," Dieter's father observed, gesturing to the beautiful day around him.

"Yes," I said, not having enough international experience to form an opinion. "Have you been here before?"

"Oh yes," Dieter's father replied. "My wife and I both read Greats up at Oxford."

Which shut my mouth.

Dieter, meanwhile, off among the tombstones, was engrossed in animated conversation with Reggie Mould, their hands tracing out zooming, swooping angles in the air.

"We'd better go inside," I said. "Feely will be thinking we've abandoned her."

And so it all began.

A church is a wonderful place for a wedding, surrounded as it is by the legions of the dead, whose listening bones bear silent witness to every promise made—and broken—at the altar.

Dead now, every last one of them, including the man who invented the rule about not putting your elbows on the dinner table. Most of these had taken their vows at this very altar, and each in his turn reduced by life and time at first to juice . . . and then to dust.

As Daffy once pointed out to me, the Latin word *carnarium* can mean both "cemetery" and "larder," which shows that the Romans knew what they were talking about. The function of a churchyard—and the church itself, to some extent—is to digest the dead: There's no point in pretending otherwise.

After Undine's shocking outburst of ventriloquism, the ceremony itself went relatively well. Feely, although it pains me to say so, was radiant in the wedding dress that had belonged to our mother, Harriet. Radiant or not, it gave me the shivers.

When all of the proper words had been spoken, rings and vows exchanged, and the register duly signed, the vicar, Denwyn Richardson, held up a hand signaling us to remain in our seats.

"Before walking down the aisle and departing upon their newly married life, Mr. and Mrs. Schrantz," he said, "have prepared a personal thanks—a little gift—to each and every one of you, who have come from near and far to share their happy day."

It took a moment for me to realize that "Mr. and Mrs. Schrantz" meant Dieter and Feely, who were already moving toward the grand piano which had been carted from Buckshaw to the church in the early hours of the morning.

Feely, flushing furiously in her billowing white wedding dress and veil, fiddled annoyingly, as she usually does, with the height of the piano stool, twisting it this way and that in a series of ever-diminishing adjustments until it met the stringent requirements of her fastidious backside. Then she sat down and lifted the lid.

There was a long, expectant silence and then, at last, her hands fell upon the keys and she began to play.

A series of descending chords, following one upon another, joined in a melody of childlike simplicity.

Dieter stood stiffly at the foot of the piano which, to my way of thinking, looked in the shafts of light from the stained-glass windows uncommonly like a polished black coffin. He shoved a hand in the front of his morning coat, and began to sing—in German:

"*Fremd bin ich eingezogen . . .*"

It was "*Gute Nacht*," from the song cycle *Winterreise*. I

recognized the song at once as one of Franz Schubert's lieder, those songs of love and longing so popular in the last century, yet still so beloved by *The Third Programme*, on the BBC wireless Home Service.

"I came among you as a stranger," the song began, and went on to tell the sad tale of a lovestruck young man, standing in the snowy darkness at his lover's gate. He dares not disturb her dreams, but instead, writes on her gate the words "Good night," so that when she awakes, she will know he was thinking of her.

Even though Daffy had explained the whole thing to me in great detail, I didn't then—and still don't—understand how it is that love feeds so voraciously on sadness.

Come to think of it, Dieter *had* come among us as a stranger—a prisoner of war, in fact—but had long since been welcomed with open arms. He was now as much a part of Bishop's Lacey as the tower of St. Tancred's. Had he chosen to sing this particular song at his wedding as a way of expressing the fate he had so narrowly escaped?

The sound of Dieter's voice made my hair stand on end. His rich baritone filled the church with a warmth that made you turn and smile at your closest fellow man: in my case, Cynthia Richardson, the vicar's wife, who wiped away wet tears from each eye. Cynthia, too, and her husband, in the tragic loss of their first and only child, had known grief of that same intensity of which Dieter was singing.

I caught Cynthia's eye and gave her a wink. She returned a sad, wry, silly smile.

Schubert's melody line was rising like a staircase to heaven. In spite of its melancholy words, the music was that of hope, ever and ever higher, ever and ever more haunting.

It was, I realized with a gasp, the story of my life to date, and I was suddenly finding it difficult to breathe.

Great music has much the same effect upon humans as cyanide, I managed to think: It paralyzes the respiratory system.

Get a grip on yourself, Flavia, I thought.

I had heard stories of people flying to pieces at weddings but had never imagined it could happen to me.

Was it the sudden realization that after today Feely would be gone forever from Buckshaw? It seemed unthinkable.

The two of us had waged war upon each other since the day she had first overturned my pram. What would I do without her?

I twisted round in the pew and glanced back at Dogger, who had chosen to sit with Mrs. Mullet and her husband, Alf (he in a new suit with a chest full of medals), at the back of the church.

We had tried to insist upon them sitting with the family—which consisted today of just Daffy, myself, and, unfortunately, Undine.

But Dogger had demurred.

"I shouldn't feel comfortable, Miss Flavia," he said. When he saw my disappointment, he had added, "One must be free to be oneself at weddings, despite the fal-lal and flapdoodle."

I knew that he was right.

All too soon Dieter's song came to its inevitable end. It was greeted with an explosion of applause from nearly everybody, an ear-splitting two-fingered whistle from Carl Pendracka, and an inexplicable wail—that of a wolf howling at the moon—from Undine.

I was about to pinch her when she bared her sharp little fangs at me in a werewolf grin, and I let my hand fall to my side.

"*Gute nacht,*" she whispered in a rasping, guttural voice that could be heard as far away as the font.

Someone giggled, but it wasn't me.

Feely closed the piano lid, screwed down the seat of the stool, strode back to the top of the aisle, and reassumed the role of a blushing bride.

Transformations, I thought, *are everywhere. We are all of us in the process of becoming someone—or something—else. If only we knew it, there are probably people all around us who are in the process of becoming dead.*

Later, I wished I hadn't thought that.

Well, almost.

After Feely finished fussing with her dress almost as much as if it were a piano stool, she was ready to begin her walk down the aisle.

As Maximilian Brock, drafted in for the occasion, unleashed the full power of the organ upon us—something from Wagner, I think—Feely seized Dieter's arm and began her stroll to the door, taking her own good time about it. I could see that she was having her day and was going to make the most of it.

Feely had first asked Daffy and me to be her brides-maids, but we had both declined: Daffy because she be-lieved bridesmaids at a wedding to be superstitious hokum ("Originally meant to scare away spooks," she insisted) and I because I wasn't going to climb into ballet tights just to pander to a sister's whim.

"What a relief!" Feely had told us. "I didn't want either of you anyway. I asked only out of courtesy. Actually, I've promised Sheila and Flossie Foster since we were tod-dlers, and I couldn't possibly back out now—not that I'd want to, anyway."

And that was that. I have to admit that the Foster sis-ters lent glamour to the occasion. Having put away their chewing gum and tennis rackets for a few hours, they were radiant in autumn-colored faille frocks with Elizabe-than collars, sweetheart necklines, and full skirts.

And I might as well mention that, in order not to be outdone, they both also wore tiaras, with Juliet caps em-broidered with pearls and silver beads.

Not that I care a rat's rompers what they draped them-selves with, but I'm always trying to sharpen my already formidable powers of observation.

I, having fallen in behind, was able to follow the pro-cession closely down the aisle to the porch, where the Misses Puddock, Lavinia and Aurelia, perched on match-ing shooting sticks, had already staked out their vantage point.

Cameras large and small flashed and clicked as the happy couple paused in the porch and smiled out upon the assembled villagers, some of whom, although not present in the church for the ceremony, had gathered in the churchyard to cheer and tug their forelocks in respect, and as a way of getting an hour or so off work with hopes of a free drink or two.

When the wedding was being planned, the Misses Puddock had tried to horn in, as they always did, by offering to perform one of their dreary musical offerings free of charge.

"Oh no," Feely had told them. "You must be at the door to catch my bouquet."

Now, with a modest, maidenly backhand, Feely tossed her bouquet into the air. For a girl who could bowl a cricket ball with the best of them when she felt like it, it seemed a frail and puny effort.

Although Miss Lavinia and Miss Aurelia were both in their seventies, and well past the age when most females traipse to the altar, hope still burned eternal, apparently, in their respective withered breasts. These two ancient sisters shot off their respective shooting sticks like ancient skyrockets, and fell upon the flowers as hounds upon the fox, clawing and hissing at each other as if it were a catfight rather than a celebration of Holy Matrimony. Blows and several shocking words were exchanged. It was not a pleasant spectacle.

The real horror, however, was not to come until the reception.

·TWO·

DINNER HAD BEEN DULY eaten and the speeches made, including a gracious yet entertaining address by Bunny Spirling, who recalled his first meeting with Feely. "She vomited copiously on my spats and cravat," he said. "In spite of her tender years, I recognized at once that Ophelia was a most thorough young lady, and she has since done nothing to change my opinion."

There was much laughter and clinking of glasses, and then Dieter's father, with great grace and tenderness, recalled his son's childhood, including an early attempt to launch himself from the housetop in a glider made from bedsheets, broom handles, and willow branches. "The tin seat he made from our best coal scuttle. When afterward we asked him why, he replied, 'It had sufficient tensile strength to protect my *Gesäß* . . .'—meaning his bottom—'. . . in case of an unforeseen crash.'"

Even Aunt Felicity laughed at that one. How many of his listeners, I wondered, realized the irony of the tale? Dieter had, indeed, fallen to earth, not in Germany, but in England. And in another time: in a future he could not possibly have foreseen in his boyish adventures.

Dieter's father went on: "You will understand why we have always been so proud of our son, and never more so than today, when he gives to us, in Ophelia, the daughter we have always prayed for."

After a prolonged round of applause, Feely pushed back her chair and, taking Dieter by the hand, headed for the wedding cake. This creation stood on a low wrought iron table which Dogger had brought from the conservatory for the occasion, and which Mrs. Mullet had draped with white lace.

"It's me own weddin' dress," she had confided in a whisper, "for good luck and to keep down the costs."

Mrs. M had outdone herself with the wedding cake. It rose up from the table in tier after tier like the Tower of Babel in the painting by Pieter Bruegel, but not nearly so lopsided.

Because the de Luce silver had been sold up several years ago to settle my father's pressing debts, we were dining today with an array of unmatched cutlery collected from round about the parish. The knife with which the cake was to be cut had been loaned by the vicar: a wicked-looking thing more suited to the foggy back streets of Limehouse than a country-house wedding.

"It's Tudor silver," he had warned Dieter and Feely, "but wickedly sharp all the same. Belonged to Henry the

Eighth. Probably one of his hunting knives, originally, but used upon royal ceremonial occasions for the past four hundred years and more. Not really supposed to be in private hands, you know, but the hands that actually own the thing are not in effect private, if you take my meaning. Mind your fingers when you cut the cake."

Feely and Dieter had promised they would, and the nasty-looking weapon was wrapped in oilcloth and tucked away for safekeeping at the back of the handy drawer—originally designed to hold secateurs and so forth—until such time as it was required.

But now that moment had come.

Dieter reached deftly under the fringe of the lacy tablecloth and a moment later the knife was in his hands.

The bride and groom struck a smiling pose and held it, fingers entwined, the blade hovering above the cake.

Cynthia Richardson and a dozen ladies from the Altar Guild closed in with their Brownie cameras. They had worked for weeks behind the scenes to plan this reception, and they weren't going to miss an instant of it.

Flashbulbs popped as the room rang with applause, and when the moment had been stretched to the utmost, down went the blade into the rich soil of the wedding cake. With the second cut Feely seemed to be struggling a bit at the task. Laughing and tossing her head, she brushed away Dieter's hand as if to ask, "Do I have to do it myself?" and bore heavily down upon the blade.

The blood ran out of her face. I watched her go as white as her wedding dress. She screamed and dropped the knife. Dieter seized her by the elbow and guided her back to her chair, where she sank down into her seat like a sack of flour, her face pressed tightly into Dieter's breast, sobbing uncontrollably.

Had she cut herself?

Dr. Darby began making his way toward her, pushing along behind the head table. By the time he got within ten feet of her, Feely had fled.

I leaped to my feet. Everyone else in the room seemed frozen in shock. No one paid me the slightest attention as I stepped behind the wedding cake.

The knife lay on the floor where Feely had dropped it. The first thing I noticed was that there was no blood on the blade. I left it where it was and turned my attention to the cake itself.

The single slice that Feely had managed to cut lay tumbled on its side, and in the V-shaped hole which it had left lay a severed finger.

A human finger.

I reached for one of the nearby napkins which had been provided for the guests, quickly wrapped the finger in its folds, shoved it into my pocket, and left the room.

Up the stairs I ran to my chemical laboratory in the east wing of the house. Once inside, I locked the door and carefully unwrapped the dead digit.

I pulled a powerful magnifying lens from a drawer and examined my find.

Except for the cake crumbs, it was an ordinary enough finger. The nail was nicely manicured, the skin soft enough, with no apparent calluses or scars. The clean cut at the lower end indicated that it had been sliced with almost surgical precision from its owner's hand.

The finger of someone not accustomed to manual labor, I decided. Someone who worked more with their brains than with their hands.

The important thing was to take a fingerprint impression before I was interrupted. With a stamp pad of India ink and a piece of paper, this was easily accomplished. I was just washing off the inky fingertip when there came a knock at the door.

"Are you all right, Miss Flavia?" a voice called out.

"I'm fine, Dogger," I replied. "I'll let you in."

As I opened the door, I asked, "How's Feely?"

"She'll be all right," Dogger said. "Dr. Darby is attending to her. She had rather a bad shock. She claims there was a finger in the cake, but no finger was to be found."

"I brought it upstairs," I admitted.

"Ah," said Dogger. "I thought you might have. May I have a look?"

"I wonder who it belonged to?" I said.

"I expect we shall find out in due course," he replied, bending over the finger. "The philosopher Locke wondered if consciousness remained in a severed finger. If it did, it could, perhaps, even indicate to us the identity of the assailant."

"Like a Ouija board!" I said, enthusiastically. "It could spell out the killer's name by dragging itself to one letter at a time."

"Killer?" Dogger smiled. "What makes you think that

the former owner of this prize specimen is no longer alive?"

"Formaldehyde!" I crowed. "The smell of formaldehyde. This finger came from an embalmed body."

"I was wondering if you'd notice that," Dogger said. "Well done."

"What do you make of it, Dogger?" I asked. "I've already noted the manicured nail and the lack of calluses."

"Indeed," Dogger said, bending in again for an even closer look. "We shall note also the very slight depression encircling the digit at the approximate position of the metacarpophalangeal joint."

"The cut end, you mean?" I asked.

Dogger nodded. "Indicating that we are missing a ring."

"Of course!" I said. "I ought to have spotted it. Did someone remove a finger to steal a ring?"

"It is not unknown," Dogger answered, "in the slimier headlines, as well as in folklore. There have been many tales, some dating back to the Middle Ages, in which a wealthy woman is disinterred by a grave robber in order to steal a valuable ring, only to have the dead lady awaken."

"Premature burial! Do you think that's what's happened here?"

"Perhaps," Dogger said. "We mustn't discount it. But if we keep to the facts, we can be quite confident that what we have here is a fourth phalanx: a ring finger. We can still see quite clearly, in its lateral aspect, the two small distinguishing facets which interface with the third metacarpal bone."

I shook my head sagely. "Anything else?" I asked.

"A married woman," he said.

"Married because of the ring!" I said excitedly.

"Yes," Dogger said. "And a woman because of the dainty anatomy. A married woman who was proficient upon the classical guitar."

My eyebrows must have shot up like roller blinds. "Classical guitar?"

"Indeed," Dogger said. "Observe the fingernail. It is sloped across the end at an oblique angle. Professional performers, I believe, trim their nails so as to slope away from the thumb, the more correctly to strike the strings. By the fact that this nail is nicely angled from left to right, rather than the usual reverse manner, we can deduce that its owner was left-handed.

"Now, then," he added. "I see that you have already taken a fingerprint."

I nodded eagerly.

"Excellent," he said, picking up the dead digit and examining it closely. He pinched the tip beneath the nail.

"Ah," he said. "The anticipated thickening of the flesh. Produced by constant striking of the strings. Not a callus, and not visible superficially, but present and palpable nonetheless."

He held it out for my inspection. I felt the finger. Sure enough, as Dogger had observed: a definite thickening of the otherwise soft skin.

"A Spanish lady!" I exclaimed, noticing for the first time the slight olive tone to the skin.

"Well done," Dogger said, and I basked in the glow of his words, knowing that he meant it.

"Not that it helps," I said. "There are a great many Spanish ladies in the world."

"Indeed there are," Dogger agreed. "But far fewer in England, and fewer still who are proficient upon the guitar, and no others, perhaps, who have been buried at Brookwood within the past month or so."

"Brookwood?" I exclaimed.

"Brookwood Cemetery, in Surrey," Dogger said.

"How could you possibly know that?"

Although it was not like him, Dogger was pulling my leg. I was sure of it.

"You're joking," I said.

"Not at all," Dogger said, peering closely at the severed finger. "In its most recent issue, the magazine *Gramophone* carried an obituary for Mme. Adriana Castelnuovo, the noted guitar impresario. She studied under Andrés Segovia, the acknowledged master of the instrument, and made a number of pretty transcriptions for guitar of the works of the elder Scarlatti, Alessandro. I have a few of her recordings in my small collection. Mme. Castelnuovo's interment took place at Brookwood in August."

"Dogger, you amaze me," I said. I didn't bother mentioning also that I love it when someone uses the word *interment*. It comes from the Old French word *enterrer*, which means the act of placing into the earth; of burying. It's a comfortable word, all in all, since it conveys precisely the general idea of what's taking place without actually raising images of the worms and slugs and squishiness, et cetera. Personally, I delight in deliquescence, although I am aware that not everyone shares my enthusiasms.

The idea of human hearts and brains turning to cheese is not everyone's cup of tea.

"So then," I said. "The first official act of Arthur W. Dogger & Associates is to be a trip to Brookwood?"

"It would seem so," Dogger said, rewrapping the finger in the napkin. "Did you know the London Necropolis Company has its own railway? Or *had*, at least until the Blitz. They still run the occasional train from Waterloo."

Why have I never heard of this? I wondered. *Who has been shielding me?*

"A railway for the dead?" I asked. I could scarcely contain myself.

"Precisely," Dogger said.

As it turned out, we were not able to set out for Brookwood until the next day. Circumstances combined to keep us at home, the most pressing of these being the prying of Feely off the ceiling and getting her fit to depart upon her honeymoon. The plan had been to get her to London in the early evening to catch the boat train for the Continent. Dieter was taking her on a tour of musical shrines in Germany, culminating with two weeks in Vienna, with visits to the State Opera and the birthplace of Mozart.

With Feely still sobbing madly in her bedroom, and now refusing to admit even dear old Dr. Darby, it seemed unlikely that my sister would make it even to the W.C., never mind the former haunts of Wolfgang Amadeus Mozart.

Dieter was at his wits' end. He had begged, he had pleaded, he had hugged and cooed and coddled her, but Feely was having none of it. Save for an occasional retching scream, she refused to communicate.

"She's had a very bad shock," Dr. Darby said. "I've seen many such instances."

I was longing to ask him where and when, but I managed to restrain myself.

The vicar and his wife were huddled in a corner with Dieter and his parents. Dieter had the look of a man whose cat has been skinned. "In these cases, time is the great healer," the vicar was telling him, which may have been comforting to some, but not to Dieter.

"I have the tickets," he said. "We booked them months ago. I cannot possibly change them."

Poor Dieter! I could have cried for him. Was there nothing I could do to ease his agony?

"I'll talk to her," I said, making a sudden decision. I had taken several steps toward the door when Dr. Darby seized my arm.

"Hold on," he said, and then in a low voice, he added: "What did you actually see in that cake? There's no use denying it: I saw you at the table."

"Nothing," I told him. "There was nothing remarkable in the cake."

Which was partly true. There *was* nothing remarkable

in the cake—at least, there hadn't been after I wrapped the severed finger in a napkin and shoved it into my pocket.

I drew Dr. Darby slightly aside.

"She's under a lot of stress," I said. "First, Father; then her engagement; now her wedding. I've noticed that she's been rather nervy lately. I thought we might be able to get her away on her honeymoon before it did her in entirely."

I touched the doctor's arm, patting him reassuringly. "Which is why I've offered to go up and talk to her."

"Well . . ." he said, and before he could utter another word, I strode away with a confidence I didn't really possess—but which I hoped was convincing.

I didn't bother knocking, but barged into Feely's bedroom as if I were the Bishop's Lacey Volunteer Fire Brigade.

Feely had flung herself on a Victorian couch in front of the window, the back of one wrist covering her eyes as she sobbed great strangled sobs into a knotted silk handkerchief.

"Get up, Feely!" I commanded. "You ought to be ashamed of yourself. Get up and go back to your guests. Everyone's waiting for you. You can't let people down like that. What would Father say?"

I paused to let my words sink in.

"There was a—a—human finger . . . in the— Oh! It was—"

"It was a sausage," I said. "Daffy and I put it there as a joke. I'm sorry if we upset you."

I would make my peace with God later for such a blatant lie. He would forgive me, but Daffy wouldn't.

"A sausage," I repeated. "A stale, stupid sausage."

I sent up a silent prayer of apology to the ghost of the late Mme. Castelnuovo, wherever it might presently be. *A sausage, indeed!*

The sniveling abated slightly. Had Feely believed me? It was hard to tell.

"I told them the wine had upset your tummy," I said. "They understand."

"How dare you!" Feely hissed. "How *dare* you! All the chins in the village will be wagging now."

Already she was more like her old self.

"Off you go," I said, planting my hands on my hips to make myself appear larger. "Your bridegroom awaits you."

Feely mopped at her eyes with the soggy handkerchief. "You've made me ruin my makeup."

"Oh, bosh," I told her. "It was ruined before I came upstairs. They've already taken the photos, so who cares. Smile through the old tears. Off to Vienna with you. And don't come back until your disposition has improved."

Feely tried to catch my eye, but I wasn't having any of it.

"Don't bother with the basilisk look," I said. "I've been vaccinated against them. Now shoo!"

And to my utter amazement, she obeyed me.

"Have a happy honeymoon!" I shouted after her, but she either didn't hear me or decided I didn't deserve an answer.

The life of a go-between is not an easy one.

And so, in due course, and just in the nick of time, Feely and Dieter were carried off in Bunny's car in a shower of confetti, tears, and old boots.

There was a long, awkward silence among those gathered at the front door. No one seemed to want to be the first to speak.

My own first thought was one of relief that she was gone: that Feely no longer lived at Buckshaw.

No, that's not true. That's what I *wanted* to think.

In truth, it hit me like a hod of bricks that I was now alone in a way that I had never been alone before. Of course, I still had Daffy and Dogger and Mrs. Mullet, but Feely was gone. Feely, with whom I had been engaged in an eternal joust since the day of my birth; Feely whom I always loved; Feely whom I sometimes hated.

But it is not easy to keep alive a grudge against a person who has written music in your honor, even if it was only a short piano piece: a cascade of vividly ascending octaves, composed to commemorate the dramatic and unforgettable outcome of an occasion when I had unwisely gobbled down a few too many of Mrs. Mullet's Cornish pasties. Feely called the piece "Whoops-a-Daisy!" and would perform it for visitors at the drop of a hat or—as Daffy liked to say—at the rise of a gorge.

"Beast!" I would hiss, whenever she tortured me like this, but she would merely transpose the melody into an even more upward-tending key and start over from the beginning.

But yet, although we three despised one another, there

were certain occasions when we could be, suddenly and surprisingly, as thick as thieves.

There were those instances, for instance, such as the Christmas Eve service at St. Tancred's, when Daffy and I would stand shoulder to shoulder with all the other parishioners, caroling our hearts out, but inserting the wrong words.

"Braise my soul the King of Heaven," we would bellow. That and "While shepherds washed their socks by night . . ."

And at the conclusion of every hymn, we would sing "Ah, men!"—as if we were despairing of every male who had ever drawn breath.

With practice, and a good bit of nerve, you could pull this off while smiling broadly at your neighbors across the aisle and they would smile back, never for an instant detecting the difference.

And then there had been the year all three of us had contracted mumps at the Christmas Concert. Confined strictly to the house, we had given one another names: I was Mumpso, Daffy was Mumpsis, and Feely was Mumpsissimus. Never had we been so close as we were then, howling with swollen glands and laughter.

Feely, especially, had been a rock. But as Dogger once told me, every rock has its underside.

Still, I was going to miss her.

It was Daffy who broke the silence at last.

"Now, then, Helmut and Inge . . ." (She meant Mr. and Mrs. Schrantz. Daffy was never one to stand on ceremony.) "Let's go have a look at those first edition *Pick-wick Papers* I promised to show you. You'll find Dickens's signature especially suggestive. It's in green ink on the title page of each number."

"Nineteen signatures of the divine Dickens," Helmut marveled. "Remarkable. Lead on, dear Daphne."

And with that, they were gone.

Mrs. Mullet was already bustling about, cleaning up. It seemed a good time to tackle her.

"Take a break, Mrs. M," I said. "You must be exhausted. Let's go into the kitchen and I'll make you a nice cup of tea."

Mrs. Mullet beamed upon me like the sun. "You know me like a book, don't you, dear?" she asked.

"I try," I said. "One must always keep one's dearest hearts happy."

All right, I was pandering, I admit it. But a little of that goes a long way when soliciting tittle-tattle.

"Poor Feely," I continued. "Her nerves gave out. I thought they might. She doesn't like having strangers around at the best of times."

"But most of them were 'er friends!" Mrs. Mullet protested.

"Most," I said, "but not all. I've been drawing up a list of everyone that's been in the house. You know—in case we're missing any of the family jewels."

Making a joke can sometimes produce unforeseen results.

Mrs. Mullet laughed.

That was step one.

"With strangers, you never know which are the good ones, and which the villains," I added.

"They ought to 'ave 'ats," Mrs. Mullet said, getting into the spirit of things. "Like in the cinema. Alf always likes a good western at the cinema, Alf does. Roy Rochester or Gene Artery, or one o' them. Alf says you can always tell 'oo's got the best 'earts by the color of their 'ats an' 'orses."

"He's very observant, your Alf," I said. "He ought to have been a tec rather than wasting his time in the army."

Mrs. Mullet drew herself up to her full height, which was very little when she was seated.

"Alf is very proud of 'is military detachments," she sniffed. "'E 'as the Military Cross, you know. 'E says 'e wouldn't trade it for all the tea in China."

As a matter of fact, I didn't know. Alf had never mentioned being the recipient of such a distinguished medal. The Military Cross was awarded for acts of great gallantry against the enemy, and I couldn't help wondering what he had done to deserve it.

"I was teasing, Mrs. M," I said, and she eventually broke into a grin.

"Well," she said, "you'll 'ave to jot down the ones as brought the chairs from the parish 'all, them as brought the flowers, the one as came to fix the telephone, the one as came six times with telegrams, the milk float man, the butcher, the baker—"

"And the candlestick maker," I added with a smile to show that I was joking.

"No. 'E didn't come. We 'ave enough candles left over from the war, in the pantry."

"Was Feely's wedding cake in the pantry?" I asked, suddenly inspired.

Mrs. Mullet nodded. "You saw me put it there yourself, remember?"

I did remember. Dogger had helped her roll the heavy cake into the pantry on a tea trolley, where it had languished for weeks under a tent of netting, waiting to be iced at the last moment.

"'Member I said what a waste it would be if they called the whole thing off?" She laughed. "That we should 'ave to eat the 'ole blessed thing ourselfs?"

"So you did, Mrs. Mullet. I recall it perfectly."

I also remembered that Mrs. Mullet guarded her pantry as jealously as the Beefeaters at the Tower of London guard the Crown Jewels.

Who, then, had had access to the cake between the time it was iced and the time it was cut? It seemed evident that the finger in question had been thrust into the cake at some point in between those two events, and the hole patched by smearing a bit of icing to conceal it.

"Excuse me, Mrs. M," I said. "I think I'll go see if there's anything else I can do to help."

I left her alone with her cup of tea and a look of utter fatigue on her face.

There was little left of the wedding cake but wreckage. Somehow, the slice that Feely had cut had been left untouched, as if out of respect. A fresh incision had obviously been made in the opposite side of the cake, and the tall tower gutted.

Which made no difference to my investigation. Feely's

preliminary slice still lay on its side exactly as it had fallen. I examined the curved edge of the piece, which appeared to be pristine.

To one side, though, just where the knife had gone through, was a small, dimpled depression in the icing.

Someone had shoved the finger—either deliberately or as a way of quickly disposing of it—into the side of Feely's wedding cake.

Who could have done such a thing, and how? Was it a cruel joke—or part of a larger, darker tale? How had an embalmed finger found its way from the hand of a dead woman in a Surrey cemetery into the heart of a wedding cake at Buckshaw?

It was promising to be a very pretty puzzle.

·THREE·

IT'S AMAZING WHAT A wedding can take out of you, even if it's not your own. I had gone to my room to lie down and collect my thoughts. The past few days had been like being thrown into a millstream, tossed and buffeted by other people's plans, like a cork in the millrace.

I must have nodded off for some time when I was awakened by a knocking at the door. I managed to work myself up onto one elbow, my brain groggy with sleep.

"Wha—" I managed, the inside of my mouth feeling like the newspaper in the bottom of the canary's cage.

"It's Dogger, Miss Flavia. May I come in?"

"Of course," I said, clawing at my hair to make it look decent as I sprang up from the bed and took up a pose at the window, gazing reflectively out upon the garden as if I were Olivia de Havilland.

"Sorry to disturb you, miss," Dogger said, "but I believe we have a client. Where would you like to receive her?"

Her? My heart began to accelerate. Would our first paying client turn out to be some mysterious woman in black? A woman who was being held to ransom by a coven of witches? But witches didn't usually blackmail, did they? Weren't they far more likely to seek revenge by black magic than by black*mail*?

"Show her into the drawing room, Dogger," I said, trying to calm my breathing. "I shall be down directly."

As soon as I heard Dogger's departing footsteps on the stair, I dashed next door into my chemical laboratory and grabbed a pair of glasses, a notebook with a professional-looking marbled cover, and one of my late uncle Tarquin's Waverley fountain pens, which had once been advertised everywhere with the jingle: "They come as a boon and a blessing to men, the Pickwick, the Owl, and the Waverley pen."

Uncle Tar had owned several of each model.

After changing my wedding outfit for a more business-like skirt and blouse, set off by a pair of ghastly oxfords left over as a grim reminder of my detention at Miss Bodycote's Female Academy, I counted slowly to one hundred and eighty and then began my leisurely descent.

"Mrs. Prill," Dogger said, as I entered the room, "I should like to introduce Miss Flavia de Luce. Miss Flavia, Mrs. Anastasia Prill."

"Pleased to meet you," I said, removing my glasses and giving her a firm, businesslike handshake.

With her prim gray suit and a dove-winged gray hat on her head, she looked like a cross between a Trafalgar Square fountain pigeon and the winged god Mercury.

I was expecting her voice to be a harsh, birdlike cry, but when it came, it took me by surprise, for it was a voice like old mahogany polished with beeswax: rich, warm, and surprisingly deep. The voice of a trained vocalist. A contralto. An opera singer, perhaps?

"I'm very happy to meet you, Flavia," she said, which was probably an appropriate way of addressing me, given that she was considerably older than I was, but still, I didn't want a too-easy familiarity to ruin our relationship. She needed to keep in mind that *she* was the client, and Dogger and I the consultants.

Accordingly, I kept my gob shut, and began to leaf quickly through the pages of the notebook as if seeking to remind myself of some important fact. That done, I replaced my spectacles and waved Mrs. Prill to a nearby chair.

"Would you care for a cup of tea?" I asked. The business of Arthur W. Dogger & Associates would be, if nothing else, conducted in a civilized manner.

"No, thank you," she said. "Tea is not among my weaknesses."

So there was I, put firmly in my place.

"Well then, how may we assist you, Mrs. Prill?" I asked.

She colored slightly. "Actually, I've come upon a quite delicate matter."

"It's all right, Mrs. Prill," I reassured her. "Mr. Dogger

and I are quite accustomed to delicate matters. Are we not, Mr. Dogger?"

Dogger made a slight but beautiful bow from the waist. What a joy he was to work with!

"Well, you see, certain letters have been stolen and—"

"And they are of a nature such that their loss cannot be reported to the police," I finished for her.

I believed my train of thought was obvious, but Mrs. Prill sucked in her breath.

"Amazing," she said. "You're uncanny. Just as they told me you would be."

"And who are *they?*" I asked, trying to crinkle the corners of my eyes to make myself appear a little more human: a little less like a thinking machine.

"I'm afraid I'm not at liberty to say," Mrs. Prill said, biting her lip.

"Not that it matters," I said, hoping to leave the impression, without actually saying so, that I'd find out anyway.

Dogger stepped into the uneasy silence. Good old Dogger!

"I believe that what Miss de Luce wishes to stress is that, if we are to look into this matter on your behalf, we must establish, at the outset, a basis of perfect trust and frankness."

I couldn't have said it better myself.

"Very well," Mrs. Prill said. "I presume that all communication between us is in the strictest confidence?"

I nodded discreetly, as if the walls had ears.

"Well then, the 'they' to whom I refer are Dr. Darby and the vicar, as well as their respective wives. They all told me that your abilities are quite remarkable."

I nodded again. *Why hide your light under a bushel?* is—or will be—my motto.

"Go on," I said, opening the notebook and taking up my fountain pen. "Please begin at the beginning."

She took me literally. "My name is Anastasia Brocken Prill, and I was born at Boswell Magna, in Kent, the only daughter of a successful medical man. After a private education, I—"

"Ah! Your father was Dr. Augustus Brocken, the noted homeopathic practitioner," Dogger interrupted. "Yes, I see the resemblance. Dr. Brocken was a very famous man in his day."

"And still is," Mrs. Prill said. "Although no longer active, he remains—he is—"

Her face clouded over.

"In the care of others," Dogger suggested.

"Precisely," Mrs. Prill said. "Precisely the phrase I was searching for. Thank you, Mr. Dogger."

Seemingly renewed, she went on: "These letters of which I speak had to do with my father's medical practice. You will understand, of course, why I cannot allow them to be made public."

"Just a moment," I said. "Involving the police in stolen letters is hardly the same as making them public."

"It may as well be in a village as small as Bishop's Lacey, where secrets are no more sacred than sieves."

I knew she was referring indirectly to our village policeman, Constable Linnet, who was said to have suffered a serious loosening of the lips on more than one occasion in the public bar of the Thirteen Drakes.

"When did you first notice these letters were missing?" Dogger asked.

"On Friday. Friday evening. I came down from London after a day of committee meetings. I found Stars and Garters outside in the garden."

"Stars and Garters?" I asked.

"My cats. They're named for their markings. I had locked them in the house when I left in the morning."

"Does anyone else have a key to your house?" I asked. "A neighbor? A relative?"

Mrs. Prill shook her head vigorously. "I am extremely attentive to my own security and that of my possessions," she said.

Why? I wondered.

She must have read my mind.

"I have been aware of certain . . . threats in the past."

"Could you give us a few details?" I asked.

"Certainly," she said. "The field of homeopathic remedies is a fiercely competitive one. It can also be unbelievably bitter. Patents, and so forth. Legal wrangling. I'm sure you understand."

"Of course," Dogger said. "Brocken's Balsamic Electuary. *The Best Balm for Man or Beast.* One used to see the advertising everywhere: railway platforms, omnibuses, newspapers, hoardings, even men with sandwich boards in the street."

Mrs. Prill seemed to preen a little.

"Ours was a household name." She smiled smugly.

"We understand perfectly your wish for privacy," Dogger said. "Pray, continue."

"Well, as I've said, I arrived home at 9:50 on the dot. I remember glancing at my wristwatch as I opened the gate. I make a point of recording my comings and goings in my diary."

"Indeed," Dogger said. "Very wise. Very useful."

He beamed upon her and she beamed back.

"I let Stars and Garters into the house—"

"Did you find the door unlocked?" Dogger interrupted.

"No. I should have noticed if it were," Mrs. Prill answered. "I have something of a ritual of checking it scrupulously—twice, in fact—whenever I leave."

"Very wise," Dogger said. "Security of possessions."

He smiled at me and I wrote it down.

"In hindsight," she continued, "I ought to have noticed. Stars and Garters seemed restless and did an inordinate bit of sniffing round the house. I put it down to their having been outdoors all day. Reclaiming their territory, that sort of thing.

"It wasn't until after I'd eaten and was preparing to make up a few notes that I noticed my desk had been disturbed."

"In what way?" I asked.

"Well, I always leave the corner of a sheet of writing paper sticking out of the top drawer. Very inconspicuous, but unlikely to be disturbed by the cats."

"Was the desk locked?" I asked, without looking up from my notes.

"No. But the box of letters at the back of the drawer most definitely was. It had been forced open with a pen-knife, or something similar."

"A wooden box," I said.

"Yes."

"And the letters were missing."

"Yes."

"On Friday evening."

"Yes."

"Then why did you wait until today to bring the matter to us, Mrs. Prill?"

"You may not believe it, but I thought they'd turn up. I thought I might have opened the box and put them aside in a distracted frame of mind, and simply forgotten about it."

"You would not have pried open the box, though, would you?" Dogger observed.

"No. There was no need to do so. I carry the key round my neck."

She rummaged at her throat and excavated a gold chain from which was suspended a small silver key.

"You see? It's been here all along. It hasn't been out of my hands."

Or your bosoms, I wanted to add, but I didn't.

"Another reason I didn't come at once," she continued, "was that I wanted to seek the advice of Dr. Darby and the vicar before consulting you. I still wasn't sure of your . . . your . . ."

"Bona fides," Dogger supplied, giving her a comforting smile.

"Just a few more questions," I said. "If you don't mind. Were there any other signs of an intruder? Locks, misplaced objects, footprints, and so on?"

"None," Mrs. Prill said. "It had rained for an hour or so in the early evening, and any footprints would have been washed away."

So it had, but I'd forgotten about it. A question popped into my mind.

"I hope you won't think me impertinent, Mrs. Prill, but how did you know how long the rain lasted, when you yourself were up in London?"

"I asked Mrs. Richardson, the vicar's wife. It was the first thing I thought of."

"Excellent," I said, rather condescendingly.

"Very well then," Dogger interposed. "Let me summarize: former threats, missing letters, jimmied box, but no sign of forced entry."

"Correct," Mrs. Prill said. "I should be very obliged if you could get to the bottom of this matter."

"We shall, of course, want to have a firsthand look at the earliest convenience," Dogger told her. "If you'd care to leave us your address."

"Balsam Cottage, Mincing.

"You must come for tea," she added, as if to relieve the tension in the air.

I recognized Mincing as a hamlet between Bishop's Lacey and Hinley.

Dogger went to the door and opened it as a signal that she ought to leave.

"Oh, I almost forgot," Dogger said.

I smiled. Dogger had never forgotten anything in his life.

"Could you leave us the address where your father, Dr. Brocken, is being cared for?"

Mrs. Prill's voice, which had been until now as warm and comforting as honey on toast, turned suddenly to ice.

"No!" she snapped. "I cannot. He is not capable—"

As if realizing what she had said, she smiled. "I'm sorry," she told us, "if I seem fiercely protective, but my father is of advanced years and is not quite compos mentis, if you take my meaning."

Dogger put his hand lightly upon Mrs. Prill's arm, his face a study in sculptured grace.

"We understand perfectly, Mrs. Prill. We shall be in touch."

"Rats!" I said when she was gone. "We might have got more from the father than from the daughter."

Dogger smiled. "There is, I recall, only one private hospital in England which assures highest security for its private patients. Because of the costs involved, it is restricted to those of considerable means."

"Such as Dr. Brocken," I said.

"Such as Dr. Brocken." Dogger smiled again. "It is called Gollingford Abbey.

"*And,*" he added, "it is conveniently, and most happily, located on the outskirts of the village of Pirbright: a stone's throw from Brookwood Cemetery."

· FOUR ·

THERE IS NO COZIER place on earth to discuss body-snatching than a gently rocking railway carriage in the rain. The constant jostling to and fro over the rails seems to shake loose the mind and send it into channels one would never dream of at the fireside.

Each rivulet of water racing down the glass suggests a river of thought: a branching Amazon, with countless tributaries of deduction and speculation.

"Do you think we shall find Mme. Castelnuovo's grave disturbed?" I asked.

"Perhaps," Dogger said. "Perhaps not. The odds, I should say, are slightly in favor of 'not.'"

He saw my puzzled look.

"It is a far easier matter to purloin a finger *before* burial than afterward. Think of the sheer logistics, and of the chances of being caught."

I *hadn't* thought of that, and I must admit I felt slightly cheated. I had been quite looking forward to a jolly good old-fashioned case of grave-robbing. Reading the blood-curdling tales about Burke and Hare at night in bed by the light of an electric torch had given me an unquenchable appetite for ghastly goings-on at the graveside.

Oh, well, I thought. *One can't have* everything.

We had taken the 11:27 from Waterloo to Brookwood, in order to match, as closely as possible, the daily funeral trains, which had departed, in their day, at 11:20. The mourners could bid their farewell to the loved one at Brookwood, gather for the regulation funeral feast (consisting of ham sandwiches and fairy cake), and be back home in London in time for tea.

How civilized it seemed! And how British.

The rails upon which we were riding today were, for the most part, the same rails that had carried those cargoes of corpses to their graves on the London Necropolis Railway.

A delicious shiver shook my spine.

Dogger glanced at his pocket watch.

"We are dead on time," he said.

Was he joking? His face gave nothing away.

"We have just entered the cutting between Walton and Weybridge, which puts us precisely eighteen and a quarter miles from Waterloo. We shall be at Brookwood in less than ten minutes."

In order to exercise and stretch my mental capacity, I had been memorizing the stations and junctions through which we had already passed after making our departure from Waterloo: Vauxhall, Queen's Road, Clapham Junction, Earlsfield, Wimbledon, Raynes Park, Malden, Berrylands, Surbiton, Esher, Hersham, and, of course, Walton. Weybridge, West Weybridge, Byfleet, and Woking were still to come before we would step down from the train and set foot in the streets of the city of the dead.

What wonders could we expect to find there? Or what horrors?

As if reading my mind, Dogger put away his watch and settled back into his seat. "It's quite remarkable, when one comes to think about it. Even today, when so much else remains rationed, there are still more than sixty trains a day calling at Brookwood. Think what it must have been like in Queen Victoria's time."

I had no trouble whatsoever in doing so. In my mind, horse-drawn hearses of black veneer, their etched glass panels eerily reflecting the mourners' faces, like mirrors that could show the future, drew slowly up to the narrow premises of the London Necropolis Company, a private station in the shadow of Waterloo. Here, among milling mutes and mourners, surrounded by nodding black plumes of ostrich feathers and inhaling the sickly, overpowering odor of funeral flowers and engine smoke, the mourners filed in somber silence to the waiting train, boarding the appropriate carriage according to the class of funeral they had purchased: first, second, or third.

Meanwhile, the coffin and its occupant were being whisked by steam lift to the rail platform where (under a glass roof to prevent suggestive and disturbing shadows from falling upon the coffin) they would be loaded aboard the appropriate carriage: foremost, behind the engine for the mourners, with the hearse van with its first-, second-, and third-class compartments, like horse stalls, for the coffins bringing up the rear.

The black-faced locomotive, as if in permanent mechanical mourning, and its gleaming carriages were kept always at the ready to transport the dead, six days a week at 11:35 A.M. and 11:20 on Sundays, with a muffled and respectable huffing and puffing, and discreet emissions of steam, to the waiting Underworld.

Much as I was enjoying bringing defunct Victorians back to life, something was nagging at the back of my mind: a dog snapping at the heels of my prefrontal cortex (if the prefrontal cortex has heels, which, now that I come to think about it, I somehow doubt).

"Dogger," I said. "We ought to have gone at once to examine Mrs. Prill's house. Whatever evidence may have been there has probably been disturbed—or worse, removed."

"There was no evidence," Dogger said.

Was I hearing things?

"I beg your pardon?"

"There was no evidence. Mrs. Prill was not, as she stated, up in London on Friday at the time of the so-called burglary. She was purchasing leeks at the market in Bishop's Lacey. I saw her with my own two eyes."

"Which means?"

"She fabricated the tale. Possibly to provide a plausible

excuse for certain embarrassing or incriminating letters to vanish. Such sleights of hand often happen when an elderly, wealthy parent is ill. It's an old, old story."

"Is Dr. Brocken in danger of dying, do you think?"

"All of us are in danger of dying." Dogger smiled. "Some of us more than others. It would not be unreasonable to deduce that Dr. Brocken is in the latter category."

"Is he in danger?"

"We must assume he is, but make certain that he is not," Dogger said.

A delicious shiver ran down my pigtails. I savored it for a moment, and then said: "Mrs. Prill's consultation with us was meant to provide her with an excuse, and to involve Dr. Darby and the vicar as witnesses to the fact that she was seeking our assistance."

"Precisely," Dogger agreed. "She intended to make us part of her alibi."

"So there *were* no missing letters?"

"No." Dogger shook his head. "There are almost certainly letters; otherwise this whole exercise would be pointless. They are not, however, missing. Mrs. Prill—or perhaps someone else—has almost certainly hidden them well. However, since she has retained us to find them, find them we shall."

"So there's no rush," I said.

"None whatsoever," Dogger said. "And now, if I am not mistaken, that is Knaphill Common on our right. Let us prepare to disembark."

Moments later, we were standing on the platform, watching our train vanish toward Farnborough and the southwest. During our journey the skies had cleared, and we were bathed now in glorious and unexpected autumnal sunshine.

Across the tracks, to the south, lay Brookwood Cemetery, and I must admit that I was disappointed.

Brookwood was not at all like Highgate Cemetery, with its mossy, tottering angels and tumbled tombs, where Death had become a work of art.

No, Brookwood was, by contrast, as flat as a farmer's field, broken only by the odd patch of tall conifers or hedges, with here or there a fake classical rotunda to make it seem vaguely interesting. Thirty-odd acres of shop front: thirty-odd acres of, so far as I was concerned, bad taste.

We set out on foot along the nearby layby or siding, passing the refreshment room and the mortuary, which were surprisingly close together, I thought.

"In former days," Dogger told me, "the engine backed the funeral trains onto the private branch line, from which point the carriages were uncoupled and pulled into the cemetery by horses."

"And the locomotive?" I asked.

"Steamed back to London to haul the living until it was time for the return trip from Brookwood."

"Were the living aware that the train had just carted a load of dead bodies to the grave?"

"Public discussion was not encouraged," Dogger said. "Sanitary issues, and so forth."

"It all sounds so dry and clinical," I said. "Timetables and tickets."

"Death's like that," Dogger said. "When you stop to think about it."

And then, almost as an afterthought, he added, "The London Necropolis Company used to have as their telegraphic address *Tenebrio, London.*"

"Meaning?" I asked.

"It's one of those substantives so beloved of Cicero, but almost no one since. Not quite an infinitive and not quite—"

"A gerund!" I exclaimed. I had been lectured without mercy on gerunds by Daffy, who lived and breathed such treacly trivia. A gerund, I recalled, was a verbal noun, such as the word "poisoning."

"Quite," Dogger said. "It is derived from *tenebrae*, the Latin word for 'darkness,' and means a darkening, or obscuration."

Referring to the loved one, I presumed. Perhaps even a pun upon their complexion, which has been so entertainingly described by Mr. Waugh in his novel of the same name, which was now one of my all-time favorite books.

"They might as well have put, 'Becoming shades,'" I said.

"I agree," Dogger said. "The *Tenebrio* is somewhat self-consciously literary. Devised, I suppose, by some former public schoolboy who had taken up the funeral trade."

We walked on in silence.

After a while the tracks we had been following were intersected by a broad avenue which had been given the name "Cemetery Pales."

"That way toward the South Station, and that way for the North," Dogger said, pointing.

"What's the difference?" I asked.

"South Station for the Church of England, North Station for Dissenters."

As we stopped at a fingerpost which pointed to the Military Cemetery, Dogger seemed suddenly to have fallen into a deep reflection. Sharply etched lines had become suddenly visible upon his face as if at the wave of a wand by some malevolent magician. I knew what he was thinking: Dozens of his fallen comrades-in-arms lay in that direction. The war had been exceptionally cruel to Dogger, as it had been to my father. Both had survived, but both had been marked forever and forever. It was not a topic for discussion.

Walking along these railway tracks must surely catapult him back to his wartime captivity: to the time when he and Father were made to work as slaves on the Thailand Burma Death Railway.

How brave he was to travel with me upon another railway of death, even though this one was in England and in another time. Even so, it must be sheer torture.

I needed to distract him.

"Look, Dogger," I said. "There's the Cemetery Office. They'll be able to direct us to Mme. Castelnuovo's grave."

Dogger turned slowly, as if seeing me for the first time: as if I were a stranger who had approached him in the street asking for directions.

"Excellent idea," he said with great effort, seeming to

haul himself back from distant and dangerous foreign shores. "Timely assistance is always most welcome."

The office was a white brick building which had surely seen better days. Rainwater runoff of a hundred years had left trails of vivid green moss.

Dogger held the door open for me, and we passed through to the dim interior.

There was an air about the place—I could not quite put my finger on it—not so much of death as of stale commerce. Framed posters lined the walls, like railway travel posters advertising destinations from which there was no return.

There was a stirring in the room behind the desk, and after a minute or so a tiny man produced himself from among the dark cabinets. He was dressed in a tight black suit and a tall celluloid collar of a slightly yellow shade. He blinked at us through his silver pince-nez spectacles as if we were apparitions. One of his eyes was ringed by a black bruise. I wondered if he had been in a fight, or whether the black eye was purely decorative: an ornament of the trade.

I must have been staring, because he touched a forefinger to the injured eye. "Coffin shifted," he mumbled, as if that explained everything.

Since I had been in exactly the same predicament myself, I understood perfectly, putting him at ease with a quick and sympathetic puckered nose and upper lip, as if to say, "Ouch! I share your pain."

"Well then, welcome to Brookwood," he said in a new

and surprisingly chirpy voice. "I hope you're not planning on staying?"

Could he be joking? I glanced at Dogger to judge his reaction, but his face was as straight as that of any Friday night whist player back home at St. Tancred's.

Even as I watched, his expression softened just enough to indicate that the witticism had not gone over his head.

"We are seeking the grave of Mme. Castelnuovo," Dogger replied. "I understand she was interred here in August."

"Family, are you?" the little man asked, putting on a sad face, just in case.

"Admirers," Dogger said.

"Ah! Musicians, then?" The sad face was replaced by that of an opera buff waiting for the curtain to go up.

"Something of the sort." Dogger bowed his head slightly in deference.

"Well then," said the little man, rubbing his hands together. "We shall see what we shall see. It wasn't all that long ago, was it?"

"August," Dogger repeated.

The man looked from one of us to the other, as if to find in our faces some mislaid index card containing the required information.

The moment was frozen in time.

And then, having reached some sudden decision, he turned away and scurried off into the depths of the shadowy cabinets, where we could hear him pawing through papers and giving off the occasional exasperated sigh.

After what seemed to me like an eternity, he came forth from his wooden den clutching a fat register with marbled edges which he banged down on the counter.

"Yes, here it is," he said, licking a finger and using the moistened digit to claw open the page he had inadvertently allowed to turn over.

The ancient sheet of letterhead which he took up was, I noted with pleasure, printed with the logotype of the London Necropolis & National Mausoleum Company: a snake swallowing its own tail, encircling a skull and crossbones and an hourglass, with a banner reading MORTUIS QUIES VIVIS SALUS.

I pointed to it and raised my eyebrows at Dogger.

He gave me a slight smile, which meant "Later."

We looked on as the bruised man drew laboriously, with pencil, a sketch map of the part of the cemetery we were seeking.

"Plot 124," he said, marking it on his map with a large X. "Roman Catholic section. It's near the chapel."

Which made sense. A Spanish lady would be far more likely to be found resting in the arms of her mother church than in a plot bursting with Dissenters.

"Happy hunting," the little man said cheerfully as we made our way to the door.

Behind Dogger's back, I gave the man a maniacal grin and shot him between the eyes with a revolver made from my forefinger and thumb. He grinned back as if we were long-lost twins who had been separated in the nursery.

"Now, then, Dogger. That Latin motto. You promised."

"*Mortuis Quies Vivis Salus*," Dogger said. "Which means, more or less, 'Safe rest of, or for, the living dead.'"

My eyes widened.

"Vampires?" I breathed, looking round to see that nothing spectral or hairy was stalking us behind the nearby tombstones.

"Not quite," Dogger said. "Although it would be exciting if it were, wouldn't it?"

I nodded breathless agreement.

"More like another infelicitous schoolboy effort. I'm sure that the sentiment intended was that the dead who rested in safety remained alive in memory."

"I should hope so," I said.

A moment or so later I found myself whistling Mozart's *Requiem*:

Eternal rest grant unto them, O Lord,
And let perpetual light shine upon them.

Just in case.

The Mozart *Requiem* has long been a favorite of mine. What better piece of music to put on the gramophone as one stretched out on one's bed, eyes closed, breathing slowed, hands folded prettily upon one's breast, preparing for sleep? All that was missing was the lily.

The rest of the household at Buckshaw didn't appreciate it much. A funeral mass at bedtime can be upsetting to people who are uncomfortable with the dead: people who haven't the grit of Flavia de Luce.

Daffy used to try to jolly me out of these moods by making jokes about Wolfgang Amadeus Nose-Art, referring to the scantily clad pinup girls the Americans loved to paint on the nose of their bomber aircraft.

Feely, who had too much respect for music to make cheap jokes about composers, concentrated on the gramophone itself.

"What kind of product attempts to curry favor by portraying a dog listening to a needle running round and round in a wax groove? Recorded music is painful to a dog's ears. Their range of hearing is far beyond that of humans. Animal cruelty is what it is."

I tried to point out to her that it really didn't matter, since we didn't own a dog, but Feely was having none of it.

We do not have an easy life, those of us who dote on death.

Dogger and I were now approaching the section of the cemetery where Mme. Castelnuovo was buried.

"Just here," I said, pointing at the scribbled map. "Plot 124."

It wasn't difficult to find. A mounded grave with month-old flowers among the older burials was a *dead* giveaway.

Sorry.

Two workmen were wrestling an elaborate granite tombstone into position. The empty wooden crate lay off to one side.

"Good morning, gentlemen," Dogger said, tipping his hat. "That is surely as fine a piece of Triassic marble as I have ever seen. From Almería, on the Andalusian Peninsula in Spain, if I'm any judge."

The men put down their tools and gaped at him.

"Let me guess," Dogger went on. "From the village of Macael. Yes, surely there is not anywhere in the world marble more white than that quarried at Macael. Do I win my bet?"

He beamed down upon them.

The smaller of the two men, obviously the foreman, got up from his knees and ripped off one of his workman's gloves.

"You have been to Macael, señor?" he asked, in a noticeable accent, giving Dogger a crushing handshake. "My mother she still lives there, in Macael."

Dogger smiled one of those smiles of his which makes a person feel that their question has been answered, but which, in fact, has done nothing of the sort.

"And your name is?" he asked, cocking his head.

"Diego," the worker said. "Diego Montalvo."

"Very pleased to meet you, Mr. Montalvo," Dogger said. "May I congratulate you on a very fine piece of craftsmanship?"

Flustered, Montalvo introduced his partner, who turned out to be Roberto (no last name), and we were soon shaking hands all round and grinning at one another like idiots as we chattered away about Almerían marble.

Inevitably, the conversation turned to Mme. Castelnuovo's tombstone, which the two men had been putting into place until we happened along. It was a flat oblong slab of blindingly white marble.

On it were given her names and dates: *Madame Adriana Castelnuovo, 1917–1952*, and beneath that a tasteful engraving of a guitar with a broken string.

"She wasn't very old, was she?" I observed.

"No," Dogger said. "As Wordsworth noticed, 'The good die first and—'"

He broke off abruptly.

"And?" I prompted softly.

"'. . . and they whose hearts are dry as summer dust burn to the socket.'"

Tears sprang to my eyes, even though I wasn't quite sure why.

Diego and Roberto crossed themselves, and I did the same.

Dogger cleared his throat. "Well then," he said, bringing the conversation back to more worldly things, "I expect it's a bit of a job to get it perfectly level, what with the loose earth, and so forth."

"No loose earth," Roberto said. "Hard like steel."

"Ah," Dogger said, nodding sagely. "Concrete. The family were very wise. Very wise, indeed."

It was a well-known fact—at least to me—that the famous are often tucked away immediately after interment beneath a substantial layer of concrete, simply to prevent the taking of trophies.

Which told us what we had come to find out.

Mme. Castelnuovo's digit had been detached before the burial.

We exchanged secret smiles.

"One box ticked," Dogger remarked, after we had

made our farewells to Diego and Roberto and strolled off along the Cemetery Pales. "One box to go. Gollingford Abbey, if I am not mistaken, lies in this direction."

"I'm curious, Dogger," I said. "How could you possibly have known that Mme. Castelnuovo's tombstone had been quarried at the village of Macael, in Almería, on the Andalusian Peninsula in Spain?"

"Ah!" Dogger said. "One must have one's secrets."

"You're pulling my leg," I said.

"Indeed I am, miss. The truth is, if you must know, that it was stenciled on the end of the shipping crate."

·FIVE·

I<small>T WAS NO MORE</small> than a pleasant stroll along the cemetery's main avenue to the village of Pirbright.

A couple of helpful soldiers in an army lorry were kind enough to stop at a crossroads and point us on our way.

"Gollingford Abbey? Can't miss it," they said, pointing. "Huge old place. On the hill. Oak avenue in front."

Dogger thanked them and gave them a smart, professional salute, which they returned with interest.

"Carry on, Major!" one of them shouted back, leaning out the window as the lorry ground into gear and roared off in a cloud of dust and dry leaves.

I rubbed at the grit that had been thrown up into my eyes.

"Sandy soil," I remarked, trying to make the best of it.

Dogger dabbed at my eye with the corner of his handkerchief. "So beloved by the military for maneuvers and shooting ranges," he said. "In former years, the parish was noted for its barren heath and moorlands."

"Strange place to put a private hospital," I said.

"On the contrary. Pirbright was once considered so secluded a place that the villagers would turn out and join hands to dance a circle around any stranger who might happen to make his way here. 'Dancing the Hog,' they called it."

"I wonder if they'll dance round us?"

"I shouldn't think so," Dogger said. "It's a different world than what it used to be."

I threw my arms up over my head into something like a Highland fling and circled him as if I were picking my way between crossed swords.

"Oink! Oink!" I cried, pointing my toes prettily.

Dogger pretended to smile indulgently. "I believe that is Gollingford Abbey just ahead."

A discreet signboard confirmed his words. We were at the bottom of a sloping avenue of tall oak trees which led directly up the hill to the hospital.

Even from the road, the place was impressive: a country house in the style of the Gothic Revival, simply crawling with cunning crenellations and pointed arches; spires, lancet windows, and tourelles; finials, scalloping, wedges, and pyramids; traceries and niches; a forest of tall, corseted chimneys; and here and there, a watchful gargoyle.

Gollingford Abbey had all of those and more. It looked like nothing so much as a London railway station that had hoisted its skirts one night in the dark of the moon and flounced off for some rustic haven, and was now caught nestling with quiet innocence in the countryside as if to say, "Who, me?"

"Do you think they will let us see Dr. Brocken?" I asked Dogger.

"It will depend."

"Upon what?" I was nothing if not keen.

"Upon us," he replied, holding open the door for me to pass through.

We found ourselves standing in a vast, empty foyer, our feet on the glossy tiled squares of a black-and-white checkerboard floor. The place smelled of wax and something far, far worse. In the distance was a desk at which was seated an imposing woman in white, shuffling papers, or pretending to.

As we set out across that immense expanse, Dogger paused to swipe a forefinger across a fluted pillar and examine it closely for dust.

I saw immediately what he was up to: We were sanitary inspectors, perhaps, and certainly not to be trifled with.

As we reached the desk, he pulled from his pocket the sketch map the little man at Brookwood had drawn for us. Looking at it closely, he pretended to read: "Dr. Augustus Brocken," he said briskly. "Is there someone here by that name?"

"Are you relatives?" the woman asked.

That made twice within the hour we had been presented with the same question.

"No," Dogger told her.

"Then I'm afraid I can be of no assistance. Good day to you."

"We are the representatives of Dr. Brocken's daughter, Mrs. Anastasia Prill." His voice hardened. "Did you not receive her letter, telling you to expect us?"

"Well . . . no," the woman stammered. I could see her rethinking her brusqueness. "I suppose it's possible—"

"I am not interested in possibilities, madam," Dogger said, and I almost cheered. I had never seen him so forceful—or so magnificent.

And as I looked on, she relented. I could see it in her face: a weakening of the hard lines around the mouth, an ever-so-slight sagging of the muscles around the eyes, her chin retreating slowly but relentlessly, like the ebbing tide.

"I shall inquire," she said, and as she picked up the telephone handset, I thought I heard Dogger sniff.

After a lengthy conversation with someone at the other end, which consisted mostly of "Yes . . . yes . . . yes . . . no . . . no . . ." and so forth, with the receiver cup pressed tightly to her ear to prevent us from hearing the other party, she hung up the phone.

"Nelson," she said, her finger jabbing toward the heavens.

I looked at her blankly. Dogger didn't move.

"Nelson," she repeated. "It's the name of the wing. Upstairs. First floor. Use the lift."

And with that she nodded toward an ancient carriage which seemed to be constructed mainly of string and wire. It reminded me of one of the early airplanes in which fearless flying aces risked their lives daily with grim resignation.

We stepped into the cage and Dogger operated a brass lever in a black iron quadrant. With an alarming squeal, the lift jerked into action, and up we shot like a squadron of Sopwith Camels, howling, into the heavens.

As the infernal device ground to a juddering halt, we stepped off hastily into a broad hall which was filled with unexpected light.

Dogger tilted his head toward a framed portrait of a uniformed naval officer with one sleeve pinned prominently to the front of his blue coat, which was papered with gaudy orders of chivalry.

"Admiral Nelson," he said.

"He looks as if he was thinking more of Emma Hamilton than of battle tactics," I whispered. Daffy had described to me that famous love affair after sneaking to the cinema with Feely to see the film *That Hamilton Woman*.

"Or roast beef," Dogger suggested.

A short walk down an echoing hallway brought us to a crossroads: Painted arrows on the walls pointed the way to Corridors A, B, and C.

How were we to proceed?

The problem solved itself when a nurse in a crisp blue-and-white uniform came bustling toward us.

"Yes?" she said, making one eyebrow into a question mark.

"Dr. Brocken," Dogger said.

The nurse looked us—one at a time—in the eye.

"I'm afraid you're too late," she said, shaking her head, and my stomach sank.

But Dogger was made of sterner stuff.

"Too late?" he replied, as if he hadn't heard properly.

The nurse made an elaborate show of hauling up, and consulting, the watch which was hung from her chest by a lanyard.

It was a magnificent performance, punctuated by numerous small hesitations, wrinklings of the brow, and examinations of the soul: a performance which would have been showered with awards on the West End stage.

"Too late," she repeated, letting go the watch. "Visiting hours are from eleven till two, no exceptions. It is now half two. You must make arrangements to come another day."

"I'm afraid that's impossible," Dogger said and then, lowering his voice, he added, "Confidentially, it's a grave legal matter. All rather hush-hush, I'm afraid. I represent Dr. Brocken's daughter, Mrs. Prill. She would be most upset to hear that we had been turned away after coming such a great distance."

"And this young lady?" she asked, redeploying the old eyebrow.

"Ah." Dogger put a protective hand on my shoulder. "As I say, it's all rather hush-hush."

You could see the wheels turning. Who could I possibly be? It was evident that I was not a barrister or solicitor. Who, then? A granddaughter? A legatee? A child offering whose blood was to be transfused into the old goat?

I could see the possibilities racing through the nurse's mind like some infernal Rolodex.

"Room 37," she said. "That corridor. On the left. Ten minutes. Not a second more."

Having put us in our place, she sailed off to find some fresh skirmish.

Room 37 had sticky linoleum; the walls were a shade of vomitous green. You could have cut the atmosphere with a pickax; I could feel it clogging my pores. The staleness of the place suggested that the doors and windows had not been opened in living memory.

An ancient human being was sitting propped up in a wingback chair in front of the window, although it could not be said that he was looking out of it.

His mouth hung open by force of gravity and I would have sworn he was dead, save for the minute pulsing of his glazed eyes. His skin had the appearance of having been removed and crumpled into a ball, like yellowed tissue paper, then roughly flattened and pasted back on.

"Dr. Brocken?" Dogger said.

There was no reply.

"I've told your daughter I'd look in on you."

The old man didn't move a muscle. Perhaps Mrs. Prill had been right after all: Her father was not compos mentis.

I caught Dogger's eye and shook my head.

Dogger had taken up one of the old man's hands, holding it tenderly in his own.

How kind, I thought. *The reassurance of human touch.*

The old man twitched and went on staring.

"Time for your medicine, Dr. Brocken," Dogger said, reaching into his pocket and pulling out a green glass pyramid of what appeared by its label to be patent medicine.

From another pocket, Dogger conjured a spoon.

"Brocken's Balsamic Electuary," he said, as if to me, as he uncorked the oddly shaped bottle and decanted a dark ooze into the spoon. "The stuff's full of laudanum."

And then in a louder voice he added, "Open up, Doctor."

If I hadn't been watching for it, I should have missed it. Dr. Brocken's mouth clamped tightly shut: only a whisker's breadth, but still, discernible to the observant eye.

"Take your medicine, Doctor," Dogger said quietly, "or I shall have to send for Mrs. Prill."

The ancient eyes shifted ever so slightly, jerking by one or two degrees at a time, as if unaccustomed to moving, until at last, they came to rest on mine.

Dr. Brocken's ancient tongue made its appearance and licked the ancient lips.

Dogger made no move to bring the spoon toward his mouth.

"Your daughter has told us about the letters," he said to the doctor. "There is no longer any need for secrecy. Who wrote them?"

A tremor began at the old man's fingers and worked its way up to his elbows and shoulders. Moments later a single tear appeared in the corner of his rheumy eye.

Dr. Brocken was crying.

"Just the name, Doctor. Tell me the name and we shall be gone."

As he spoke, Dogger leaned in so that his ear was at the old man's mouth.

All that came out was drool.

Dogger produced a white handkerchief and wiped gently at the doctor's mouth.

"Just the name," he said again, in a voice so soft I could hardly hear him: a voice that might be saying a few last words to a child being coaxed back into sleep after a nightmare.

"Just the name. That's a good lad."

The mouth of Dr. Brocken convulsed, folded in upon its wrinkled self, the lips trembling. "Proteus," he whispered.

"Proteus," Dogger repeated, turning to me. "Write that down if you please, Miss Churchill."

Miss Churchill? Very well then, I would play along.

I pretended to rummage for a writing tablet and made a scribble in my palm with an imaginary pencil.

"An ingenious attempt, Doctor," Dogger told the old man. "I congratulate you."

Again, speaking to me, he said, "Proteus: one of the early Greek sea gods, said to know everything, past, present, and future, but reluctant to divulge any of his knowledge. He was able to assume whatever shape he wished. The only way of extracting information was to surprise him during his nap. How clever of you to have thought of it, Dr. Brocken. How very clever indeed. Now, then . . ."

The spoon was moving again, remorselessly, toward

the doctor's mouth. The smell of balsam—and something else—hung in the air.

Turning his head away, his hands and arms thrashing feebly, the old man sputtered, and a name came bubbling out.

"Gabriel!"

"Thank you," Dogger said. "And good day to you."

Emptying the spoon into a nearby aspidistra, he wrapped it and the recorked bottle in the same soiled handkerchief with which he had wiped the old man's lips, then strode toward the door.

I, naturally, followed.

"What did you make of him, Dogger?" I asked, trying to sort out my own thinking.

We were strolling slowly back toward the railway station at Brookwood.

"The eyes gave him away," Dogger said. "Given his supposed condition, one would have expected dilation of the pupils, but they presented nothing remarkable."

"Malingering?" I asked. I remembered it was a subject upon which Sherlock Holmes had thought of writing a monograph.

"Exactly," Dogger said. "Feigning a condition which does not exist. And I must say that he seems to have been remarkably successful at his game. It was a question of catching him out."

"*You* smoked him out!" I said, clapping my hands in delight. "I wonder why no one else ever thought to do it?"

"Perhaps because it wasn't in their best interests to do so. Great wealth can buy great oversight."

"But not from us!"

Dogger smiled. "A thumbnail applied sharply beneath the fingernail of an apparently unconscious subject can be a remarkably useful tool of detection."

"We're breaking new ground in criminal investigation," I said proudly, touching his sleeve.

"Not really," Dogger replied. "Still, as Francis Bacon once said, 'To go beyond Aristotle by the light of Aristotle is to think that a borrowed light can increase the original light from which it is taken.' What he meant is that we must strike our own match and venture forth into our own darkness."

"We must be prepared to improvise!" I said. It was a thought I had already formulated many times in my chemical laboratory.

"If we are to keep up with Dr. Brocken, I suppose we must," Dogger agreed. "His telling us that Gabriel wrote the letters is most helpful."

"I'm afraid I don't follow," I admitted.

"He claimed at first they were written by Proteus, a sea god. Then, by Gabriel, an angel noted for his announcement of the birth of Christ. Two things are perfectly clear: that he is not telling the truth, and that behind his façade of helplessness, there still whirs an active and scheming mind. Our Dr. Brocken is an uncommonly cunning individual."

We walked for a while in silence. Dogger's words had embedded themselves in my brain.

"Dogger," I said. "May I ask you something? I hope it's not impertinent."

It was a question I had been meaning to ask him for ages and ages, but until now, the moment had never seemed right.

"Of course you may, Miss Flavia."

I screwed up my courage. This wasn't going to be easy.

"Do you believe in angels?" I blurted.

I instantly regretted it. My question was too personal. It was none of my business.

Time slowed in an instant to a horrific crawl.

I was biting my tongue when Dogger replied.

"Yes, I do, most assuredly. They are invisible, of course, but we humans know them as thoughts."

Somewhere, a corner of the universe clicked into place, and the day brightened. I knew that things hereafter were never going to be the same.

"Thank you, Dogger," I said. "I've always suspected that."

And we both laughed.

·SIX·

We were, as the London Necropolis Railway had promised its passengers a century ago—the living ones, at least—home in time for tea.

Clarence Mundy had picked us up at the train and was now dropping us off at Buckshaw. Mrs. Mullet met us at the door.

"You've got 'ome just in the neck of time," she said. "That woman was 'ere again. I told 'er you wasn't in, but she pushed 'er way in any'ow. Said she left 'er purse 'ere last time."

"And did she manage to find it?" Dogger asked.

"No. But I kept a close eye on 'er all the same."

"Did she leave a message?" I asked.

"No. She just kept sayin' over and over she needed to see you and Mr. Dogger. Wouldn't believe you wasn't 'ere. Must've thought I was 'idin' you behind the AGA, or some such foolishness. Wants to see you at 'er place at once. At once, mind! I kept a close eye on 'er for finger-prints, but she never touched anythin'. I'd stake my life on it."

"Excellent, Mrs. Mullet," Dogger said. "Well done. Would you care to join us for tea before we set out?"

By her expression, you'd think Mrs. M had just been crowned Queen of Heaven.

She poured the tea with a blissful smile on her face and a sturdy forefinger on the lid of the teapot to keep it from tumbling into someone's lap, and passed the sugar as daintily as if it were live ammunition. She cut the Victoria cake and passed round the slices with silent pride.

"I called Miss Daphne, but she says she doesn't want 'er tea. She's got 'er nose stuck in a book. *Useless*, I think it's called, by some woman named Joyce. It isn't right. But 'oo am I to say? We'll take care of 'er share, won't we? 'Ave another piece of cake, dear."

Fed to the gills and awash in hot tea, we set out at last for Mincing, and Balsam Cottage, in my late mother Harriet's Rolls-Royce, which Dogger was gradually coddling back to its full functional glory after years of near-abandonment in the coach house.

"We shall examine the empty box," Dogger told me, "making note, of course, of anything else of interest we observe in the house."

"Check," I said. It was an American expression I had learned from Carl Pendracka, but it seemed apt in the circumstances. "Do you suspect that she knows that we know? About the letters not being stolen, I mean?"

"We must assume that she does. Dissemblers often have a keen nose for that same trait in others."

"Liars recognize liars," I said.

"Precisely," Dogger said.

"Then why," I wondered, "did she make a second trip to Buckshaw?"

"Two reasons come to mind: to reinforce her fib, and to find out what we have uncovered so far. I favor the former."

And so did I. As no mean dissembler myself—oh, all right, as a downright filthy fibber when the occasion and circumstances required—I knew all too well the liar's tendency to stitch and embroider the truth until it resembled the winner of the Best Tea Towel Award at the church fête.

Lies and needlework skills have much in common.

Lost in my own thoughts, I did not notice that we had reached Mincing, and Balsam Cottage.

I knew it was Balsam Cottage because the name was marked on a discreet sign attached to one of the stone pillars that marked the driveway.

The house itself was not visible but was hidden behind a dense hedge of conifers.

"Balsam firs," Dogger said, following my gaze. "*Abies balsamea*. Brought, no doubt, from North America at great expense, and the source, as it were, of Dr. Brocken's wealth."

"Brocken's Balsamic Electuary," I said. "Do you still have that bottle of the stuff in your pocket?"

Dogger dug deep in the pocket of his coat and produced his handkerchief, which he unrolled carefully.

"Sticky stuff," he said. "I must confess that this isn't
the genuine article. It is, rather, something I concocted
myself on the hot plate: a mixture of friar's balsam and
bitter aloes from the medicine cabinet. Vile, should the
good doctor have been so foolish as to swallow it."

"Bitter aloes?" I said. "Isn't that the stuff Dr. Darby
gives Mrs. Gull to discourage thumb-sucking?"

I didn't need to add that whatever it was, it didn't
work, since Mrs. Gull's eldest son, Gregory, who was now
almost twenty, was still to be seen occasionally wandering
round Bishop's Lacey with his thumb planted firmly in his
face. "A village tragedy of the first water," Daffy called it.

"That's the stuff," Dogger said. "Antifungal, antibacte-
rial, anti-inflammatory, and can also be used to purge
horses. Bitter aloes is the jack-of-all-trades in every doctor's black bag."

I knew, of course, that, chemically, aloes could be iden-
tified with either borax or a solution of bromine or nitric
acid, to produce, respectively, a green fluorescence, a pale
yellow precipitate, or a yellowish brown passing rapidly to
a vivid green. Its crystalline principal was *aloin* or *aloi-
num*: a name I could always remember by thinking of Ha-
waii, or, as it was formerly called, the Sandwich Islands.

We left the Rolls parked on the grassy verge outside
the gate and headed up the gravel path on foot.

Because it lay in the shadow of several large trees, the
house was not visible at once. Only bit by bit did it reveal

itself as we approached: a window here, a gable here, a glimpse of timbering somewhere else.

The final surprise was that Balsam Cottage was not a cottage at all, but rather an imposing two-story house in the Arts and Crafts style: a place that had been built by meat-and-potatoes carpenters who had learned their trade by studying sturdy chalets in the Swiss Alps. All wood, plaster, and whitewash, the place fairly oozed respectability.

"Just as one would expect," Dogger said, reading my mind.

The front of the house was crawling with Virginia creeper, now in the full red blaze of autumn. Round the front door, like a wreath, another vine was simply swarming with startling berries of lilac, turquoise, and blue, each shining pearly globe spotted like the eggs of the song thrush. The leaves were a leprous variegated green.

"Ampelopsis," Dogger said. "Sometimes called the porcelain vine."

"Poisonous?" I asked hopefully.

"No," Dogger said. "Merely decorative."

I lost interest instantly.

Dogger operated the bellpull, and from somewhere inside the house came a distant pealing.

We waited expectantly, but there was no answer: no sound of approaching footsteps, no curtains twitched aside—at least those visible from where we stood.

Dogger rang again.

"Perhaps she forgot she sent for us," I suggested.

"Unlikely," Dogger said. "She hardly seems the type. If

she were called away unexpectedly, she'd have left a note on the door."

I had to admit he was right. Whatever she was, Mrs. Prill was no flibbertigibbet.

I cupped my hands against the small diamond-shaped panes of the front door window, hoping to see if someone was coming.

To my surprise, the door, without a sound, swung inward.

"It was off the latch," I said.

Dogger said nothing but pulled from his pocket a pair of white cotton gloves he had used for polishing the family silver, before Father had been forced to sell it to settle his debts.

"You were expecting this," I said.

"Not exactly," he answered, "but I had my hopes."

"Shall we go inside?" I asked.

"It would be unneighborly not to," Dogger said. "It would not be out of order to see that the unlocked door has not been taken advantage of by some wandering tramp, or that Mrs. Prill has not suffered a fall in her bath.

"Mrs. Prill?" he called out loudly, in case she hadn't heard the doorbell.

"I'll leave you to check that," I said eagerly. "Meanwhile, I'll have a quick look round the outside, and then we shall have done our duty."

To be perfectly honest, the gloom of the overhanging balsams gave me an edgy feeling. I wanted to be certain that the coast was clear before venturing inside.

I made my way quickly round the house, to the garden

and back, keeping an eye peeled for anything out of order.

The grounds, which were well kept, lay in perfect silence, and no birds sang. The tail of a calico cat vanished in silence among the shrubbery, but no gloved and trench-coated killers lay in wait among the last, lingering hollyhocks.

I was simply doing my civic duty, I told myself.

How easily housebreaking can be justified when you put your mind to it!

Returning to the front door, and ever conscious of fingerprints—even in a good cause—I pushed against it with my elbow to open it fully.

The house lay in stillness.

With a brisk nod to Dogger, who was halfway along the front hall, I crossed the foyer to the stairs and started up them to the first floor.

"Mrs. Prill?" I called up, not wanting to be startled by her sudden appearance.

The W.C. and bath were not difficult to find. They were, as usual in these large houses, located at the top of the main staircase so that visitors needn't invade your privacy when all they required was a quick piddle.

The room was simply functional with no frills: W.C., tub, and washbasin. Not even a medicine cabinet in which to snoop.

"Mrs. Prill?" I called again. Perhaps she was having a nap.

I strode swiftly along the hall, opening the door of each bedroom and peering in to make sure that it was empty.

Relieved, I skipped down the stairs, glanced into each of the two reception rooms and the dining room, then made my way back to the kitchen, which was at the rear of the house.

"It's all right, Dogger," I said. "She's not at home. We can leave her a note and say that we called."

"That won't be necessary," Dogger said, as I came round the door.

He was squatting beside a Windsor chair in which sat Mrs. Prill, her head slumped grotesquely forward onto the tabletop, her chalky face openmouthed in a pool of her own vomit.

The contents of an overturned mug merged with the late contents of Mrs. Prill's gastrointestinal tract.

"Is she dead?" I asked. I already knew the answer.

"Yes," Dogger said.

"Recently?" I asked.

"Quite recently," Dogger said, removing his forefinger from Mrs. Prill's dead dewlaps. "Within the past hour, I should say. We had best call the police."

Call the police!

My mind and body thrilled at the words. Suddenly, I was alive again—fully alive, as if some energy which had been leaking unnoticed from my body for the past few months had been miraculously restored.

Call the police!

"I'll do it," I said. "I know Inspector Hewitt's number off by heart."

"Very good," Dogger said. "But before you do, let's have a quick dekko at the place. This lady isn't going anywhere."

It was a moment right out of Philip Odell, the famous wireless detective, and I'm afraid I clasped my hands together under my chin. Such moments of bliss were few in my life and I needed to savor them the moment they occurred. At my age, there might never be another chance.

First things first. I pulled out my white handkerchief and immersed a corner of it in the liquid that had spilled from the mug. With the diagonally opposite corner, I sampled a bit of Mrs. Prill's tummy turbulence. That done, I isolated the two corners from each other and rolled the whole thing into a compact—if slightly damp—ball, which I shoved into my pocket.

One of the ten commandments of criminal investigation is this: last in, first out. Meaning, of course, that in the absence of external wounds, the last thing taken by mouth, either food or drink, ought to be the first thing analyzed.

Dogger looked on approvingly.

"Smells like coffee," Dogger observed, pointing at the cup. I hadn't noticed until he mentioned it.

"Let's begin with the pantry," he said, and I agreed. He had already had an opportunity to examine the body while I was on my useless mission to the upper regions of the house.

The pantry was what you would expect to find in the house of a lady who lived alone: bread, jam, a few bottled preserves, tinned meat (ugh!), butter, a quart of milk in an ancient icebox—in which the ice was almost completely melted—a few stalks of rhubarb wrapped in newspaper (*The Times*, dated ten days ago), a cabbage, and three windfall apples, judging by their skin.

On the wall was mounted a coffee grinder: a glass globe atop a metal mill with a wooden cranking handle, and a calibrated glass cup below for the grounds. Beneath it was a bag of coffee beans, which made sense: Mrs. Prill had made it quite clear at Buckshaw that she didn't drink tea.

With a fingernail, I pried up the top of the coffee hopper. Dogger reached into the lining of his coat and produced—was it with a bit of a flourish, or did I imagine it?—a pair of silver-plated butler's tongs.

With a nod of gratitude, I took these from him and, with their claw-shaped ends, lifted one at a time from the open hopper a small pile of the beans, which I wrapped up in a twist of paper torn carefully from an inside corner of *The Times*. With a second screw of paper, I sampled a half ounce or so of the ground coffee from the lower glass cup.

After checking the back door and windows (all locked from the inside), examining the floors for unusual scuffs or footprints (none), and finding no signs of a struggle, Dogger said, "I am quite convinced the woman died alone."

"No second coffee mug," I said, glancing at the corpse. "Chair pulled firmly up to the table; her legs completely underneath the table. No sugar or cream as might be required if she had company. A woman alone."

"Agreed," Dogger said. "Which indicates that it was premeditated. And now, I think, you ought to ring up your friend the inspector."

I made my way to the telephone, which I had seen on a table in the hall.

Too excited now to remember the number, I took a deep breath and, using the hem of my jumper, picked up the handset.

"Hello? Miss Runciman? This is Flavia de Luce speaking. Please connect me with the Hinley Constabulary."

There was a quavering but almost audible silence, like duckweed shimmering sinuously beneath the surface of a country stream.

"Not again!" Miss Runciman said.

I was put through to Inspector Hewitt with remarkable speed. Was the Hinley Constabulary becoming accustomed to my calls? It would be flattering to think so.

"Hewitt," said the familiar voice.

"Inspector Hewitt," I said. "This is Flavia de Luce speaking."

"So I've been informed," the inspector said in rather a dry voice. "To what do I owe the pleasure?"

Was he twitting me? If he was, he'd soon regret it.

"I'm calling to report a suspected murder," I said. "At Balsam Cottage, Mincing. The apparent victim is a Mrs. Prill, the daughter of Dr. Augustus Brocken. Mr. Dogger and I are on the scene and shall remain here until you arrive."

There! I had done it. I had reported the crime and at the same time managed to insert ourselves into the investigation, all in one clear and remarkably concise statement.

Take a bow, Flavia!

"You say you're presently on the premises?" the inspector asked.

"Yes," I said. "I'm in the front hall at the telephone table."

I heard a muffled grunt at the other end of the line.

"Don't worry, Inspector," I said. "I'm using an article of my clothing to prevent fingerprints."

Another muffled grunt, and then the inspector said, in what seemed to me a resigned voice, "If both of you will be so good as to step outside, I shall have someone there shortly. Don't touch anything."

There was a haughty *click* as he hung up.

"They're on the way," I told Dogger.

"Excellent," he said. While I was on the telephone he had been using the time to give the corpse—the late Mrs. Prill, I mean—a final once-over.

We let ourselves out the door and stood in companionable silence on the step.

A sudden thought occurred to me.

"Did you examine her fingernails?" I asked Dogger. If he hadn't, it was probably too late now.

"I did, indeed," Dogger said. I needn't have worried.

"And?"

"The fingernails were normal, if slightly gaudy. No signs of excessive guitar use."

Well, there went that theory.

·SEVEN·

TEN MINUTES LATER, A familiar blue Vauxhall saloon turned quietly in at the driveway and rolled up to the door. Dogger and I stood in menial attitudes as Inspector Hewitt hauled himself out of the front seat, closely followed by Detective Sergeants Graves and Woolmer.

"Nice to see you again, Mr. Dogger," Inspector Hewitt said, strolling over to where Dogger and I stood waiting. He offered his hand.

"Had a good look round, have you?" he asked, turning to me.

"Inspector Hewitt," I said, pressing my lips together and thrusting out my hand so that he could hardly ignore it.

I gave him a brief, businesslike shake, resisting the urge to ask how his wife, Antigone, was doing, and if they were enjoying their new role as parents? And had the baby cut her first tooth yet? Or shown any signs of taking her first step? Or learned to say "Mama" or "Papa" in Greek?

I'd teach the man to be saucy with *me*.

Meanwhile, his two subordinates were unloading their gear from the car.

Sergeant Graves gave me a shy smile behind Inspector Hewitt's back, as if he didn't want to be caught. The sergeant had once been keen on Feely, but with my sister now successfully married off, his ardor had probably cooled.

I smiled back.

Sergeant Woolmer, as usual, ignored me. The man had no human feelings whatsoever. His eyes were anastigmat lenses with an f-stop of 3.1, able to gather, with astonishing resolving power, the smallest detail of a crime scene; his heart was a focal-plane shutter with speeds calibrated in the thousandth parts of a second. I shouldn't have been surprised to learn that he stopped regularly at his local after work to order a pint of Kodak Developing Solution.

Even before Inspector Hewitt reached the spot, Sergeant Woolmer had already begun dragging his heavy photographic kit—rather sourly, I thought—from the car.

Well, good luck to him. It was not my nature to wish anyone ill, but if ever I did, I might consider practicing upon Sergeant Woolmer.

"Well, we might as well have a look-see," Inspector Hewitt said, and I couldn't help wondering if his use of such an informal term meant that he viewed us as almost equals.

"Wait here," he added. "I shall require a statement from each of you."

And with that, he vanished suddenly inside the house. *Like a cuckoo into a clock*, I thought.

Flavia! I also thought. *How uncharitable. Just because the poor man hasn't dragged you into the house for advice— and besides, he is probably forbidden by statute, or something like that, to allow any civilians, no matter how well qualified, to set foot upon the scene of a crime. It would be as much as his career was worth to—*

And besides, we had already had a good old squint anyway.

While we were waiting, Dogger and I had a look at the balsam trees.

"The foundation of the family fortune," Dogger said. "As I have already remarked. And remarkably good cover for anyone who wanted to spy on the house, or to use as cover for their escape."

I thought of how quickly the cat outside had vanished.

"Did she live here alone?" I asked.

"As far as I could see," Dogger said. "Single toothbrush, which is very often the prime indicator of occupancy."

"You *were* busy," I marveled. "You must have had a look upstairs even before I came into the house."

"I wanted to be sure the coast was clear." He smiled.

Meaning, of course, that he wanted to be certain that there was no maddened ax murderer waiting behind a door to dispatch poor Flavia with a single swipe to the gizzard.

"Thank you, Dogger," I said.

I was itching to hear his analysis of Mrs. Prill's body,

and, even more, dying to hear his deductions, but now was not the time or place.

While we waited, we spoke instead of other things and Dogger, as he often does, turned the topic to practical matters. In this case, using the brickwork of Balsam Cottage as an example, he explained why it is that, because of the golden mean, the number of bricks used around the perimeter of a building can never come out evenly.

I pointed out that a similar instance was to be found in chemistry, in the radicals of cyanogen and the cyanides, and the combinations of methyl, cacodyl, and so on. I had, several years ago, conducted researches into cacodyl oxide, one of the most vile and toxic substances known to man, of which I was quite proud.

"I'm quite sure you're correct," Dogger said. "In any case, I defer. Ah, here comes Inspector Hewitt now."

The inspector was walking briskly toward us, opening the flap of his notebook as he came.

"I'd like a complete account of your movements from the time you arrived," he said. "Room by room."

I tried not to smile.

"We checked, of course," Dogger told him, "that there was no one else in the house requiring aid."

"Of course," the inspector said drily, making a note.

"I determined also that life was extinct," Dogger said.

"Before deciding whether to call us or the ambulance first," Inspector Hewitt finished for him.

"Of course," Dogger said.

It was a game of chess, and so far, my player was winning.

We went on to give a brief outline of our movements up to the inspector's arrival, all of which he duly noted.

"Very well," he said. "Thank you. If there's anything further, we shall be in touch."

After quick smiles all round, we turned and walked away down the drive.

"Oh, Flavia," the inspector called, and I turned back expectantly. "My wife and I would like to—"

I was already aglow. Antigone must have forgiven me for whatever *faux pas* I may have unwittingly made in the past. It was now only a matter of time before I was invited back to their little cottage for tea, for a shopping expedition in the Hinley shops, or—joy of joys—to be appointed "Auntie," or Belated Godmother to their little girl.

". . . to congratulate your sister Ophelia upon her marriage," the inspector finished.

I contrived a quick backward wave over my shoulder so that he wouldn't see my burning face.

"Decent of him," Dogger remarked as he steered the Rolls off the grassy verge and onto the road.

"Mm," I managed.

Daylight had already begun to fade, and by the time we reached Buckshaw, it was sunset. I could see that Dogger was tired and needed to rest.

He accepted without argument my suggestion that he take time to put his feet up.

"A very successful day, don't you think, Dogger?" I asked.

"Very," he replied, and I left him to retire.

But for me, in a way, the day was just beginning. My laboratory awaited above, and I could not resist its almost animal call.

I flew up the stairs, switched on the lights in the laboratory, locked the door, and rolled up my sleeves.

One would suppose that coffee, being such a common presence in nearly every household—except for the rationing, of course—would be easy to analyze. But one would suppose that incorrectly.

The humble coffee bean contains more than a thousand aromatic compounds, of which the alkaloid caffeine is, of course, the best known. The remainder of the bean is a treasure chest of alcohols, aldehydes, esters, hydrocarbons, ketones, lactones, phenols, and so forth, to list just a few.

The standard analytical test for caffeine, as every schoolboy knows (or ought to), is called the murexide test.

I lit a Bunsen burner and brought a pint of distilled water to the boil. When it was bubbling and steaming furiously I decanted a few ounces into each of three clean beakers.

Into the first, I inserted the knotted corner of my handkerchief with which I had soaked up the spilled liquid on Mrs. Prill's kitchen table. I draped the diagonally opposite corner of the handkerchief—the one soaked with her vomit—into the second beaker.

While I awaited the infusion, I carefully untwisted the paper scrap I had torn from *The Times* ("Sir, I must object strenuously to your recent—") and tipped out the roasted beans from the kitchen coffee mill into a glass petri dish, sorting them, with tweezers, by size.

I would not, of course, be making the laughably common mistake of employing Dragendorff's reagent, which, although often used to detect alkaloids, does not respond to caffeine.

Taking a pipette, I drew off a small amount of the brownish liquid in the first beaker and ejected it into a clean petri dish. To it, I added one half grain of potassium chlorate and a single drop of hydrochloric acid. I set the dish to dry over a very low Bunsen flame.

I now repeated these steps precisely, using the liquid from the second beaker: the one containing the infusion of the late contents of the late Mrs. Prill's stomach.

With the two glass dishes warming gently over the flame, I turned my attention to the coffee beans.

I chose first one of the smaller beans, which I placed in a stone mortar and crushed with a pestle. What I had now—or ought to have—was finely pulverized coffee.

I reboiled what remained of the distilled water, and to it added the oily residue of the beans. And again, the potassium chlorate and the tiny drop of hydrochloric acid.

This I placed on a wire mesh screen with the others, over the low flame.

Patience now was needed. I could proceed no further with the test until all liquid had completely evaporated and the residues dried completely.

Then would come the moment so popular in cinema thrillers: the moment when the detective would hold the test tube up to the light, and announce to his awestruck companion, "*What we have here, Watson* (or Jones, or Gilhooly, or whatever surname had been chosen for the dimwitted sidekick), *is a poison previously unknown to man.*"

Except in this case it wasn't cyanide.

I amused myself for a while by tapping out in Morse code on the countertop with my fingernails the names, in order, of the periodic table of the elements, from hydrogen all the way up to the recently discovered californium, which had the atomic number 98.

One of the radioisotopes of californium, called californium-251, has a half-life of 898 years. We should all be so lucky.

And I thought for a moment of the late Mrs. Prill, who had come nowhere near that age.

To cheer myself up a bit, I began to whistle that silly song about whistling while you work. But I found myself wondering if, by whistling about whistling while you work while you were actually working, you would cause some odd bit of the universe, in some unknown dimension, to fold in upon itself—rather like a Klein bottle, which has no inside or outside—causing you to disappear up your own posterior in a cloud of probably invisible orange smoke.

By now, I saw with relief, the residue was dry.

The answer was at hand.

I scraped a small bit of each of the two samples onto a strip of filter paper.

From a shelf, I brought down a bottle of ammonia and removed the glass stopper.

Phew! What a stench it made. No wonder they used to use it to revive faint maidens who had swooned at an uttered *Damn!* in the drawing room. This stuff was enough to awaken the Seven Sleepers of Ephesus.

Holding the paper in the rising fumes above the unstoppered bottle, I watched closely for any change in the color of the respective residues.

There went the first one: *pink!*

And there went the second: *pink!*

Which proved beyond much doubt that the spilled black liquid beside Mrs. Prill's cup had been coffee, and that coffee, too, had been in her vomit.

Ergo (as Uncle Tarquin used to write in his notebooks), Mrs. Prill had consumed coffee before she died.

Now for the second part of my experiment.

With the mortar and pestle thoroughly scrubbed, I took two of the larger beans and reduced them to dust. Again, I added to them boiled water from a fresh flask.

It would not be out of order to remark here that a chemist's work is never done. Those choosing it as a profession ought to know at the outset that most of their lives will be spent washing up.

Unless, of course, you are Sir Bernard Spilsbury or Professor Keith Simpson (the pathologist in the notorious Acid Bath Murders) and have your own adoring laboratory assistant to clean up your messes.

With the grounds of the larger beans (anything ground in a mortar and pestle can be considered "grounds," I suppose) I repeated the procedure I had used with the first part of my experiment: infusion, addition of potassium chlorate and hydrochloric acid, followed by warming to dryness, and exposure to the fumes of ammonia.

I watched expectantly, waiting for the tattletale pink that would indicate the presence of caffeine.

But nothing happened. The dried sludge remained the same color as it had been before: a miserable and, quite frankly, depressing brown.

But wait! If no caffeine was present, this could not possibly be a coffee bean. It might well have all the appearances of being a coffee bean, but as Macbeth so aptly remarked, "Fair is foul, and foul is fair," and "nothing is but what is not," both meaning that appearances can be deceiving.

Macbeth, incidentally, ought to be essential reading for anyone who wishes truly to understand British family life. It has helped me to understand many people, including myself.

But back to the beans. If this second sampling were not coffee beans, then what could they possibly be?

The answer came as it so often does, like a fizzling bolt: a thunderclap from the blue.

Physostigmine!

Calabar beans!

Of course! Why hadn't I thought of it until now? As any student of poisons knows, the ordeal bean of Calabar (*Physostigma venenosum*), which is almost indistinguishable from the coffee bean, was formerly used by superstitious tribes on the west coast of Africa to detect witchcraft or determine guilt. An innocent man accused of theft would vomit up the bean and live, whereas a guilty man would retain it and die.

The active alkaloid, physostigmine, which was also known as eserine, had been first separated by Jobst and Hesse in 1864 and given the chemical formula $C_{15}H_{21}N_3O_2$.

The stuff could be violently poisonous. I remembered from my bedtime reading that seventy children had been poisoned in Liverpool in 1864, having eaten some of the beans, presumably thrown on a rubbish heap by the crew of a cargo ship from the west coast of Africa. One poor little lad, Michael Russell, had eaten just four beans and died.

Almost unbelievably, the same thing had happened again in the same city only six years later.

At the time of the first inquest, a chemical analyst had testified that he had extracted the physostigmine with alcohol, which he had then purified with ether. After observing the various color changes made by caustic potash, chloroform, and various solutions of sulfuric acid, he had applied a few drops of the ethereal solution by insertion under the skin of a frog, which soon died.

I would not need to go to such extremes. In fact, I rather fancied frogs, and would take great pains to find a more humane solution.

The answer was close at hand.

The very Dragendorff's reagent I had shunned to test for caffeine would now be the ideal means by which to identify the presence of that other alkaloid, physostigmine.

To refresh my memory, I reached for one of Uncle Tar's fat volumes of *Tables of Chemistry*, and soon found what I was looking for.

Dragendorff's reagent was produced by mixing two solutions, A and B.

A was obtained by dissolving two grams of bismuth subnitrate in just under a fluid ounce of glacial acetic acid and adding three and a half ounces of water, while B was even simpler: an ounce and a half of potassium iodide to three and a half ounces of water.

The final reagent was produced by mixing equal amounts of A and B with twice the amount of glacial acetic acid and ten times that amount of water.

I did so and *"Viola!,"* as Mrs. Mullet, who had honeymooned in France, always says.

Here was my Dragendorff's reagent.

All that I needed to do was apply it to a fresh bit of the infusion I had extracted from the larger beans.

As the residue dried on the petri dish, I saw that it had begun very slightly to glaze into a brittle-looking mass: an early sign, perhaps, of a crystalline alkaloid.

Time, in all the history of the world, had never passed more slowly. I was tempted to hurry the stuff by heating it over the flame, even though I knew that doing so would incinerate and destroy the alkaloid I was so eagerly seeking.

Anticipating the outcome of a chemical experiment is the sure sign of an amateur. I knew that perfectly well. The true professional stands impassively by awaiting the evidence of her eyes, ears, and nose.

"Patience is paramount," said a quiet voice, somewhere back behind the curtains of my brain.

And I knew it was the truth. In fact, I jotted down the words in the margin of my notebook. Later, I would purloin Daffy's calligraphy set and letter it on a card, which I would frame and hang in a prominent place.

Before I knew it, the residue was dry. In just a few more heartbeats, all would be revealed.

It was with hands that were trembling only slightly that I picked up a pipette and drew up into it a few drops of Dragendorff's reagent.

I released the solution onto the dried residue.

At first . . . nothing. And then . . . like the sun crawling its way up above the eastern horizon, the matter in the petri dish began rapidly to change color: pink, orange, and finally a deep red.

Physostigmine. Calabar beans.

Someone had put the ordeal beans of Calabar into Mrs. Prill's coffee grinder.

I couldn't wait to tell Dogger.

It was too late tonight. He needed his rest. And so, to think of it, did I.

I switched off the lights and went to my bedroom. I sat on the edge of my bed reviewing the events of a hectic day.

But even before I reached the London Necropolis Railway, sleep fell on my head like a sackful of anvils, and I did not move until morning.

·EIGHT·

SOMEONE WAS HAMMERING ON my bedroom door.

"Flavia! Wake up! Wake up! Let's all sing like the bird-ies sing! Rise and shine!"

"Go away," I muttered, and covered my head with a pillow.

But the little swine was not giving up that easily. Like all great torturers, Undine had learned to save the worst till the last.

"Come on, Flavia. Up and at 'em! Tallyho! You're wanted on the telephone."

Even through a bundle of goose down her voice grated upon my tired ears.

Telephone? I thought. *Who would be calling so early in the morning?* I glanced at my clock: It was just past eight.

"Telephone, Flavia! I think it's the garbage collectors. They want to pick you up in ten minutes."

This was followed by an utterly despicable, throaty gurgle of a laugh at her own witticism.

"Come on, Flavia. Mrs. Richardson wants a word with you. I told her you were awake."

Cynthia Richardson—the vicar's wife. What can she possibly want? Has something horrible happened?

"Tell her I'll be there in a minute," I grumbled, hauling myself out of bed and sliding my arms into one of Father's old bathrobes.

And just for an instant, Father was there. Just for an instant I was in his warm embrace.

Not that that had ever happened in real life, of course. We de Luces are far too reticent to allow such familiarity.

The moment passed, and I was glad of it as I hurtled down the stairs and slipped into the cubicle that lay beneath.

"Flavia speaking," I said, picking up the telephone handset, which Undine had left dangling, writhing at the end of its cord like a tree snake.

"Flavia, dear," Cynthia began. "Sorry to bother you at such an ungodly hour, but it's an emergency."

I was all ears. The only things that came close to poisons, in my estimation, were emergencies.

"I'm all of a dither," Cynthia said, and I could tell by her voice that she wasn't exaggerating.

"How can I help?" I asked, as Anglicans have been taught to do—and in spite of the fact that our family have been Roman Catholics since Saint Peter was a sailor.

"You might recall that Denwyn has his Vicar's Vestry

this week. Hordes of young men will be coming down from Christ Church and of course we have to put them up."

"I remember it from last year," I said. "It was a madhouse."

"Yes, well," Cynthia said, "it had completely slipped my mind that we were also expecting our Missioners, and there simply isn't room for all of them.

"Besides," she added, "it wouldn't be right to expose the dear ladies to a houseful of—"

Hooligans, I almost said, but I managed to hold my tongue. Hooligans might be too powerful a word, but there was no denying that a host of Divinity students could sometimes be full to overflowing with the Holy Spirit.

"Healthy horseplay," I said, letting her off the hook.

"Perfectly put," Cynthia said. "Thank you, Flavia. Now, about the rooms . . ."

"Yes?" I asked. I could see what was coming, and I wasn't sure that I liked it.

"Well, Buckshaw *is* quite spacious, isn't it? Much more so than the vicarage, where we're always under one another's feet. I thought that if you'd be so gracious . . ."

She left the last word hanging in the air. *Gracious?* I thought. *As if I were royalty?*

Even though Buckshaw now belonged solely to me, it wasn't just a matter of throwing open the doors and allowing the general public to come tramping through. Dogger, for instance, would need to be consulted. It would be wrong to saddle him with further duties. I was keenly aware of his need for—

"Flavia? Are you there, dear?"

"Yes," I said. "I was just thinking."

"If it's Dogger and Mrs. Mullet you're worried about, you mustn't give it a minute's thought. Doris and Ardella are used to fending for themselves under the harshest of conditions. They're just back from Africa, you know."

Her voice dropped to a confidential whisper. "They were both with Dr. Schweitzer at Lambaréné for a time. In spite of his being a Lutheran, I'm given to understand that they all got on swimmingly."

I had heard of Albert Schweitzer, of course. Who hadn't? His hospital in French Equatorial Africa was featured regularly in the pictorial magazines, popular for their portrayal in glossy portraits of poor people suffering the most appalling diseases.

I remembered, too, that because he was a fellow organist, Feely had a large framed newspaper photograph of the good doctor on her bedroom wall: a charming shot of Dr. Schweitzer in a railway carriage, practicing diligently upon a dummy organ keyboard he had caused to be specially made.

Too bad Feely was now off somewhere in a state of matrimonial bliss. She would have loved a good old chinwag with Doris and Ardella.

"Flavia? Are you there, dear?"

"Yes."

I let the silence lengthen. If I waited long enough, Cynthia might sense my reluctance.

"So, it's all settled then? I'll send them along to you

directly after breakfast. I'm sure they will be no trouble at all."

I was speechless.

"Oh, and Flavia—"

"Yes?" I asked. I could feel my breathing tightening.

"Thank you. You're a brick."

And she rang off.

If I *were* a brick I'd have thrown myself through Cynthia's kitchen window, vicarage or no.

I was thinking of banging my head against the wall when a strange voice drifted into the telephone cubicle. Although difficult to tell where it was coming from, it seemed to be seeping in through the crack under the door.

"Flavia!" it said, in a hollow, mocking rasp. "This is your Conscience speaking."

It was, of course, Undine.

"Go away," I said.

"You ought to be ashamed of yourself," the voice went on, now changing to a peevish whine. "You promised to buy a bottle of ginger beer for your poor, deserving little cousin Undine."

It was true enough, I had. In trying to talk her out of putting a white mouse she had bought at Woolworth's into Aunt Felicity's handbag, I'd rashly promised a treat.

"For heaven's sake, Undine," I said, "the shops aren't open yet. Let me at least have breakfast."

"Mrs. Mullet's given your kippers to the cat," the voice replied in a surprisingly menacing whisper.

Even though we didn't have a cat, there was something undefined in Undine's tone that chilled my marrow: some icy blast from the Arctic wastes. Was it possible that she had inherited from her late mother, Lena, some embedded evil in the blood?

There's no escaping such a curse if it runs in the family.

"All right, Conscience," I called out loudly. "Tell my poor, deserving cousin Undine to get herself ready. We'll leave as soon as I have a bite of toast."

Outside the door of the telephone cubicle, my Conscience gave a mad giggle and went scampering away with cries of "Yee-haw!"

It was going to be one of those days. I just knew it.

We were flying into the village, Undine and I, on my trusty bicycle Gladys. I stood on the pedals, pumping for all I was worth, while Undine sat behind me, clinging tightly to my shoulders, her legs thrown out on both sides, half singing, half chanting at the top of her lungs:

Nellie ate some marmalade, Nellie ate some jam.
Nellie ate some oysters, Nellie ate some ham.
Nellie ate some johnnycake, drank some ginger beer
And then Nellie wondered what made her feel so queer."

"Where did you learn that?" I shouted over my shoulder.
"In Singapore. Ibu used to sing me to sleep with it.
"When I was a child," she added.

Ibu was the Malay name for "mother," I recalled. It was what Undine had called Lena before that ghastly—

"Ibu learned it from the Aussie soldiers," Undine shouted. "The Australians. There were hordes of them in Singapore. They taught her all their best songs."

Undine resumed her banshee screeching:

"Oh! Up came the marmalade
And up came the jam.
Oh! Up came the oysters
And up came the ham.
Oh! Up came the johnnycake.
Up came the ginger beer.
And then Nellie knew what made her feel so queer."

Under my breath, I apologized to Gladys, who had rather a delicate constitution when it came to sick-making songs. I patted her on the handlebars.

"This, too, shall pass," I whispered.

"Someone's gone off the road!" Undine shrieked into my ear, pointing to the lane ahead, where a car lay canted to one side on the verge, half on and half off the sandy track.

I applied Gladys's brakes and we juddered to a stop.

Two women were bent busily over the front of the car. In spite of Undine's caterwauling, they had not heard us approaching.

"Hello," I called out. "Is everything all right?"

As the taller woman of the two swung round, I could see that she had been operating a jack. She raised one hand to shade her eyes against the morning sun, the better to see me.

"Morgan F-4 three-wheeler," Undine observed matter-of-factly behind me. "Thirty-six horsepower Ford Side-valve engine."

I find it annoying when someone younger knows something that one doesn't know oneself.

"Enthralling," I said. In spite of not being on a first-name basis with the beast, I recognized the disabled car as the old clinker that Bert Archer kept at the garage for hire to the occasional tourist. Half automobile and half motorcycle, it looked like a gargantuan green grasshopper that had lost a back leg in a fight to the death.

The woman had spotted me at last.

"Oh, look, Ardella," she trilled to her companion, who was disconnecting an air pump from one of the front tires. "Our prayers have been answered."

Ardella looked up and I wished she hadn't. To be charitable, she had a fierce face that could probably convert French Equatorial Africans to Christianity simply by glaring at them: bringing them down with her divine dart gun. Her complexion could be best described as not merely spotted, but positively polka-dotted.

"Do you live nearby?" this apparition asked.

"Yes," I said. I had been taught to be cautious with strangers.

"We were looking for a house called Buckshaw, when we seem to have incurred a puncture. We've changed the tire, but now the blessed thing won't start. Maddening."

"Infuriating," she added.

"Hmf!" Undine said. She climbed down from the seat behind me, marched straight over to the car, climbed into the cockpit—there's no other word for it—and began to fiddle with the hand controls.

"Undine!" I called out, but she ignored me. She had switched on the ignition and was turning over the engine.

"Undine!"

"Don't worry," Ardella called out to me. "It's dead as a dodo." (I deduced that *she* was Ardella since her companion had called her by that name.)

"Because you've flooded it," Undine announced in a rooster cackle. "You ought to have used the choke."

She adjusted something on the instrument panel and pressed again on the starter button.

With a happy *whirrrppp* the engine burst into a rude burble. Both women applauded as Undine gave the throttle a couple of fearsome revs before stepping out into the grass, closing the door, and taking a deep, sweeping, dramatic bow.

"How do you do?" Doris said, sticking out a hand. "I'm Miss Pursemaker, and this is my friend Miss Stonebrook."

It was obvious that, because of my age, she wanted to keep things on a formal basis.

"How do you do, Miss Pursemaker—and Miss Stonebrook. My name is Miss de Luce. And this is my cousin, Miss de Luce the Younger."

Undine hooted at my witticism.

"But you can call me Sticky," she told them with a toothy grin. "I'm called that because I'm a terribly tenacious person."

Awkward handshakes were made all round, after each of which Undine wiped her hands on her skirt.

"You must be the Missioners," I said. "Cynthia Richardson told us to expect you."

"Ah," said Miss Pursemaker. "So you are *that* Miss de Luce. Flavia, I believe. We were given to understand that you would be willing to provide us with lodgings. To be a Good Samaritan, so to speak. Ha! Ha!"

I decided there and then on the spur of the moment that if ever I were given the opportunity to compose my own epitaph, I would have engraved upon my tombstone: *Here lies Flavia de Luce—A Good Samaritan So to Speak,* followed by the dates of my birth and death.

"It's a bit chilly, in spite of the sun," I said, hugging myself. "If you'd care to follow, we shall lead you."

"What about my ginger beer?" Undine wailed. "You promised me a ginger beer!"

"Perhaps another time," I replied cheerily. "But for now, we must do our Christian duty."

So with me pedaling in a leisurely manner, Undine pouting thunderclouds on the seat behind me, and the two Missioners rattling along behind like a green clockwork dragon, we made our way back to Buckshaw.

Dogger was not surprised to see us.

"Mrs. Richardson rang up to see if the ladies had arrived safely," he said as he met us at the door. "I've prepared rooms in the north wing."

"Excellent," I said. I needn't tell our guests that their quarters had last been occupied by a murder victim. "I'm sure they will suit them perfectly."

Leaving the ladies to work out whether I was referring to the rooms or to themselves.

·NINE·

"Work, work, work," Mrs. Mullet said. "We just gets rid of one and two more takes 'er place."

I could tell by the way she was flailing the AGA with her duster that she was thoroughly enjoying herself.

"I don't know what we'd do without you, Mrs. M," I said.

"You'd die," she shot back, but with a twinkle in her eye. "Die like dogs. The 'ole lot of you. And I shouldn't be sorry."

"Of course you would," I said. "You'd visit our graves and strew them with pale primroses."

Suddenly, Mrs. Mullet's arms were around me, and she was hugging me so tightly I couldn't draw a breath. Tears were streaming down her face.

"Oh, Miss Flavia," she sobbed. "What are we going to do without 'er?"

It took me a moment to realize she was referring to Feely.

It would have been oh so fatally easy to make a flippant remark, such as "Extra bacon for everyone," but now was not the time. Only the right words would do.

"I don't know, Mrs. Mullet. We shall have to cling to one another and do our best."

I was thinking, I suppose, of the film *Lifeboat,* which Mrs. Mullet had taken my sisters and me to see at the cinema in Hinley. The way in which a small group of people of all races, all classes, and all temperaments had come together so magnificently in the face of tragedy had obviously made a deep impression on me because, before I knew it, I had thrown my arms around her in return, and the two of us were howling unashamedly.

We, too, were survivors, weren't we? Left bobbing adrift in the dark by death, grief, and shock in a frail little shell.

When the sun came up, what would we find to be the name painted on the gunwales of our lifeboat? Was it *Buckshaw*? Or would it be *Flavia de Luce*?

Only the coming of daylight would tell.

I am not a person given to glum thoughts, but the day seemed to have dawned with the promise of thunder and lightning.

Perhaps the storm had begun with Feely's wedding, and the realization that I had lost another member of my family.

It was all so infernally complicated. The wish to be surrounded by those of the same blood made me want to be alone. It didn't make sense.

I'll admit I was being hard on myself, and consequently, on others around me.

How, for instance, could I have been so insensitive to drag Dogger with me on the rails of the London Necropolis Railway? Why hadn't I been more sensitive to the fact that the trip would trigger horrific memories of his own forced labor on the Death Railway in Burma?

What was happening to me? Why was I suddenly a hornet's nest of emotions?

These questions and others were shooting like bolts of lightning through my mind as Mrs. Mullet and I hung on to each other for dear life.

For dear life.

Yes, that was it! Life *was* dear, in every sense of the word. You just needed to remember it in the dark.

I was trying to think of a way of breaking the clinch without embarrassment when the kitchen door swung open and Dogger appeared.

"I beg your pardon," he said quietly when he saw us, and turned to leave.

"It's all right, Dogger," I said. "We were just congratulating each other on a job well done."

Which didn't explain the tears, but Dogger was a rock of discretion.

"I've made up the two rooms on either side of the Blue Bedroom for Miss Pursemaker and Miss Stonebrook," he said. "I thought they might appreciate private accommodations."

"I'm sure you're right, Dogger," I told him. "They're probably tired of shared tents."

The Blue Bedroom on the north front of the house was reserved for Aunt Felicity when she visited. All of the other rooms in that long, dark, private wing were preserved in mothballs, their furniture draped in dusty bedsheets for as long as I could remember.

Even after all these years, the rooms still reeked of naphthalene and para-dichlorobenzene: the stuff used by entomologists in their killing jars, which came in colorful tins and boxes labeled with such charming names as Paracide (I'm not making this up!) and Krystal Gas.

Needless to say, there were no moths at Buckshaw.

For anyone with eyes to see, the place was a poisoner's paradise. Even my late mother Harriet's fur coats were kept in perpetual storage in the museum that had been her bedroom, having been carefully washed with a mixture of water and corrosive sublimate: mercuric chloride, which was also used as a preservative bath for railway sleepers (the wooden ones under the rails, not the rolling ones such as those travelers on the Orient Express).

Thomas Tusser, that great—and underrated—poet of the sixteenth century, a man ahead of his times in matters of poison, had warned of the dangers to a household:

> Take heede how thou laiest the bane for the rats,
> for poisoning servant, thy selfe and thy brats.

Actually, distant diggings such as the north front of the house might make our lady Missioners feel more at home, being nearly as far off the beaten track as French

Equatorial Africa, although Buckshaw was certainly much colder and more drafty.

Even our antiquated plumbing would be a dream of splendor to ladies accustomed to powdering their noses in the underbrush.

"I'd better go up and give them the old formal welcome," I said.

It was difficult to realize that I was now the Chatelaine of Buckshaw, and that onto my shoulders fell all the necessities of civility. I'd have to be a quick study.

"Shall I ask them down for tea?" I asked, giving Mrs. Mullet a cautious glance.

"Bit early for that, dear," she replied, glancing at the kitchen clock. "It's barely gone ten. P'raps a potluck elevenses. They'll 'ave to take their chances along with the rest of us."

"Welcome to Buckshaw," I said in a loud, official voice, showing an unnecessary amount of tooth. Having reached the stage of needing to wear my braces only at night, I was no longer ashamed to display my mouthful of dental artistry.

I had taken up a position at the bottom of the west staircase, the better to welcome our unwelcome visitors.

"And how did you find your rooms?" I demanded.

"Quite commodious," Ardella said (she of the hatchet face). "We've opened all the windows."

"Ah!" I said, making a tent of my fingers under my

chin. "To let out the ghosts, of course. They appreciate a chance to float across the Visto now and then. They're awfully fond of fresh air."

I said this in a jovial voice with just enough lightness to make them think I was joking. But, nevertheless, the seed was planted.

"Ghosts?" Miss Stonebrook asked, grasping the banister.

"Oh, don't worry," I told her. "They're actually quite harmless. The most recent exorcism has reduced them to no more than nuisances.

"No more dragging chains," I added, with a slightly mad chuckle. "No more icy hands at the throats of sleepers."

"Nonsense," Miss Pursemaker said loudly, taking a step down toward me. "There are no such things as ghosts."

"Well," I said with an indulgent smile. "We mustn't forget that the Witch of Endor called up the ghost of Samuel for Saul. It's in the first book of Samuel. Chapter twenty-eight, I believe."

As if I could ever forget it. On a winter night at Evensong, the vicar had preached a sermon on the text which had left me shattered. There in the darkness of St. Tancred's, lit only by the light of the flickering candles, with the wind howling outside at the ancient stones and the stained-glass windows, his hovering words had confirmed my worst fears: The dead are never truly dead. They never leave us.

"Nonsense," Miss Pursemaker repeated. "Certain tales are meant to be taken only as parables. They are instructional in nature."

"Ah, well then!" I said in a cheery voice, plastering a look of idiot relief onto my face. "Who's for elevenses? Unless I'm mistaken, the good Mrs. Mullet has laid on scones and tea."

"And gin!" shouted Undine, who had appeared suddenly at my elbow.

I spun her round and marched her out of the room, her arm twisted up behind her back just far enough to know I meant business.

Whatever had become of maidenly modesty?

In the drawing room, we sat in a civilized manner, cups balanced on laps, as if we had evolved eons since our days of swinging from the trees.

Dogger, who had strategically reverted to his role as butler, stood silently by with the slightest of smiles on his face.

"You simply *must* tell us about Africa," I said to the ladies. "You must be so awfully brave to have gone there, mustn't they, Undine?"

Undine peeled back her upper lip and let out an alarming gibbering noise.

"You mustn't pay her any attention," I told the Missioners. "She has seen too many Tarzan films at the cinema."

With wrists bent inward almost to breaking, Undine scratched herself vigorously under both armpits.

"I understand you were with Dr. Schweitzer in Lambaréné," I said, pronouncing the name of the place as if it rhymed with "gabardine."

"In *Lom-bar-EN-neh*, yes." Miss Pursemaker curled her lip and put the full French accent on the name.

"And how was it?" I pressed. "Not that you'll want to tell us, of course. You must have seen some dreadful things."

Miss Stonebrook was already nodding vigorously in agreement with my words.

There are people on this planet who live for the approval of others, but I am not one of them. I personally don't give a rat's ruby eyes what other people think, but I can readily slip inside the skin of those who do.

I smiled at Miss Stonebrook.

Encouraged, she leaned forward and shrilled in a confidential tone, "Although, if the truth be told, the doctor *could* be something of a martinet."

Miss Pursemaker glanced up sharply, skewering her companion with a look that might have handled a whole hog on a spit.

"Nonsense," she said. "The man was a saint, and like all saints, he had his trials. You exaggerate, Ardella."

Put in her place, Ardella retreated into her teacup.

"What I meant was," I said, "you must have had to deal with some of the most horrid tropical diseases: leprosy, malaria, river blindness, and so forth. And you must have had to battle the dreaded Congo floor maggot fly."

Dogger had described to me in detail these remarkable creatures that extracted blood from their sleeping victims.

"And of course," I said, abruptly changing the subject, a tactic I had picked up from the unwitting Inspector

Hewitt, "you must have come across many of the quaint native customs?"

Of course, I didn't want to give the thing away by mentioning the ordeal beans outright. I would let them lead me to the topic of their own accord.

But Miss Pursemaker was not to be led.

"Hardly fit for drawing room discussion," she said, with another warning glance at Miss Stonebrook. "Needless to say, we look forward to a restful stay at Buckshaw. You must entrust us with your recipe for scones, Mrs. Mullet. It's been simply ages since we feasted in so grand a fashion."

She made an elaborate sign of the cross over her third scone and jammed it into her mouth.

"And where is your sister Daphne?" Miss Stonebrook asked. "Mrs. Richardson said we would quite enjoy meeting her."

"Oh, she's in the library," I replied. "Working on her memoirs."

"Her memoirs?" Miss Stonebrook was agog.

"Yes. She decided that, with our sister Ophelia married, she would concentrate full-time on her book."

This was quite true. Daffy had determined to write one of those partially factual and partially fabricated autobiographies about her eccentric family.

"I already have a working title," she had told me: "*Horseflies in the Mayonnaise*. I shall become filthy rich and be interviewed on the wireless, wearing tinted glasses. It's all very well if you want to spend your life sitting around on sodden churchyard moss, but if I don't escape from this damp pile I shall have to have my bones replaced before I'm twenty."

"Fancy that," Miss Stonebrook said, referring to Daffy's memoirs.

"She doesn't like to be disturbed," I told them. "Authors can't stand anyone's words but their own."

I gave a rueful little grimace, as if I were an insider.

"Well then," Miss Pursemaker said, setting her cup and saucer on the table with a distinct clatter of china on wood. "We shall retire to our rooms for a rest. We had barely any sleep last night at the vicarage, what with the choir practice and so forth."

"And none whatsoever the previous three nights at Balsam Cottage," Miss Stonebrook bleated, determined to have the last word. "We are quite unaccustomed to the din of ringing telephones, aren't we, Doris. Altogether barbaric, when you come to think of it."

· TEN ·

I COULDN'T WAIT TO be rid of them. I wanted to shoo the two Missioners up the stairs and into their beds like a gaggle of geese, but as Mistress of Buckshaw, I had to maintain a veneer of polish. My questions about the ordeal beans would have to wait until another time.

"Sleep well," I managed, as their feet vanished up among the banisters.

I went back to the drawing room where Dogger was waiting. We pulled up a couple of chairs and tucked into what was left of the food.

"Did you hear what she said?" I asked, meaning Miss Stonebrook. "They stayed overnight at Balsam Cottage for three nights before moving to the rectory."

"So it would seem," Dogger said. "And yet there was no trace of them when we—ah—reconnoitered the place."

"What kind of missionary takes care to erase their tracks when they change sleeping places?" I wondered.

"In the jungle, probably all of them," Dogger replied. "In Bishop's Lacey—well, that does present a pretty problem."

It was fortunate that we were such keen trackers, I thought. But hold on! Had we forgotten something?

"Did you check the rubbish bins?" I asked. I had completely overlooked them.

"I did indeed," Dogger said. "The debris was that of a single inhabitant, Mrs. Prill. Single tins, single newspapers, single envelopes. No sign of communal feasting or otherwise."

Whatever he meant by that.

"Single envelopes?" I asked, my ears perking up. "Were there letters in the rubbish bin?"

"Envelopes only," Dogger said. "Two from Dr. Brocken, at Gollingford Abbey. Consecutive dates."

"Hold on!" I said, leaping up out of my chair. "Wouldn't these prove beyond a doubt that he wasn't gaga?"

"Even if he were"—Dogger smiled—"he must have been in remission four and five days ago. Those were the dates postmarked on the letters addressed to his daughter, in what I take to be his handwriting. Elderly, but certainly not incompetent."

"You left them for Inspector Hewitt to find, of course?"

Dogger nodded.

"I wonder what he'll make of them."

"He'll have no trouble tracking down the sender," Dogger replied. "I should think we have less than twenty-four hours."

I couldn't have agreed with him more—but where were we to start?

"Two letters in two days," I said, "suggests a regular communication between Dr. Brocken and his daughter. And Miss Stonebrook, you will remember, complained about telephones ringing in the night at Balsam Cottage. Are Mrs. Prill and her father still involved in an ongoing business? And if so, what?"

"We might begin," Dogger said, "by assuming that the two letters from her father are among those Mrs. Prill wished to pretend had been stolen."

"That sounds reasonable," I agreed. "I wouldn't expect that a lady in her circumstances receives bags of mail."

"A good point," Dogger said.

"But where ought we to begin?" I asked. "Balsam Cottage is out of bounds for as long as the police wish it to be. Which leaves another visit to Gollingford Abbey."

Although it may make me sound ghoulish, a return visit to Dr. Brocken—under the pretense of offering our condolences, of course—would perhaps allow us to obtain a sample of his handwriting, even if we had to rummage without mercy through his personal belongings.

But much as I would welcome another chance to snoop around the dismal abbey, there was one great drawback: I didn't want to subject Dogger to the mental tortures of another trip on the former London Necropolis Railway. Memories, I was coming to realize, can be sharper than daggers.

The answer came to me instantly. I would make the journey alone.

"Or perhaps," Dogger said with a slight smile, "the information we seek—or at least some of it—can be found a little closer to home."

I gave him a puzzled look. And then the sun broke through the clouds.

"Of course!" I exclaimed. "The two Missioners. Miss Pursemaker and Miss Stonebrook! They spent several nights at Balsam Cottage. They left nothing behind. Therefore, if they didn't dispose of anything at the vicarage, they brought it with them and it is now here at Buckshaw. Tallyho, the north front! Tah-rah!"

"Excellent," Dogger said, and I glowed like the summer sun.

"We'll have to wait, of course, until they're well away from their rooms. And we'll need to be certain when they're coming back."

"I've always believed," Dogger remarked, "that a nice drive in the country is a most healthful restorative."

"Would you?" I cried excitedly. "Oh, Dogger, you are— you are—"

I ran out of words.

"Something historical, I fancy," Dogger continued. "Ahab's Tower, perhaps, which has the great advantage of being an hour away by automobile."

"Two hours to have a good old rummage!" I said, clapping my hands together. "That ought to be more than enough time."

Ahab's Tower was a Georgian folly near Churningham, built to mark some remarkable but long-forgotten occasion. It had been owned more recently, in Victorian

times, by an acolyte of David Livingstone of "Dr. Livingstone, I presume" fame. (To which question, I remembered, Livingstone's less-than-inspired reply had been
"Yes.")

The ladies, when they came downstairs from their
naps, seemed remarkably refreshed.

"The quiet," Miss Stonebrook said.

"The *blessed* quiet," Miss Pursemaker added.

"Miss Flavia has suggested a drive in the country,"
Dogger told them. "I have taken the liberty of bringing
the car to the door. Ahab's Tower has interesting connections with Dr. Livingstone. I am given to believe that the
additional decorations on some of the later crenellations
contain certain oblique or obscure references to his missionary work in Africa. Perhaps you would be good
enough to explain them to me? I should be greatly in your
debt."

I had seldom heard Dogger utter so many words at one
time.

"Ah," said Miss Pursemaker, rubbing her hands together with cheery enthusiasm. "A student of Equatorial
Evangelism, are you?"

"A student of tropical medicine," Dogger said, and I
gasped at his frankness.

Somewhere in Dogger's past, a first-class medical education lay in ruins. Much of the mystery was shrouded by
the mists of war and time, and I had realized not long ago
that I would probably never know the entire truth of it.

"Excellent," Miss Stonebrook said, actually patting
him on the arm. "Our sorry world could use more enthu-

siasts of your particular breed, Mr. Dogger. And so, shall we away?"

She was almost dancing now on tiptoe.

Was she flirting with Dogger? I couldn't be sure, but the possibility was there. Perhaps she had visions of setting up a little hospital in the jungle, up a cozy river somewhere away from the hustle and bustle of civilization; a place where she could park her Bible and her blackboard in the shade of a rainproof canvas canopy and read to the natives about the conversion of Saint Paul on the road to Damascus as Dogger injected them with chloroquine against malaria.

Oh, well. Never mind. Dogger was more than capable of looking after himself.

As soon as they were out the door, I was up the stairs like a freshly lubricated thunderbolt.

With Daffy at work on her memoirs in the library, Undine off stalking rabbits on the Visto, and Mrs. Mullet gone for the day, the house lay in an utter hush. Only the occasional unsettling gurgle of the plumbing system broke the silence.

Fortunately for me, people who live in country houses don't generally lock their bedroom doors. In fact, they probably couldn't even if they wanted to. The keys to the various Buckshaw bedrooms had likely been lost back in the days of my ancestors Antony and William de Luce who, after a sharp difference of political opinion at the time of the Crimean War, had caused a black dividing line to be painted across the vestibule. It was a line which was not, ever, under any circumstances, to be crossed by the other: a situation which, although less evident, still divided our family in one cruel way or another, down the years to this very day.

I opened the door of the bedroom immediately to the east of the Blue Bedroom and stepped inside. I went at once to one of the tall Georgian windows. At the far end of the avenue of chestnuts, the Rolls was just disappearing through the Mulford Gates.

I had all the time in the world.

First things first, I thought. Luggage, with its locks, could be most potentially time-consuming. And besides, one piece of the ladies' luggage had been placed conveniently on a mahogany stand at the end of the bed.

As an adept picker of locks, an art learned from Dogger with both of us on our knees in front of countless doorjambs, I was ready for—in fact looking forward to—a jolly good tweaking of the old pin tumblers, but it was not to be. The suitcase, a large, battered thing of soft leather hide, enmeshed in sturdy straps, had a pair of sliding chromium-plated lever locks, which sprang open at a touch. I undid the buckles and lifted the lid.

Curses! It was completely empty. The suitcase had already been unpacked.

With my fingertips, I felt the lining carefully for hidden pockets, but without success. There were no irregularities in the surface beneath, which was as smooth as the heavy watered silk that lined it.

I crossed the room and opened the clothespress. In it were hanging a nightdress of white Dorcas cambric in the style so favored by governesses, a blue-patterned dress, and a weather-worn mackintosh. At the bottom were neatly arranged a pair of carpet slippers and a pair of sensible brown oxfords, which I examined carefully. There were, to my disappointment, no hollow heels, no retractable linings, and no stowage for valuables in the toes.

"Cranberries," I said under my breath, and turned my attention to the dresser, beginning with the bottom drawer, because of the old saying "Always save the best for last."

In spite of that, I couldn't help letting out a low whistle as the contents came sliding out into the light of the room: in the drawer was folded a wire and wicker framework of such savage corsetry as might once, in ancient times, have been applied in dungeons to damsels in distress.

Who, in their right mind, would strap themselves into such an instrument of torture? And, more important, *why*?

The dress in the clothespress had already told me that I was looking at the belongings of Miss Stonebrook. Why would a woman of her already substantial heft add to it by climbing into such a suit of hidden armor? It didn't make sense.

In circumstances such as these, the mind runs riot.

Could Miss Stonebrook possibly be an imposter? Had she added to her bulk in order to pull the wool over the keen eyes of His (or was it now Her?) Majesty's Board of Customs and Excise while disembarking from French West Africa? Had the woman lined her linens with bags of smuggled dope, hanging beneath her skirt and bodice like Christmas turkeys in a poulterer's window?

Might she have contracted some horror of a subequatorial plague which had turned her bones and muscles to a quivering jelly, making her able to walk only with the support of this dreadful makeshift outer skeleton of wire and cane?

Or was she suffering from some other loathsome tropical disease? Some blackwater fever that covered her skin with bloody blisters that burst at the very touch of fabric?

I examined the contraption closely for further clues. In spite of its cobwebs of struts and stays and lacing, there appeared to be no parts of it hidden. The thing was like nothing so much as a dirigible with the skin off, or a bird-cage from an alien world.

For now, it must remain a mystery. The search must go on.

The more obvious spots—such as under the mattress, behind the curtains, under the rug, and in the chamber pot—yielded nothing. I checked for loose bed knobs, overturned chairs to examine the upholstery, and took down pictures from the wall.

And then I spotted the Bible: hidden in plain sight on the bedside table. I fell upon it like a wolf, riffling through the crisp pages in search of telltale markings, remembering that a well-thumbed Bible is most worn away at its owner's worst sins.

But something wasn't right here. I knew it instinctively before the rational part of my brain stepped in. It took a moment for the truth to hit me: The book was too new.

A missionary's Bible ought to be read to ribbons, the

pages tattered and torn, the binding loose, with penciled notes illuminating the text from beginning to end.

But the leaves of this book stuck together as if with static electricity, due to the electrical charge between the paper and the ink. It had barely been opened.

I turned my way back to the title page:

The HOLY BIBLE [it said]
Containing the
Old and New Testaments
Revised Standard Version
Translated from the original tongues
Being the version set forth A.D. 1611
Revised A.D. 1881–1885 and A.D. 1901
Compared with the most ancient authorities
And revised A.D. 1952

The book had been published by Thomas Nelson & Sons, of Toronto, New York, and Edinburgh.

At the bottom of the page, just above the name of the publishers, had been written in black ink: Presented to Ardella Stonebrook by her friend, Dymphna Locke and the date August 17th, 1952—not much more than a month ago!

Scribbled underneath this inscription, in pencil, was the message: Ardella: Under strict embargo till publication date Oct. 8th /52. Keep for personal use only until then.

Following this were the initials D.L.

Dymphna Locke. Whoever she may be.

I read the date again: Oct. 8th/52.

Which wasn't for another ten days or so. This book had not yet been published!

It was what Daffy would call an "advance copy," for internal circulation only before the official publication date.

What could I deduce about the mysterious Dymphna Locke? Well, to begin with, she was probably American or Canadian, given the probable origin of the book and the style in which she wrote the date. Had she been British, she'd have written *8th Oct.* rather than *Oct. 8th.*

A small point, but a telling one, nonetheless.

How had an as-yet-unpublished American Bible come into the hands of a woman freshly returned from French Equatorial Africa? Had she used it at all? Or was she obeying strictly the command to wait until the 8th of October?

Why would she do so? Was she afraid of something? Perhaps she was just too busy.

Still, most missionaries would make daily use of a Bible.

It was then that it came to me: a trick Daffy had taught me one rainy afternoon in the library at Buckshaw. It was this:

A new book has a memory. While the pages are stiff and fresh, it will open naturally—if one is careful—to any page or pages to which it has previously been opened.

It was necessary to do this with great care, letting the book itself decide.

I took a deep breath and relaxed. Holding the Bible as

lightly as possible in both hands, I ran a forefinger across the edges of the pages, trying to sense any lessening of resistance. With one thumb on the front cover and the other on the back, I applied a minuscule amount of outward pressure.

Did the book open more easily? Perhaps it was my imagination, but I felt it had. I was almost afraid to read the page.

This whole technique was perilously close to the method used by some to tell the future, or to act as an oracle: the sticking of a finger into a random page at a random line and taking the resulting text as gospel.

Because prognostication was frowned upon in the Church of England, I kept my forefingers out of the way and let my eyes fall upon the page.

I needn't have bothered. Two of the verses were already underlined powerfully in pencil:

2 Samuel 5:23: *And when David inquired of the LORD, he said, "You shall not go up; go around to their rear, and come upon them opposite the balsam trees."*

2 Samuel 5:24: *"And when you hear the sound of marching in the tops of the balsam trees, then bestir yourself; for then the LORD has gone out before you to smite the army of the Philistines."*

Hold on a minute, I thought. *What in heaven's name is going on here?*

Balsam trees? Since when were there balsam trees in Samuel? And what did the author mean by God marching in the tops of them? Was He weightless whenever He wanted to be, or was He an accomplished ventriloquist, like Undine?

That would have to wait till another time.

I thought I knew my Samuel as well as any reasonably attentive Sunday School and Bible Class student. And there *were* no balsam trees in Samuel. *Mulberry* trees, yes. Balsam trees, no.

I had already cited 1 Samuel to Miss Pursemaker and Miss Stonebrook as evidence of the very real existence of ghosts.

Ghosts, yes: but balsam trees, no.

Could this mean that Samuel was mistaken also about the ghosts?

In any case, it was immediately obvious that this so-called Revised Standard Version of the Bible was in powerful disagreement with the King James Version.

A balsam is not a mulberry, take my word for it. I have extracted the essential oils of both, and I know the difference, both chemically and otherwise.

In the first place, it is a simple matter of fact, in spite of Samuel, that there are no balsams and no mulberries in the Holy Land. The tree mistaken by our Bible translators for mulberry is probably an aspen of the willow family with the name *Populus euphratica*, which contains— besides diterpenic acids, hydroxy fatty acids, triterpenic alcohols, and phenolic glycerides—a substantial amount of cinnamyl cinnamate ($C_{18}H_{16}O_2$), whereas balm of Gilead, *Commiphora opobalsamum*, contains a resin resembling bassorin, or tragacanthic acid, which is the water-insoluble component of gum tragacanth—the other being, of course, tragacanthin.

The word "tragacanth," for what it's worth, comes from two Greek words meaning, respectively, "goat" and "thorn," which tells one all one really needs to know about this otherwise dreary plant.

The point, though, was this: Why were passages referring to balsam underlined in a Bible belonging to a missionary from French West Africa who had recently spent several nights under the roof of a woman—now deceased—whose father had made his fortune from the stuff?

Phew!

It was enough to put kinks in your brain.

The connection, though, seemed to me beyond coincidence.

I replaced the Bible on the table, taking great care to align it precisely as it had been beside Miss Stonebrook's battered alarm clock, a timepiece with a luminous dial about the size of a pocket watch but standing up on cleverly contrived little legs that reminded me of the dish running away with the spoon.

Just to be sure, I had the back off the thing in a flash, but other than the silently whirring clockwork mechanism, there was nothing to see. I wanted to hurl it at the wall.

Time was flying and there was still another room to search.

I had already looked in all the usual places: underneath the mattress and pillows, under the carpet (the usual place to hide letters, except in springtime when floor coverings were taken outside for their annual beating), behind the draperies, and so forth, but nothing of interest had come to light.

After a quick review and a close look at the tooth powder (Thymol—"Specially recommended to arrest the germs of dental decay") and the toothbrush itself (an Army & Navy Perfected model, with Xylonite handle, which was designed no doubt to resist jungle rot), it was with some relief that I closed the door and made my way past the Blue Bedroom to the chamber assigned to Miss Pursemaker.

·ELEVEN·

As did the previous room, Miss Pursemaker's bed-room looked north over the forecourt to the avenue of poplars and the Mulford Gates beyond. Although it was too early for the return of the Missioners, when you're on the snoop, it never hurts to check.

It was good, in a way, that the window had been left wide open. In case of their sudden or unexpected return, I would hear the tires of the Rolls on the gravel sweep at the front door in plenty of time to make my escape.

Which was ironic, when you came to think of it. Because Buckshaw now belonged to me, I had every right to be anywhere I wanted to be within its walls—decency and common courtesy aside, of course.

Why sneak about in my own house? Besides, if I were caught out unexpectedly, I could always claim I had smelled smoke: a cover-all excuse that would provide an alibi for even the worst nosy parker. Be prepared, as the Boy Scouts are so fond of saying.

Although I had never been a member of that organization, I *had* for a time, before being drummed out, belonged to its sister group, the Girl Guides, just long enough to realize that most of the arts and skill taught to their young members were nothing new: They were merely updated refinements of the wily tricks known to every tight-corseted Georgian lady and every Victorian spinster. Knowing precisely when to smell smoke, when to faint, when to see your dead Auntie Winnie in the drawing room, and when to hear a cat walled up behind the bricks is a set of tricks that desperately needs reviving. I have often thought that I ought to open a school.

In Miss Pursemaker's room, although I began with the Bible, it was a rich disappointment: no names, no earnest inscriptions, no underlining. It was a plain black Bible of workmanlike construction, King James Version, in an English Revised Version with no visible publication date, but it smelled as if it had been absorbing its surroundings since the later part of the last century.

Reluctantly, I moved on to the drawers of the dresser, which contained just what you would expect: a selection of severe pieces of underclothing of an old-fashioned nature: bloomers, stockings, garters (industrial grade), and so on. A pair of hunting breeches and a wool shirt, a silk blouse of ecclesiastical blue: nothing to excite my interest. The clothespress was hardly more revealing: a Norfolk jacket; a pair of brown brogues, or walking shoes; and two umbrellas, one white, the other black. I opened them wide (bad luck be hanged) to check for contraband and found nothing but the usual wire ribs.

On the washstand: toothpaste, toothbrush, brush and comb set (again, like Miss Stonebrook's, backed with some kind of black material, gutta-percha, perhaps, or even India rubber. There is no call for silver—even of the electroplated variety—in the jungle.).

I examined the brush and comb for hairs, but they were hopelessly clean.

After giving the room a thorough turning out, I had found nothing more than a pair of small surgical scissors which I had lost a couple of years ago when examining the wallpapers at Buckshaw for arsenic.

How frustrating it was! These two women were no more than they appeared to be: a couple of Missioners home on furlough from the tropics.

That was when the brainwave struck. I hadn't checked their car.

It made good sense that if anything were to be kept from prying eyes, the best spot for concealment was not necessarily in the house of a stranger. A hired car, on the other hand, had lockable compartments in which private belongings could be safely stored.

Dogger had parked the Morgan three-wheeler out of sight in the coach house.

There was a sudden crunching on the gravel outside. A vehicle had stopped at the front door. Curses! They were back far sooner than I had anticipated. A hurried glance out the window revealed Dogger already out of the

Rolls, holding open the back door, and Miss Pursemaker helping out a shaky Miss Stonebrook.

I bolted for the west wing and clattered down the back stairs. With only moments to spare I made for the kitchen just as the front door opened, and I heard Miss Pursemaker's voice in the foyer saying, "Steady on, Ardella. We're almost there."

If I were speedy enough, I could get to the coach house and back before anyone realized I was gone. Through the kitchen garden I fled, as if the Hounds of Hell were after me, even though it wasn't strictly necessary. Still, it is a sign of maturity to be able to motivate oneself, as Aunt Felicity never tires of telling me.

The coach house lay, as it always has, in gloom and shadows beyond the garden. It was here that Harriet's Rolls had lain in state on wooden blocks, before Dogger had, not so long ago, resurrected it in the dead of night to save my life. Time here seemed to have stopped, and in the heavy silence, it seemed always that some defunct de Luce was about to glide soundlessly out of one of the empty horse stalls to tap me on the shoulder.

There had been a time when Father had come to this place to sit in mourning and reflect upon his unhappy state, and I had found that, since his death last winter, he was more present here than he had ever been in life.

I shivered at the thought.

I wasn't proud of what I was about to do. And yet, if I was being called by my profession to rifle someone else's belongings with my father's ghost, like Hamlet's, peering peevishly over my shoulder, then so be it. In view of his own life experiences, I was sure he would understand.

The Morgan lay in shadows in the farthest corner. With its canvas roof folded down into the convertible luggage rack, there was no need for a door key. I could simply reach inside.

The glove box was just an open hole in the walnut dashboard. I could see at a glance that it was empty. There were no elasticized pockets in the doors.

Because of the scarcity of hiding places, my search was going to be a relatively straightforward one.

Where, I wondered, *would I hide my belongings in such a simple machine?*

The answer seemed obvious: under the seats.

I opened the door—which groaned a horrible metallic groan—and squeezed a hand under one of the bucket seats.

It was a tight fit. My fingers crept across the wooden floorboards like an exploring spider. They touched upon something hard and solid. I seized it between fingers and thumb and gently pulled it forward from beneath the seat.

A box! By all that was holy, a tin box!

Well done, Flavia! Go to the top of the class.

Even in the gloom of the coach house I could see that the box was one which had originally contained tablets of quinine dihydrochloride: five hundred of them, in fact, with a strength of five grains each.

Although I was familiar enough with this alkaloid in the laboratory, I had no idea whatsoever of its uses in medicine. I knew only that it was extracted from the bark of the *cinchona* shrub. For further enlightenment, I was going to require a consultation with Dogger.

As I gave the tin a shake, it made a slight rattling noise: nothing at all like the clatter you would expect medicinal tablets to produce.

Carefully—because it had been in the jungle, and you never knew—I lifted the lid.

Inside was a packet of darning needles, a couple of cards of Chadwick's black mending cotton, a small pair of surgical scissors (not unlike those of my own which I had just rediscovered in Miss Pursemaker's room), a half dozen safety pins in assorted sizes, a couple of buttons (likewise black), and two mummified cigarettes (which by their vile smell—yes, I sniffed them—could only have been made of the stalks and roots of *Datura stramonium,* the deadly thorn apple). I had once found a tin of these cigarettes—produced for asthmatics—at the back of a drawer in my chemical laboratory. My late uncle Tarquin had cured himself permanently of asthma immediately after his father died.

Until then, Uncle Tar had grown the deadly poisonous stuff in the kitchen garden, where it was still to be found if you knew where to look. I had once pointed it out to Daffy, who remarked that Uncle Tar wasn't the only one: Marcel Proust had written to his mother of having such a severe attack of asthma that he was obliged to walk doubled up, with his nose running, from one tobacconist's shop to the next, lighting an antiasthma cigarette at each stop.

"With Uncle Tar, the *father*," she said with a knowing look. "And with Proust, the *mother*."

At that point she had fled a hornet that emerged from an apple tree, and our first civilized conversation in years had been left hanging in midair.

I returned my attention to the tin box.

Folded in the bottom, underneath the miscellaneous bric-a-brac, was a single sheet of water-stained cigarette paper. I extracted it carefully with two fingers and flattened it out.

On it was written, in pencil:

Dr. Augustus Brocken, Gollingford Abbey, Pirbright.

I was fairly bursting at the seams to share my find with Dogger, but when I walked into the kitchen, he was not alone. He was handing Miss Stonebrook a cup of black coffee. She was sitting straight-backed in a kitchen chair, clutching her chest and wheezing heavily, with Miss Pursemaker standing behind her.

Miss Stonebrook's lips were going blue. Our conversation would have to wait.

"Caffeine is said to be helpful," Dogger was saying. "It will provide temporary relief until Dr. Darby arrives."

But rather than being grateful, Miss Stonebrook roughly shoved Dogger's hand away.

"No," she said in a strangled voice. "No coffee."

"She never touches the stuff," Miss Pursemaker told us. "Her family forbade it."

Was Miss Stonebrook a Mormon? I wondered. I was too polite to ask. Tea and coffee were forbidden by the Latter-Day Saints: that I had learned from a remarkably informative article in *The Strand Magazine.*

Still, I thought, *it's like Jack Sprat and his wife, isn't it; he*

could eat no fat and his wife could eat no lean? Mrs. Prill re-
fused tea and Miss Stonebrook would not take coffee. Signifi-
cant? Only time would tell.

At that very moment the doorbell rang, and Dogger moved soundlessly out of the room. Moments later he was back with Dr. Darby.

As the senior partner in the sole medical practice in Bishop's Lacey, Dr. Darby was everything a country practitioner ought to be: round, red, and possessed of many chins. Confidence radiated from his person as heat radiates from a kitchen cooker.

"Um . . . what's all this, then?" the doctor said jovially, producing a crystal mint from somewhere about his ample person and popping it into his mouth as he placed his black medical bag on the kitchen table.

"Bronchial asthmatic attack," Miss Pursemaker said. "She's had them before."

"Recently?" Dr. Darby asked, examining the patient.

"In Africa. Perhaps two months ago."

"And the treatment?" Dr. Darby inquired. "Would you happen to know?"

"I *ought* to know." Miss Pursemaker sniffed. "I was with her in the infirmary. It was Arsenicum album."

"Ah," said Dr. Darby, ignoring Miss Pursemaker and addressing Miss Stonebrook directly, "you are a disciple of the late Dr. Hahnemann."

Miss Stonebrook nodded, gasping for breath.

"Dr. Hahnemann," Dr. Darby said, addressing us as if he were a drawing room entertainer, "believed that like cures like. That arsenic, because it causes convulsions, may be used to *treat* convulsions, if diluted, of course, to a ten-thousandth or a trillionth of its original strength."

I could read nothing from his tone. Dr. Darby was a charming conversationalist, no more.

"And what is this?" he asked, lifting between finger and thumb what looked like a black shoelace that encircled Miss Stonebrook's neck. As the cord came away, a small black sack rose up out of her cleavage.

Miss Stonebrook snatched at it, but a sudden paroxysm of wheezing caused her hand to fall aside as Dr. Darby whisked the bag out of her reach.

"If I'm not mistaken," he said, "this will be the very substance of which we were just speaking: Arsenicum album, which is a dilution of what the *British Pharmacopoeia* delights to call Arseni trioxidum—arsenic trioxide to the likes of you and me."

What a joy it was to hear someone speak my language! Like meeting a fellow earthling on the far side of Jupiter.

Miss Stonebrook, showing the whites of her eyes, glanced guiltily at the little sack.

"How long have you been toting this about?" Dr. Darby carefully but firmly removed the cord from around her neck and placed the little black sack in his medical bag.

Miss Stonebrook shrugged.

"Well, no matter," Dr. Darby said. "It's a shot of aqueous epinephrine for you, old girl. Adrenaline. Don't worry, it's as natural as the nose on your face. It'll soon set you right."

He reached into his bag and the injection was given in the blink of an eye.

"And," Dr. Darby added, "for the rest of us—umm . . . a crystal mint."

He handed round his bag of sweets, watching each of us intently as we helped ourselves.

"You may take her up to her room," he told Miss Pursemaker. "Bed rest is advised. I shall leave a prescription."

Dogger offered his arm as Miss Stonebrook arose slowly from her chair, giving each of us a grim smile.

"Come along, Ardella," Miss Pursemaker said, and the two of them shuffled from the room, Miss Stonebrook now hanging heavily upon her companion's arm.

"What was the inciting incident?" Dr. Darby asked Dogger, as soon as the door had closed.

"We had stopped at Moleslip," Dogger replied, "on our way to Churningham and Ahab's Tower. Miss Stonebrook felt suddenly unwell and insisted that a bottle of smelling salts would set her right. Next door to the chemist's shop was a newsagent, *The Hinley Chronicle* prominently displayed in the window. The headline concerned the death of Mrs. Prill."

"Ah, yes," Dr. Darby said. "I saw it. Rather garish. *Foul Play Suspected in Death of Local Woman*. Intended to be titillating. They have people who stay awake nights to dream up these things, you know."

"But was it?" I said excitedly. "Foul play, I mean?"

"Ah, Flavia." Dr. Darby frowned. "You know better than to ask me that."

When the doctor had gone, Dogger and I sat at the kitchen table, alone at last.

"Quinine dihydrochloride tablets," I said. "What are they prescribed for?"

"Ah," Dogger said. "I deduce that you've searched the ladies' Morgan. Well done."

My jaw fell onto my chest.

Dogger smiled. "We would not be amiss," he continued, "to assume that the tablets, if actually taken, were self-prescribed for malaria. The tin which once contained five hundred tablets would suggest that it came from a hospital dispensary. Such quantities are seldom put directly into the hands of a patient."

"And the fact that the tin was emptied, and is now being used as a housewife's kit . . ."

"Indeed." Dogger nodded. "We have no notion of whether she still keeps a supply."

"Not in her room," I said. "I searched it."

"Excellent." Dogger smiled. "I trusted you would.

"Oddly enough," he added, "in practice, quinine is best given as a mixture, since all the salts of quinine, however administered, are reduced to the base in the duodenum before being absorbed into the bloodstream."

"Do you think Miss Stonebrook may still be suffering from malaria?"

"It's quite possible," Dogger said. "Even treated professionally, the relapse rate is fifty or sixty percent. Dr. Darby will no doubt have questioned her closely."

"It's not contagious, is it?" My arms were growing goosebumps at the thought.

"No," Dogger said. "Malaria can only be contracted

from the bite of the *Anopheles* mosquito, a most interesting parasite, which exists in at least fifty known species, none of them, fortunately, resident in this scepter'd isle."

"John of Gaunt's speech in *Richard II*," I said. I prided myself on spotting Dogger's reference. The BBC wireless is useful for more than just farm operas.

" 'This fortress built by Nature for herself,' " I said, continuing the quotation from Shakespeare, my blood thrilling at the words. " 'Against infection and the hand of war.' "

Dogger applauded.

"Well done, Miss Flavia. Well done, indeed."

I was hot with blushes. Dogger seldom gave praise, and when he did, it was like rain after an age of drought and famine.

I made a vow that instant, that I would memorize every word of every play and every poem of Shakespeare, even if it took me a lifetime. It would be more than worth it!

Besides, Daffy would be livid.

"It has occurred to me," Dogger said, "that with Miss Stonebrook left to the care of Dr. Darby, and Balsam Cottage off-limits for the time being, we might again turn our attention to Mme. Castelnuovo's finger."

Mme. Castelnuovo's finger? Tucked into a stoppered test tube for safekeeping, it had completely slipped my mind! Swept away into the tide of murder by the suspicious death of Mrs. Prill, I had let the Curious Case of the Clue in the Cake slink off into the far corners of my memory. Being reminded of it now was oddly refreshing, though with a tinge of guilt: like finding, years after the giver was dead, a ten-pound note in the pocket of an unspeakably ugly Christmas jumper.

"I must have got sidetracked," I said. "I'd almost forgotten about Mme. Castelnuovo."

"So had I," Dogger confessed.

I almost clasped my hands together. This amazing man was so noble he might have been born in armor and on horseback, ready-equipped with shield and lance.

"Tell me," I asked. "Do we need to keep investigating Mrs. Prill's missing letters? After all, the client is dead."

Dogger looked at me.

"And besides," I said, "she didn't pay us anything. Not even so much as a deposit."

Dogger continued to stare at me.

"All right," I said. "Where do we begin?"

·TWELVE·

WE HAD SET UP a desk, Dogger and I, in my chemical laboratory. Actually, it had been there all along: a Victorian partners' desk in whose drawers Uncle Tar had kept his notes on the first-order decomposition of nitrogen pentoxide—which would lead, incidentally, to the atomic bomb—many of which documents, according to Aunt Felicity, had been confiscated after his death by silent men in black trench coats.

After cleaning out the remaining papers, we had packed them away in a wooden tea chest and stored them in the attic, there to await the arrival of History. In a great stroke of good luck, the same attic had given up a pair of cast-off Windsor chairs, which we brought happily down and positioned on opposite sides of the desk.

Arthur W. Dogger & Associates was officially—and physically—in business.

With order restored, we now sat facing each other across the desk.

But where to begin? Each of us seemed reluctant to be the first to speak.

I picked up a pencil—put it down—picked up a pen.

Something was weighing heavily on my mind. Before we began anew with the stolen finger of Mme. Castelnuovo, I needed to satisfy my curiosity.

At last, I broke the silence. "Tell me, Dogger," I asked, "when you found her, were Mrs. Prill's eyes contracted to a pinpoint?"

"Remarkably so," Dogger said.

"Ha!" I said, making a note. "And were there other symptoms?"

"There must have been copious salivation, although it would have been carried off with the vomiting. There would also likely have been seizures, although, of course, no one but her killer was there to see them."

"Anything else?" I asked.

"There are several other unpleasant effects, which one needn't go into."

"The loss of control of bowels and bladder, you mean," I said. "It's in Taylor's *Medical Jurisprudence*."

The eighth edition of Taylor, edited by the legendary Sydney Smith, of the Hopetoun Quarry Murders fame, was never out of reach on my bedside table.

"So it is," Dogger said.

"Wouldn't she have noticed the extreme bitterness of the physostigmine? I should have spat it out, myself."

"The bean is virtually tasteless," Dogger observed. "And the quantity of the alkaloid too little to be detected. The coffee would have masked it, in any case."

"Anything else?" I asked.

"Not without autopsy," Dogger said. "The pathologist will find traces of the bean in the stomach and the vomit, and in the chemical analysis of the viscera. He will test for the presence of physostigmine by means of either the ammonia test or the rubreserine test."

"Of course! With potassium hydroxide and chloroform, the red becomes orange-red."

I waited for Dogger's congratulations, but they were not forthcoming. Perhaps I had received enough praise for one day.

"And the results?" I asked.

"May or may not be released until after the pathologist produces his report. And perhaps not even then."

"Why not?"

Dogger picked up the pencil I had absentmindedly put down and waved it so quickly between his thumb and forefinger that it appeared to become invisible.

"Silence may speed an arrest," he said.

I hadn't thought about it until now, but Dogger was right.

"Because her killer is still at large," I suggested, "and Inspector Hewitt thinks they might strike again, using the same poison."

"Not necessarily," Dogger said. "One of the rules of in-vestigation is to keep mum about what you know. We ought to write it into our Standards and Practices."

"I didn't know we had a Standards and Practices," I said.

"We shall have, henceforth," Dogger replied.

Because it was still early afternoon, we had decided to begin the Castelnuovo Case by answering a very basic question: How had a famous guitarist's finger found its way into my sister Feely's wedding cake?

"It would be easier," I suggested, "if we determined when the deed was done. It might have been well before the event. Mrs. Mullet made the cake ages ago. But she didn't apply the icing until the morning of the wedding. When I examined the cake at the reception, after Feely found the finger, there was a small depression in the edge of the slice containing the finger."

"Which wasn't there when I brought the cake out of the pantry," Dogger said.

My eyes widened.

"Are you sure?" I asked.

"Positive," Dogger said with a small smile. "I was rather anticipating something in the nature of a practical joke by Miss Undine, and accordingly, I kept the cake locked up from the day it was baked until it was iced. And from the moment Mrs. Mullet finished icing it on the morning of the wedding, until it was brought out for the reception, the cake in question was again under lock and key—*my* lock and key—on the trolley in the butler's pantry."

"Hmmm," I said. "What about *during* the icing?" Might there have been even a single moment when the cake was left untended?

"Under my eye from A to Z," Dogger replied. "I took the cake out of the safe, watched Mrs. Mullet apply the icing—in fact, I assisted her in a trifling way—and locked it up again as soon as she had finished."

"And there was no dimple on the side," I said.

"None, I can assure you," Dogger said.

"So you're saying that no one could have tampered with the cake between the time it was iced and when it was brought out from the pantry for the reception?"

"No one but me," Dogger said. "I transferred it to the bridal table myself."

"Then the finger must have been put into the cake *during* the reception."

"It would seem so," Dogger said. "That, at least, is the most likely possibility."

"Which means that the guilty party was at Feely's wedding."

That narrowed our list down to only about a thousand suspects.

All right, I'm exaggerating, but most of Bishop's Lacey and half the county had been there, to say nothing of those who came from out of the county: those who had traveled down from London and those who had come from abroad.

Such as Dieter's parents, who had traveled all the way from Germany.

"I have an idea," I said. "Let me talk to Cynthia Richardson. She was in charge of all the arrangements for the reception. She's very organized. She'll have lists and so on."

"Good idea," Dogger said. "I shall leave you to it."

And so, here was I, pedaling Gladys madly into the village. Gladys was quite fond of Cynthia, and gave off little squeaks of metallic anticipation as we sped along between the hedgerows.

I was looking forward to chatting with Cynthia. It was ages since we'd had a good old gab.

But there was no answer at the door of the vicarage. I turned the knob and stuck my head inside.

"Cynthia?" I called. "It's Flavia."

Nothing but silence from within. I called again, but there was no reply. Cynthia must be out.

By the way she leaned against the gate, I could see that Gladys was disappointed, too.

"Never mind," I said, seizing her by the handlebars. "We shall go home and gorge ourselves upon gear oil and graphite grease."

Gladys loved nothing better than having her joints rubbed with these lubricants, especially when, with a bit of wire, I worked it into all her ticklish places. She almost purred.

Afterward we would glide in near-perfect silence up and down the avenue to the Mulford Gates. We were a submarine: *H.M.S. Unspeakable*, on the hunt in the

North Atlantic for enemy battleships. In spite of her official name, we secretly called ourselves H.M.S. *Gladiola*
(a clever combination of our two names).

"Slow ahead. Up periscope. Stand by one, two, and
three. Steer one hundred and ten degrees. Stand by. Fire
one! Fire two. Fire three. Down periscope."

Kaboosh! Kabloom! Kablooie!

"Medals all round," I would say, as Gladys glided on in
proud silence.

Excited voices came echoing from behind the church.
A regular uproar, from the sound of it. What could possibly be going on?

I leaned Gladys back against the gate and hurried
round the north side.

A herd of young men in black shorts, long hose, and
striped rugby jerseys were galloping wildly among the
tombstones, bearing down upon a ball which seemed to
have a mind of its own as it tumbled end over end through
the grass.

A shrill whistle blew and a small figure in a housedress
and cardigan waved her arms at them.

"Knowles!" Cynthia shouted. "Forwards should keep
their heads *down*, not up. Line out toward the center of
play, for heaven's sake. Paget! Keep onside. Don't over-
run the ball! Follow it up when it's worked through the
scrummage by the forwards. Now their halfbacks have got
away with it. You ought to have tackled them or passed it
out to your own three-quarters. You really are most exas-
perating. Never mind, you'll get on to it eventually.
Hullo, Flavia."

"I see you're busy," I said. "I'll come back later."

"No, no, dear," she said. "It's quite all right. I wanted to speak with you anyway."

"About what?" I asked.

"Go for his legs, Beaufort!" she shouted. "Too late. He's leaped over you! Well done, Pemberton. Well done!"

"About the Missioners," she added in a more restrained voice.

"Yes?" I said. As this was now a professional matter, I was giving nothing away.

"How are they doing?" Cynthia asked me. "I assume they found their way to Buckshaw with no trouble?"

I nodded. "Dogger took them for an outing to Ahab's Tower. Miss Stonebrook had an attack of asthma and they came home straightaway. Dr. Darby has made her comfortable."

"Oh, I'm so glad to hear it. Not the asthma attack, of course, but that she's in the care of Dr. Darby. *Chadwick! Never* run back toward your own goal! And *Blandings!* When playing on your own twenty-five yards, never, ever, by any chance pass the ball from the sides to the center. Get it away to touch. Let the *forwards* work it out of danger.

"Great Caesar's ghost," she added. "How is she?"

"She's resting," I replied. "Don't worry. We're keeping an eye on her. By the way, I need to talk to you about Feely's reception. I'd like a list of everyone who was present."

"Why on earth—?" Cynthia said. "*Collier!* Get the cork out! Sorry, dear, but sometimes you have to speak the language of the trade, so to speak. Now, then, why on earth would you need a list like that?"

"I was thinking of writing up an account for *The Hinley Chronicle*," I lied.

Much as I hated fibbing to Cynthia, my professional reputation was at stake. Even if they *were* dead, I couldn't go blathering the business of our clients all over the countryside.

"You'd never fit them all in, dear," she warned. "And even if you did, they wouldn't print it. There's a two-hundred-and-fifty-word limit for social notices, as I know all too well. I've written enough of them myself."

Poor Cynthia, I thought. *Wife, housekeeper, washerwoman, charwoman, counselor, vestry clerk, social organizer, accountant, florist, typist, saint, cook, and comforter. And now rugger coach. It's a wonder she doesn't wither away to nothing.*

"*Collier!*" she shouted. "Never attempt a run-in unless a try is a certainty. Remember, you're the last line of defense.

"Poor Collier," she whispered to me. "I'm trying my best to treat him like the others, but he lost his mother at the end of Trinity Term. He's putting a brave face on it, but everyone knows he's not himself."

Collier had thrown his hands up to cover his face in disgust. For a moment, his tall boyish figure looked utterly alone among the tombstones.

"I'm sorry to hear that," I said. In truth, I wanted to rush out among the milling bodies and crush this young man in a comforting embrace.

We who lose parents are one, I thought. *We all of us are as brothers and sisters of a single blood.*

"Very tragic," Cynthia was saying. "He misses her grievously. They were more like chums than mother and son."

How I envied young Collier. I had never been chums with my father, and as for my mother—well, I probably was, but Harriet had died when I was just a baby, leaving a hollowness which could never be filled.

"Don't look so sad, Flavia," Cynthia said. "He'll be all right. He's got his friends."

I forced up the corners of my mouth.

"And she's left him well off. He'll have a steady income, as well as the royalties from her recordings, and so forth."

"Recordings?" I asked.

"Oh yes," Cynthia said. "His mother was Mme. Adriana Castelnuovo, the celebrated guitarist. Her married name was Collier. He'll be very well off, indeed. *Don't freeze*, Grigson! Get rid of the blasted ball!"

I stood there with my mouth open like a coalhole.

Cynthia's whistle brought me out of my trance.

"Time!" she shouted. "Off you go. The vicar will be awaiting you in the chapel, and if I'm not mistaken, it's Ecclesiastes today. 'Dead flies cause the ointment of the apothecary to send forth a stinking savor.' Remember, lads—he's talking about rugger. Play up and play the game!"

With various hoots and whistles, the young men galloped out of the graveyard for further instruction.

Collier remained sitting on a tombstone, staring dejectedly at the ground, his hands clasped between his knees.

I walked toward him, kicking inquisitively at the grass so as not to startle him.

"Forgive me for intruding," I said, "but do you fancy graveyards as much as I do?"

Collier looked slowly up at me with his deep, dark eyes.

"You look like a person who relishes solitude," I said. "I pride myself on my ability to spot a fellow Churchyardian. Forgive me if I'm wrong."

"There's no such word as 'Churchyardian,'" Collier said.

"There is now," I told him. "I've just made it up."

Collier gazed off sadly toward the riverbank.

"So at this very moment," I persisted, "you and I are the only two Churchyardians in the world—perhaps in the universe. We ought to have jerseys made."

"What's your name?" he asked. "You have the advantage of me. You already know mine."

He was referring, of course, to the gaffe in play he had made, for which Cynthia had called him out by name.

"Flavia de Luce," I answered, placing an open hand an inch from his nose, so he pretty well had to shake.

"I'm sorry to hear about your mother," I continued. "It must have been a terrible blow. She was a very great artist."

"You heard her play?" he asked, looking up again with a sad smile.

"No," I replied. "I knew her only by reputation. I have

a very dear friend who has all of her recordings. Well, some of them, at least."

Collier nodded, gently, then looked away again, gazing off into the distance.

I held my tongue.

"You're right," he said at last. "I *do* fancy graveyards."

"Aha!" I said. I couldn't help it. "I knew I was right!"

"I suppose that's the real reason I'm planning on taking Holy Orders."

"It's as good a reason as any," I said enthusiastically, rubbing my hands together. "Just imagine—having your very own graveyard."

Collier laughed. He actually laughed!

"I like you, Flavia de Luce," he said. "Do you live around here?"

"Yes," I said, flopping a hand vaguely toward the south. Much as I liked Collier, I had been thoroughly lectured by Feely and Daffy on the perils of strangers, particularly the giving-out of personal information.

"Then perhaps you knew my late aunt," he said. "Mrs. Prill."

I gulped audibly.

"Mrs. Prill?" I said, as the image came into my mind of the woman slumped over her kitchen table, mouth in a pool of vomit and dead as a devil's doornail.

"Yes, I've heard of her," I said. "Late aunt, you say? She died recently?"

Collier nodded. "Just yesterday, in fact. She was an aunt by marriage only, but still an aunt for all that. One does become very attached when one's a child."

"I know what you mean," I told him. "I have an aunt also: Aunt Felicity. Not by marriage: She's my late father's sister. And she's still alive, of course. But aside from that, you and I seem much alike."

It's astonishing what the human heart will do to make allegiances. Loneliness is a kind of glue that can bind us to the most unlikely strangers.

Not that I'm lonely, of course, but I do like others to feel comfortable in my presence.

"*Very* much alike," I went on. "I lost my own mother when I was a child. Tragic for you to lose two of them, so to speak."

I know it sounded stilted, but conversations about death in one's own family are always like that. They are so close to the bone that we throw up a wall of words around them to deflect the arrows of hurt—guarded words like "lose" and "terrible blow"—when, in truth, we want to lie down, hug our heads, and howl.

"If you need someone to talk to, Mr. Collier, I want you to know that I'm here. It might do us both the world of good."

"My name is Colin," he said, "but you can call me Collie—or Col, as my best friends do."

"I shall call you Collie, which from this day forward shall be your Churchyardian name, which only I am entitled to use."

"Fair enough," Collie said. "And I shall call you Flea, for the same reason."

As Daffy once remarked as she soaked me with a soda fire extinguisher, turnabout is fair play, and I suppose she was right. Or as Mrs. Mullet puts it, "What's sauce for the goose is sauce for the grinder."

"All right," I said. "Flea it is. But don't you dare tell anyone. Swear it."

Collie put a forefinger to his lips and raised a hand, palm out.

"Now, then," I said, "about your mother . . ."

My words were interrupted by a fierce series of whistle blasts from the direction of the church.

"Collier!" Cynthia's voice called. "Collier? Come along, Collier. You mustn't keep the vicar waiting."

With a heartbreaking smile and a flash of dark eyes, he was gone.

I had made a friend.

By the time I got to the church porch, Collier had vanished inside. I turned away and headed for the vicarage.

"Cynthia?" I called loudly, sticking my head inside without knocking.

"I'm running the tub, dear." Cynthia's voice came floating down the stairs. "I've got a Mothers' Union meeting in fifteen minutes. Can we talk another time?"

"All right!" I shouted in a resigned kind of voice. Short of collaring Cynthia in her bath, I had no other choice.

I needed desperately to find out more about Collier and, more important, his links with the late Mrs. Prill.

I had a feeling it wasn't going to be easy.

There are times when you want to throw your hands up into the air, run around in circles, and scream curses at the sky, but it is not wise to do so in the vicinity of a church. "That way lies madness and straitjackets," as Daffy is so fond of saying after certain disagreements with Aunt Felicity.

I believe that it is wise to learn at an early age how to deal gracefully with being thwarted, rather than waiting until the arrows are already in the air.

Accordingly, I took a deep breath, inhaled the smoky autumn air, relaxed my shoulders, and strolled casually to where Gladys was waiting by the gate. I didn't want her to see my disappointment.

"Oh, what a lovely day," I said, pounding my chest in exuberance like Tarzan of the Apes. "What say to a nice run in the country?"

And off we sped, Gladys in a happy hum of spokes, and me bellowing a pirate shanty whose words I wasn't supposed to know.

·THIRTEEN·

A RIDE IN THE fresh country air can do wonders for the brain. I had gone no more than half a mile in the direction of Malden Fenwick when it came to me.

Of course! Why hadn't I thought of it before? Feely's reception had been planned and managed by the members of the Altar Guild.

Certainly, Cynthia would have been the organizing force, but the individual duties, such as the drawing-up of seating lists and so on, would actually have been carried out by the many others.

Of course, Clary Truelove came to mind.

Miss Truelove was, to put it nicely, prominent in the Church. If the Church were a pyramid being built, Miss Truelove was the Chief Overseer: the one with the whip. She made things happen.

She was the insinuating voice on the telephone when

the coffers of the Church were running empty. In *The Canterbury Tales* (which Daffy insisted was cribbed from Boccaccio, who had cribbed it in turn from Publius Papinius Statius, a Roman poet of the first century A.D.), Chaucer speaks of "the smyler with the knyfe under the cloke" and, surely, according to Daffy, he had Clary Truelove in mind, or someone very like her. Miss Truelove was the dagger behind the cloak of kindness with which Cynthia Richardson met all comers, and, when occasion demanded, the truncheon of the Church, so to speak.

For some reason or another, most of the inhabitants of Bishop's Lacey lived in fear of Clary Truelove, but I did not.

It wasn't because I was extraordinarily brave, but rather that the two of us had so much in common, so to speak:

(a) Neither of us was afraid to say what we thought.
(b) Neither of us could be intimidated.
(c) Neither of us suffered fools gladly—or at all.
(d) Neither of us curried favor—ever.
(e) Both of us were fascinated by certain aspects of the church: she with the altar and I with the graveyard.

We ought to have been friends, I suppose, Miss Truelove and I, but we weren't. Perhaps, like identical poles of two bar magnets, we naturally repelled each other.

I screwed up my courage and turned Gladys's head toward Miss Truelove's cottage.

All that now remained of Gooling Hill was a field with

a mound in the middle and a crumbling structure of stone that had once been a forge. Five hundred years ago, the place had been a small settlement bordering on Bishop's Lacey, which had specialized in the manufacture of iron shoes for horses and oxen, until it was wiped out by plague in the year 1348—a fact drummed into every young head in our village by sermon after sermon on the evils of uncleanliness.

The ancient forge had been added to and subtracted from so often that, after centuries of fiddling, it resembled nothing so much as a huddle of stones. And it was here, with her cats and carnations, that Miss Truelove lived a life of solitary splendor.

No one, as far as I knew, had ever been inside her hovel, although since she was on the telephone exchange, someone must have been, unless she had installed the instrument herself: I wouldn't put it past her.

There were two hand-lettered signs on the gate: one read *The Old Smithy*, the other *Keep Out*.

I opened the gate and followed the overgrown flagstones to the door.

There was no knocker, which made sense. If a *Keep Out* sign is doing its duty, there's no need for a knocker.

I knocked on the door. There was no answer. As I always do in such cases, I applied my ear to the wooden door panel to see if I could detect any furtive scurrying inside.

Nothing but silence.

I hammered on the door with my fist.

"Hullo, Miss Truelove," I cried. "It's Flavia de Luce. I've come to volunteer."

No organizer on earth could turn away an offer like that. For a woman who probably spent her every waking moment choreographing the comings and goings of this committee and that, plotting upon vast military charts the endless movements of volunteer silver-polishers, flower-fixers, and candle-wranglers, my offer to help must surely be seen as manna from heaven.

I knew from my own experience that to find a person's greatest weakness, you need only find their greatest charity, and appeal to it. This technique is the skeleton key of getting your own way.

I listened at the door again and was rewarded with the sound of approaching footsteps.

Taking a deferential step back from the door, I cast my eyes humbly down upon the doormat: the very image of a Christian martyr, confessed and ready for the lions.

I heard the door open.

"Good heavens, Flavia. What brings you to my doorstep? You ought to have warned me you were coming."

Why? I wondered. *So that you'd have time to hide the bodies?*

With her tiny frame, she reminded me of an elderly sparrow.

I suppose I was being harsh, but I knew that recluses have reasons. Not that Miss Truelove was a true recluse, but she was particular about privacy.

"Sorry, Miss Truelove," I said. "But I realized suddenly

as I was out for a ride that with Feely away, you'll probably be planning to have Marilyn Ferguson take over as organist, which will leave you short one person in the Altar Guild."

It wasn't a perfect excuse, but it was the best I could come up with on the spur of the moment. And I managed not to smile while mentioning the name of Marilyn Ferguson, whose clumsiness at the keyboard made even the most grim and tragic of hymns a source of open laughter from the congregation.

"How very thoughtful of you, Flavia," Miss Truelove said. "If you'd care to discuss it over tea—"

I almost tripped over her feet in pushing through the door.

"Perfect," I said. "Tea would be perfect. I'm so looking forward to chipping in: to shouldering the load."

Careful, Flavia. Don't put too much sugar in the trap!

"Come through into the kitchen," Miss Truelove said, "and don't mind the mess. I so seldom have company that I'm not really—"

"Oh, I don't mind," I said. "I'm actually quite a messy person myself. You ought to see my room. Feely always says that I have a—"

Here I broke off, pulled out a handkerchief, and gave my nose a good honk, as if suddenly stricken with the memory of my missing sister.

"There, there, dear," Miss Truelove said, pulling out a chair and waving me into it. "It must be dreadfully difficult for you after all these years. Make yourself comfortable and I shall put the teakettle on the hob."

As Miss Truelove busied herself, I had time for a good look round the kitchen. Surprisingly, for the look of the place from the outside, the interior was relatively modern and, in spite of Miss Truelove's protestations, quite tidy. Potted houseplants were clustered feverishly at the windows, giving the place the air of a greenhouse.

On the wall hung a church calendar, almost every day marked in various colors with an X.

The AGA, at which Miss Truelove busied herself, was a remarkably large, old-fashioned model, cream-colored: not as big as the one at Buckshaw, but still massive enough to chuck into it a blubbering Hansel and Gretel with room to spare for the drippings.

"Do you do a lot of cooking, Miss Truelove?" I asked, careful to make it sound like an offhand remark.

"I suppose I do," she replied. "But not in the way you might think."

Holy Hepzibah! What had I wandered into here?

Was I to be cut up with knives, rendered into suet on the back burner of the AGA, and hung out, in the form of dangling balls, to feed the winter birds in Miss Truelove's garden?

"Oh?" I managed.

"It is difficult to cook for one," Miss Truelove replied. "Especially when one eats like a bird."

Uh-oh! I thought. *A pterodactyl, no doubt. Locate the position of the nearest exit, Flavia, as you are instructed to do at the cinema.*

I could already feel her pecking at my liver, the way the eagle in the Greek myth tore out the liver of Prometheus daily—which then grew back again. The problem was that, unlike Prometheus, I only had one liver, and it wasn't immortal.

I could see just one way out of this.

"I'm afraid I fibbed to you, Miss Truelove," I said. "I didn't actually come to volunteer."

"You didn't?" she said, bringing the kettle of boiling water to the table.

"No. I came to ask you for a list of everyone who was at Feely's reception."

"Ah," she said, pouring the water into the teapot. "And what would you want with that?"

"Well . . ." I said, wracking my brain since Cynthia had already pooh-poohed my excuse of writing a newspaper article. "I thought it would be a nice gesture to write each one of them personally and thank them."

"Thank them for what?" Miss Truelove asked.

"Well, for attending . . . for their gifts . . . for their thoughtful . . ."

I was running out of ideas.

"But that is not your responsibility, Flavia. Ophelia and her husband will surely see to those formalities, if they haven't already."

"I know," I said. "But Feely hates writing. As a musician, she worries dreadfully that her hands might be affected. I don't mind. How many would I have to write?"

"One hundred and seventy-eight," Miss Truelove answered.

I had, for the first time, my number of suspects.

Besides, writing a hundred and seventy-eight letters

was not impossible: not for someone like myself who had once been forced by Miss Delaney to write, on behalf of the Girl Guides organization, letters of apology to all those whose flower, fruit, and vegetable displays had been trampled when the Scarlet Pimpernel Patrol ran amok at the Village Show. Not one of whom, I must note, had had the courtesy to respond.

"Oh, I don't mind," I said cheerfully. "It will give me a chance to repay Feely for being such a wonderful sister."

I managed to say this with a straight face and without gagging.

Miss Truelove could see by the determined look on my face that I wasn't going to give up.

"Well, all right, then," she said. "There are several lists. We divided the guests up into lots: for seating, for food, and so forth. Miss Tomlinson and Cynthia Richardson helped, of course, as did Miss Crawford and Mrs. Charmbury."

I almost leaped out of my liver as an electric buzzer went off beside my ear.

"Don't worry," Miss Truelove told me. "It's just the doorbell. I keep it on the loud setting so I can hear it when I'm working outside."

I nodded encouragingly, as if to indicate that I always did the same.

As she left the kitchen, I took the opportunity to stand up at the table, bend at the waist, and peer out through one of the windows into the walled garden.

The English cottage garden turns in autumn from reds

and pinks to blues and purples, as if Mother Nature is gently turning down the lights for winter.

Asters, crocuses, and dahlia crowded neck-to-neck with Michaelmas daisies, aconitum, monkshood (deadly poison, and one of my favorite flowers), lavender, and witch hazel.

Tucked away into a far corner at the bottom of the garden was a potting shed, and beside it, a green gate, which opened presumably onto the field that was Gooling Hill.

I didn't hear Miss Truelove coming back into the kitchen, and so I leaped guiltily as she spoke suddenly at my elbow: "No patience, these postmen nowadays. Can't wait for you to get to the door before they're off like a shot rabbit."

"Infuriating," I said, because it seemed like the right thing to say.

She went quickly to a corner of the kitchen and put away a brown-paper-wrapped package. I was not close enough to read the return address, but I didn't need to: the label was as familiar to me as the back of my own hand:

Howard, Rawson & Company, Scientific Glass Manufactory, London.

I had, myself, often enough received supplies of test tubes and beakers by mail from this old and well-established firm.

As if to confirm my thoughts, Miss Truelove's moving hand revealed a red-and-white sticker reading *Fragile— Glass—Handle With Care.*

Was she trying to hide the package from me?

It would not be polite, I knew, to comment on the parcel: too much like reading someone else's mail. There were other ways of gathering information.

My thoughts were already turning to the garden and the potting shed.

"What a lovely garden you have, Miss Truelove."

I was going to add "I love lavender," but it would have been too many loves, in too casual a remark.

"Have you ever thought of making scented waters from your flowers? It's always a pity, I think, that they die so soon. Mrs. Mullet says there's nothing like lavender in January."

In truth, Mrs. Mullet had said nothing of the sort. In fact, she loathed the smell of the stuff.

"Smells like coffins," she had once said, pinching her nose when I brought home a wand of lavender from the Goose Fair in Malden Fenwick.

"Of course I do," Miss Truelove replied. "In fact, I consider myself quite an accomplished *perfumier*."

She pronounced the word as I supposed they do in France: *par-FUME-ee-YAY*.

"Or herbalist, at any rate," she added. "I've even been known to extract a few small nostrums to ease the aches of my own ancient bones."

She glanced at me with just a hint of devilish glee, as if to say, "You naughty girl, you, Clary Truelove."

"Well then," she said, "I'd better get you what you came for."

She went to a wooden bench that stood to one side of

the fireplace and picked up a newspaper. It was *The Hinley Chronicle*, and I couldn't miss the headline: *Foul Play Suspected in Death of Local Woman*.

Miss Truelove lifted the paper just long enough to reach underneath and pull out a bundle of handwritten pages. "Ah! I thought that's where I'd left it."

I couldn't let the opportunity pass.

"Pity *that* poor woman," I said, gesturing with my head.

"What? Oh yes. Tragic, I'm sure. I believe she was related to one of the lads in digs at the vicarage."

"Collier," I said. "Colin. Yes, I've met him. Seems like a decent enough chap."

Miss Truelove, I realized, would know far more than I did. As Grand Pooh-Bah of the Altar Guild, she would be a sieve for scandal. No whisper, no twitter, no rustling of the leaves of rumor could possibly escape her ears.

"She was his aunt, I believe. By marriage. Did you know her?"

The answer was long in coming.

"I cannot say that we were friends," Miss Truelove murmured, pursing her lips as a signal that the distasteful discussion was at an end.

"Ah," I said in an understanding tone as I shoved the papers into my pocket. "Well, I must be getting along. Thank you for the list. I shall copy and return it as quickly as I can."

"Well, there's no rush, dear. The wedding and the reception are over. Your sister is now a married woman and has moved on to a new life."

"Oh, but she'll be back," I said. "She's still organist at St. Tancred's, you know."

"Is she?" said Miss Truelove with a quizzical look. "Is she indeed?"

·FOURTEEN·

HAVING MADE MY ESCAPE, I took a broad detour that took me round to the far side of the ancient settlement where, by means of an overgrown footpath, I made my way back to the mound in the center of Gooling Hill.

From its rise, I had a clear view of Miss Truelove's cottage, The Old Smithy, its roofs jutting up behind the brick wall of her kitchen garden.

I strolled casually toward the place, as if I were bird-watching, although it was certain that Miss Truelove—unless she could see through walls—could not be aware of my return.

I sidled up to the green gate, lifted the latch silently, and gave a tentative push.

Locked—blast it!—from the other side. Probably by a bolt. My lock-picking skills will be of no use whatsoever.

If I were going to capture the fort, I would need to take it like a commando: by swarming over the top.

I remembered the wise words of Mrs. Mullet's husband, Alf: "Never reckon till you've reconnoitered." That saying, drummed into his head, had returned him safely home after the war, and if it was good enough for Alf Mullet, it was good enough for me.

I drifted closer to the wall.

Like most neglected brickwork in England, this one was covered with Virginia creeper, now resplendently red in all its autumnal glory.

I reached out and touched the stuff. Beneath the bright leaves lay a mass of dark, vinous matter, dry as wicker but curiously flexible.

As I gave it a tug, the wooden netting gave off an alarming creak—or was it a groan?

My real concern was this: Would it support my weight?

Even if it did, I needed to get over the top without being seen. I had reckoned the position of the potting shed pretty accurately: a couple of feet to the left of the gate or, from my present position, to the right of it.

The first order of business would be to climb slowly until my eyes had just cleared the wall, then have a jolly good dekko, moving only my eyeballs from left to right and back again, like the animated cartoon cats in the cinema.

But first the wall.

With both hands I reached far above my head and seized on to the vegetation, but aside from a silky hiss and a slight wooden crunching—like climbing a barricade of old bones, I thought—it was satisfactorily silent.

"Over the top!" I murmured, and, placing a foot firmly into the foliage, hauled myself up.

"Take it easy," I kept telling myself. There was no point in remaining invisible if you were making more noise than a threshing machine.

Another foot . . . another hand . . . another foot . . . slowly . . . slowly . . .

Up the wall I went, wondering how I could be so calm.

As my eyes cleared the top, I took great care to limit my motions: fractions, only, of an inch at a time: ocular muscle control set to "Super-Fine."

It would be a useful lesson for later life, I decided on the spot, to teach oneself to move one's eyes in increments of sixty-fourths of an inch. Of such stuff are salamanders made, and Spartans and Stoics, to whom silent discipline is everything, and complaining unknown. I could hardly wait to get home and tell Daffy of my sudden insight.

I wouldn't tell her about climbing the wall, of course. Some things are best kept to oneself.

I let my gaze focus slowly on the kitchen window. There was no sign of Miss Truelove behind the glass. Hauling myself up half a foot, I let my chin rest on the top of the wall.

The potting shed, as I had calculated, was just to my right. If I were quick about it, I could be on the roof and down behind it before you could say "Beatrix Potter."

I hauled myself onto the top of the wall, let my legs

drop on the far side, and—*Geronimo!*—dropped onto the wooden structure, and then onto the ground.

For a moment I froze. Had I been detected?

There wasn't a sound.

Fortunately, Miss Truelove didn't keep a watchdog. If she did, I'd have already been chewed into rags and rib bones.

I flattened myself and edged along the back of the shed. Fortunately, the door was on the side of the structure and not visible from the kitchen window.

Would it be locked?

What a worrywart, Flavia! Who would bother locking a potting shed in a walled garden?

Unless, of course, they have something to hide.

The door was locked. I needed to be resourceful.

As I reached into my pocket, my fingers touched the bit of wire I carried for greasing Gladys's gears.

I offered up a silent prayer of thanksgiving to Baldo-merus, the patron saint of locksmiths, and went to work.

I have to admit it was child's play. The lock was of the old-fashioned skeleton key variety, and after a couple of deft twists, the door swung inward.

As I turned round, I let out a gasp of amazement. At the far end of the shed, under the glazed roof, lay the ex-pected plants and herbs, row upon row of them, simmer-ing in the sun. Rosemary and thyme grew in clay pots, cheek-by-jowl with deadly nightshade and datura, or jim-sonweed. Whatever else it might be, this was no ordinary kitchen garden.

At the near end, shaded with gloom, were a pair of

wooden workbenches, and upon them an array of distilling apparatus that would have warmed the heart of even the most world-weary alchemist, each with its own Bunsen burner, Liebig condenser, Kjeldahl and Erlenmeyer flasks.

A marble mortar and pestle stood at the ready.

My chemical heart gave a flutter at the sight of this near-professional setup.

The place had a heavily herbal smell, and something else, which I could not immediately identify: something earthy; something old.

But didn't all potting sheds smell like this? Perhaps they did, but the air in this one had a particular aura, which lay tantalizingly beyond recognition by the nose.

It smelled vaguely churchy.

At the end of each bench were a set of scientific cabinets, each with an array of pull-out drawers—dozens of them—none of which were labeled. On top of the cabinets were rows of apothecary bottles, their contents stated in neatly penned names: *Mentha pulegium*, *Primula vulgaris*, *Atropa mandragora*, and *Commiphora gileadensis*, which I recognized as, respectively, pennyroyal, primrose, mandrake, and balm of Gilead.

I startled slightly at the name of the last one. This was the stuff upon which Dr. Brocken had founded his fortune.

Something under the benches caught my eye: the glint of glass. By squatting, I could see that the spaces beneath the benches were taken up with boxes full of small empty bottles. And not just *any* bottles, but rather high-quality glass with decorative cut-glass stoppers, such as might have been used for expensive French scent before the war.

Surely this was not a laboratory given over entirely to the production of—what had Miss Truelove said?—"a few small nostrums to ease the aches of my own ancient bones."

I seized the brass handle of one of the drawers and slid it carefully toward me—just enough to peer carefully inside.

I didn't want any surprises.

Some object—of which I could see only one end— seemed to be wrapped in a ribbon of blue silk, as if it were somehow precious, or valuable.

As I tried to pull the drawer farther out, it jammed. Perhaps the wood had warped in the humidity of the potting shed. By sticking two fingers and a thumb into the opening, I was able to seize the object and lift it out into the light, as if with tweezers.

It was a bone. A *human* bone. A *recognizable* human bone.

It was a proximal phalanx—a human finger bone— and I almost dropped it.

But pride overcame nerves. If there were any bones in the body I was sure of—other than the skull, of course— they were the digital phalanges.

How many hours had I sat in my laboratory, holding hands with "Yorick," the complete human skeleton who had been given to Uncle Tar by the great naturalist Frank Buckland? How often had I compared my hands with poor Yorick's, bone by bone, as if our impossibly different pasts had made us next of kin?

I knew Yorick's proximal phalanges as well as I knew my own.

The puzzle was the blue silk ribbon. But why silk? Why blue?

Was it a mark of respect? Or of reverence?

Could the thing be a trophy? Had it won first prize at some nightmarish exhibition?

Put away your foolish thoughts, Flavia, said the voice in my head. *This is real. This is a finger of the dead.*

I turned it over for a closer look. Written on the underside of the white bone, in professionally small, neat letters of black ink, such as you might see on an exhibit at the Natural History Museum, were several letters: *A.C.D.*

Were they the initials of the dead man? I wondered.

Yes, it was a man's finger bone. I knew that as a general rule, the phalanges of the male were larger than those of the female and this one was no dainty digit.

Not by a long chalk. This had been the finger of a large man.

I was sure of it.

I returned the bone to its drawer and pulled open the next.

This one contained a small blue jeweler's box, which looked as if it might once have contained a ring.

Again, with great care, I lifted the lid.

Inside was a grayish powder: about a teaspoonful, I guessed. I sniffed the open box and detected at once the faint odor of burning. Was it ash?

Only taste would tell. I wetted a forefinger and touched the feathery stuff ever so lightly, raised it to my lips . . .

Hold on, I thought. *It could be arsenical ash.*

It was all well and good to put unknown substances to the taste test in your own chemical laboratory, where you had the benefit of knowing what it *wasn't*.

At home, at least, if you swallowed something dire, you would have the antidote at hand.

Frank Buckland, who presented Uncle Tar with Yorick, had, in his time, consumed everything from coprolite to sea slugs, and it was said that his father, William Buckland, had devoured even bluebottle flies and the heart of Louis XIV.

No, I decided, a strange potting shed was not a proper place for experimentation.

I wiped my finger on my skirt and examined the little box again. There were no markings, no labels.

A metallic *click* at the door froze my blood. Someone was coming!

Before I could make a move, the door swung open, and Miss Truelove stood silhouetted in bright sunlight. Lightly, she touched the lock, as if trying to remember if she could possibly have left it open.

I waited for her to speak.

And then I realized she couldn't see me. Her eyes, momentarily blinded by the outside glare, could see nothing in the darkness of the potting shed—at least, not the part of it farthest from the door, where I was standing.

Almost without thinking, I slowly lowered myself—at a glacial pace—into a squat behind the end of the bench.

Now I was looking at her knees, which began to move toward me—then stopped.

I stopped breathing as she bent over, my mind a riot of thoughts. Surely, she could hear the pounding of my heart. Surely, she would find me trembling beneath the bench. Was she listening? Had she heard me rummaging in the potting shed?

Could she smell me? Had her nostrils picked up the scent of Flavia de Luce?

I watched in horror, my eyes wide as saucers, as her hands reached toward me. They were holding something.

It was a box. A cardboard box. A box with a familiar label: *Fragile—Glass—Handle With Care.*

The same package the postman had delivered to her door.

Time did not stop, but it certainly slowed to a painful crawl as Miss Truelove reached in toward me under the bench and placed the box on top of the others.

As she straightened up, she let loose an enormous sneeze: "Ah-tish-OOO!"

Had some of the unidentified dust from the box got into her nose? Had I spilled any of it on the bench?

I dared not move a muscle.

"Gesundheit," she said, blessing herself.

A moment later, she was gone. As the door closed, I was returned to semidarkness as I heard the key turn in the mechanism.

I was locked in.

Excellent! I thought. As long as I was quiet about it, I could now have a good old rootle.

I pulled out one of the wooden drawers, and in it was a glassine envelope with a red-and-white sticker.

I tipped the contents into my hand: a twist of hair. Hair of an extraordinary grayish gold, like the hair of an elderly child.

Turning over the semitransparent envelope, I struggled for a moment with the inscription on the label. It was in a curiously old-fashioned hand.

And then I saw. *Ludwig van Beethoven,* it said.

As if it were electric, I shoved the hair back into the envelope and the envelope into the drawer, which I slammed shut with—what? Ferocity? Alarm?

Determined to banish such primitive instincts, I opened another drawer.

In it was another glassine envelope, and written upon it, another name: *C. Dickens.* I flicked it open with my thumb and into my hand dropped a single yellowed fingernail.

What was going on here? What kind of evil enterprise had I stumbled upon?

Suddenly, I thought I knew, and a kind of sick singing began in my ears.

All the tales that I had ever heard came rushing to my mind. Grave robbers! Burke and Hare. The candles in the churchyard at midnight . . . armed bullies with picks and shovels . . . the sale of corpses to the medical schools . . .

But surely not in Bishop's Lacey! Surely not in these most civilized of times.

Yet, when I was a child, Daffy had delighted to terrify me, telling by candlelight how in the days of Elizabeth I, tombs had been plundered, and hair chopped from the skulls of the dead to supply wigs for wealthy women.

"Shakespeare even mentions it in one of his sonnets," she said. "Listen, you'll love this."

She began to recite in a creaky, quavering voice, holding the candle under her chin so that her eyes, lit from below, danced like pale ghouls in their dark sockets:

"Before the golden tresses of the dead,
The right of sepulchres, were shorn away,
To live a second life on second head:
Ere beauty's dead fleece made another gay."

At which point she had whipped from behind her back a handful of musty white horsehair and shoved it into my face so that I almost gagged from claustrophobia. It was an unspeakably ancient barrister's wig.

"And they're coming for you next!" she had shouted into my tearstained face.

And although I learned later that she had found the disgusting thing in the attic, perhaps a relic of some earlier and anonymous de Luce's life on the bench, I could never quite bring myself to forgive her.

All of these things came flocking into my mind as I realized, for the first time, the horror of it all. I knew on the instant what the odd smell was in the potting shed.

I couldn't wait to get away from the place. My skin was crawling.

Although I'll be the first to admit that I love graves

and graveyards, there is something obscene about the living trafficking in the world of the dead.

Greek mythology, I remembered, had a tale of a boatman, Charon, who ferried dead souls across the Styx, the river which separated the living from the dear departed.

But once across, they stayed there. There was no galumphing back and forth by buccaneers to steal their hair and sell it in the marketplace. Charon would not have permitted such sacrilege.

And neither should I.

I needed to wash my hands. I needed fresh air.

I scrambled up onto one of the benches and put the heels of my hands against a window frame. With only the slightest of groans, it slid easily upward.

Climbing carefully over the cabinets and the rows of apothecary jars, I placed one foot on the sill, shifted my weight onto it, and wiggled my way into the opening.

From there on, it was a piece of cake. I slid down onto the ground, pulled down the sash behind me, turned, and stopped to survey my situation.

I was standing in the narrow space between the potting shed and the brick wall. The Virginia creeper was at hand. Slowly, almost casually, I made my way up the foliage, paused for a moment on the top of the wall, and dropped down onto the other side.

I could hardly wait to tell Dogger what I had discovered.

·FIFTEEN·

"IN LAW," DOGGER SAID, "there is a distinct line between trespassing and burglary. Did you bring anything away?"

"No," I replied. Although I had told Dogger the bare bones of my intrusion, I had not given him the details. After a brief reflection, I added, "Other than the ashes on my dress."

Dogger considered this seriously for a moment, and then said, "We shall make a microscopic investigation of the residue, to put our minds at ease."

Already it was growing dark outside. The days were drawing in, and once the sun went down, a chill was in the air.

And so it was that we found ourselves in the solitude of my chemical laboratory, our steaming cups of tea at our elbows, leaning in turns over the gleaming brass of the Leitz binocular microscope.

"Cremated remains, almost certainly," Dogger said. "Whether human or not is impossible to tell, although we shall, of course, make the usual titration of the primary calcium phosphate with sodium hydroxide."

"Of course," I agreed.

"The human body," Dogger continued, "when incinerated, yields up, in its ash, about half in the form of the phosphates, a quarter calcium, and lesser amounts of the sulfates, potassium, sodium, and chlorides. The remainder consists of traces of the elements: everything from aluminum and antimony to vanadium and zinc. The organic compounds are converted, largely, to the form of their metal oxides. As for the inorganic, they may remain as chlorides, carbonates, phosphates, and sulfates, depending upon, of course, combustion."

"Yes," I said, "and the carbon from the carbonates and the oxygen from the oxides go largely up the flue, although, in the case of incomplete combustion, the carbon residue would be somewhat higher, accounting for the smell of burning."

"I believe so," Dogger said. "Yes, I believe you're quite correct in that."

I loved it when Dogger talked to me like this. How cozy the world became, and how far away the troubles of everyday life. It was like being rocked in the cradle of knowledge, floating on the great calm sea of reason, suspended like a mote of dust in the sheer infinity of the universe.

A sudden thought brought me back with a jerk to the present.

"The Missioners!" I said. I had forgotten all about them.

"I have made the ladies quite comfortable in the drawing room," Dogger said. "I hope that I was not remiss. Miss Daphne has been keeping to the library. I thought she wouldn't mind."

"Her memoirs," I said. "She's going to pull the rug out from under us, Dogger. She's going to tell all. It will be like living under the same roof as Max Brock."

Dogger smiled.

Maximilian Brock, one of our Buckshaw neighbors, was a tiny gnomish creature who, after a glamorous international career as a concert pianist, had retired to "The Doldrums," as he described our neighborhood, to write—under the nom de plume Lola Lattimore—lurid tales of bloody crime, all supposedly true, for what he called "the more prurient publications."

"The ladies are preparing, I believe, for their talk at the parish hall," Dogger went on, "which promises to be inordinately interesting, as one of them seems to be cribbing her notes from a novel by Mr. Lawrence."

I didn't ask which one of the ladies it was.

"Oh, dear," I said. "Has Daffy left *Lady Chatterley* lying around again?"

Dogger gently inclined his head.

"I am given to understand that the topic is to be Christian Health," he said, "and shall be looking forward particularly to their remarks upon the subject of tropical medicine."

To think of it! Dogger, who knew more about the topic than perhaps any human being on the planet, sitting passively in the parish hall, hands folded in lap, listening quietly to a pair of missionaries prattling on about applying sticking plasters in the jungle made my heart ache—mostly for him.

How could life deal him such a rotten hand? I wanted to reach out and touch him, but I didn't. I would spare him that.

"So shall I," I said.

We turned again to our analysis of the ashes I had scraped from my skirt. The sodium hydroxide test confirmed—as we expected it would—human remains.

Whose ashes are they? I wondered. What human being had been born, lived, laughed, suffered, wept, and died, perhaps becoming famous on the way, only to wind up after all of that as a smudge on my frock?

"I think that when this is all over"—I pointed to the now slightly gelatinous matter in the test tube—"we ought to lay this to rest in a quiet corner of the churchyard."

"That would be the decent thing to do," Dogger said. "Perhaps a few prayers of the nondenominational sort would not be out of order."

A moment of reverence can often open new doors: provide new pathways which might have otherwise been left unexplored.

I realized with something of a shock that I had been avoiding a certain train of thought. Was it to shield Dogger? I wondered. Or to protect myself?

Like a sponge, the human brain can only absorb so much before it begins to leak.

Sooner or later, I had to share what I had seen.

But there was a tightness in my chest; a shortage of breath, as if the very words were unwilling.

And then, suddenly, before I could help myself, it came pouring out in all its grisly detail: The Old Smithy, Miss Truelove, the potting shed, the dust, the drawers, the blue silk ribbon, the names, the bones, the bottles . . . the whole nightmarish scene.

"What are they up to, Dogger?" I asked in a whisper. I think I knew, but I needed to hear it from a calm and critical brain.

Dogger was staring at the residue in the test tube as if his mind were a million miles away.

"It's homeopathic distillation, isn't it?" I said. "They're selling the broth of boiled-down bodies and bones—the bodies and bones of famous people!—as a kind of patent medicine. Like cures like. Isn't that what they say? The diluted dust of Dickens will turn you from a dunce into a famous author. For a price."

Dogger's eyes moved slowly from the test tube to meet mine.

"Or," I said, beginning to tremble, "an infusion of the finger of Mme. Castelnuovo will transform you into an accomplished guitarist."

"I fear you are right, Miss Flavia," Dogger said at last. "I can see no other rational explanation."

"But how did they get their hands on these . . . these . . . remains?" I asked.

"There are ways and means," Dogger said. "There have

always been ways and means. Money has always been light-fingered. Money, as they say, talks."

It more than talks, I wanted to say. *It isn't fair. It shouts from the housetops through a megaphone.*

I have been becoming more keenly aware for the past few years of the unfair cruelty of Fate. Had fairness been a fact of life, I might not have lost my mother and my father. My sisters might have loved me. I might at this very moment be—

Stuff it, Flavia, said that familiar voice, which was becoming more frequent and insistent by the day. *Stow it. Put a cork in it.*

Just like that. Three warnings for the price of one.

What on earth was happening to me?

I hadn't the faintest idea, but I'd have to admit, if subjected to an instrument of torture, such as the Iron Maiden or the rack, that, whatever this voice was and wherever it was coming from, I was beginning to appreciate its nagging.

"And is there a connection, do you think, Dogger? Between Mme. Castelnuovo's finger and the dust of Dickens?"

It was a question I hardly dared ask. If true, it would smack of some great conspiracy: some vast criminal enterprise that might well be beyond the capabilities of Dogger and me.

Perhaps we ought to dump the whole thing in Inspector Hewitt's lap, and leave it to him to deal with the evildoers.

We would wash our hands of the matter and cast around for some new case upon which to cut our teeth. A cozy blackmailing, for instance; a comfy case of arsenic in the toothpaste.

Something civilized.

Anything but these monstrous charlatans who were enticing their victims to eat—no matter how diluted—the·dead.

Dogger had still not answered my question.

I stood up and stretched elaborately.

"I'm absolutely exhausted," I told him. "Perhaps everything will seem clearer in the morning."

Dogger got up also and put on his jacket, which he had left hanging on the back of a chair.

"I am afraid," he said, "that we shall have to pay another visit to Gollingford Abbey."

My dreams were filled with phantoms: unwholesome, shapeless things that swarmed me just beyond the senses. I tossed and turned, looking at the clock from time to time, which ticked along with maddening slowness, as if it wanted the night to last forever.

After a while, I got up and slipped into Father's old bathrobe, which I kept hanging on the back of the door. I rummaged under the bed, pawing through the spilling stacks of phonograph discs, until I found the one I wanted.

It was by the American composer Samuel Barber: *Adagio for Strings*. I cranked up the Victrola and dropped the needle into the grooves. If anything could make me sleep, this was it.

The *Adagio* was composed for people who were scream-ing for sleep. It was half boxing glove and half chloral hydrate: a musical Mickey Finn.

I tucked my knees up under my chin and sat up straight in bed, listening intently to the ebb and flow of the strings: coming and going, rising and falling, ever closer, ever farther away . . .

After a couple of minutes, I realized I was humming along, and tears were coursing down my cheeks.

I leaped up, ripped the record from the spinning turn-table, and hurled it across the room, where it hit the chimneypiece and shattered into a dozen dead, dark, and accusing pieces, like the magic mirror in Hans Christian Andersen's *The Snow Queen*, whose shards got into your eyes, froze your heart, and caused you to see only the evil in the human race.

Was this happening to me?

Was that the reason I was so disgusted with the True-loves, the Pursemakers, and the Stonebrooks of the world?

And, yes, the Prills, too—and the Brockens. I might as well admit it.

The guilt was getting a grip on my throat. I had to shake it off.

Contritely, I gathered up the broken pieces of the rec-ord and carried them into the laboratory. Shellac, I knew, could be softened by the application of methylated spirits.

I sorted the shards on the work surface, then began laboriously to piece them back together again as if they were a fretwork puzzle. In the end, although there were a few chips missing, the disc seemed nearly complete. One at a time, I brushed the broken edges with the spirit and pieced them back into position. When it seemed solid, I did a few touch-ups, using a bottle of Feely's clear nail polish (which I had conveniently forgotten to return).

I nestled the disc on my open hand as gently and as tenderly as if it were an injured baby bird.

Back in my bedroom I checked the clock. The patch-up job had taken me an hour.

Taking great care, I placed the recording on the gramophone and wound up the crank.

Samuel Barber. *Adagio for Strings*.

Bliss.

Conducive to healing contemplation.

If ever I should have a daughter, I decided, *which I doubt greatly, given my solitary nature—I should name her Victrolia, for the Goddess of Music.*

I had never been wholly satisfied with my own name. *Flavia* sounds so much like vanilla extract.

If I'd been left to choose my own name, I should have chosen *Amanita*. It has such a nice ring about it, I think. And since mushrooms grow in rings . . .

"Daffy," I had once asked her, "do you like your name better than mine?"

"*Pfah!*" she had spat. "You're the lucky one. Flavia of the golden hair, whereas I'm stuck with the name of some dim-witted nymph who turned into a tree."

With precision fingers, I placed the needle in the outer grooves of the record.

And then the *Adagio* began:

Daaaa-click!-daaaa-click!-daaaa-click!-dumpf-click!
Da-click!-aa-daaaa-click!-click!-aaaa-aaaa-click!-dumpf.

I flew at the machine, ripped the record from the turntable, and flung it across the room, where it disintegrated once more against the back of the door.

I leaped into bed and covered my head with a pillow.

When I awoke, the sun was streaming in through the windows and I felt—I hate to say it—like Mary Poppins: better than ever. Practically perfect.

·SIXTEEN·

IT WAS A JOLLY good thing I'd started the day on the right foot. As I opened my bedroom door, my eye was caught by the slightest of motions in the shadows at the end of the hall.

I paused, turned myself sideways, but kept a sharp lookout from the corner of my eye. Peripheral vision is a gift from the gods that ought not to be underestimated.

Something was slithering slowly toward me in a reptilian manner. I tried not to look, but it was useless. You cannot fight ancient instinct.

But rather than fleeing, I obeyed the demands of my blood: I stood up on tiptoe, put hands on hips, and hissed through my teeth. *Make yourself as large as possible*, my million years of evolution was telling me. *Pose a threat.*

Still the thing came toward me, a slight waddle rocking it from side to side. It seemed to have a shell, of sorts. I could hear its underbelly slithering on the carpet.

Now I could see the creature more clearly: a tight, leatherlike skin with scalloped edges like the wings of some Jurassic Jabberwock; an inverted bowl animated by an ancient clockwork evil. I know it makes no sense, but that's what was running through my mind.

On it came toward me with an ominous scraping.

As it passed through a pallid beam of light from one of the clouded windows, I saw that the body of the thing was colored overall with the most peculiar markings: markings I had seen somewhere before, but which now eluded me entirely.

It was as if my brain had packed its luggage and gone off to Butlins, the seaside holiday camp where it isn't needed.

And then recognition arrived with a rush. Of course! The pattern on the shell—or skin—of the creature, whatever it was, was a pattern by William Morris, of wallpaper and upholstery fame, all twining stalks and tendrils, green acanthus leaves, and the occasional blood-red berry.

The bony back of the creature resolved itself into an opened umbrella, which was propelling itself, crabwise, along the hall and straight at me.

I stuck out a toe, hooked it under the edge of the umbrella, and flipped it cartwheeling away through the air. It fell with a hollow thump, revealing a small figure hunched up under the wicker framework of the Gothic appliance I had seen in Miss Stonebrook's room.

It was Undine.

"I'm a Bornean river turtle!" she crowed. "Did I scare you, Flavia?"

I didn't give her the satisfaction of an answer.

"Come on, Flavia, admit it. I scared the sauce out of you, didn't I?"

"All right," I said. "You scared me. My liver turned to lemon jelly."

"That's more like it," Undine said, extricating herself from the tortuous birdcage and standing up to stretch.

"You weren't present in the *now*, were you, Flavia?"

"Huh?" I said.

"Ibu always said Aristotle told us to live in the *now*. But you weren't living in the *now*, were you? That's why I was able to scare you and make your liver go to lemon jelly."

The little weasel had a point. I *hadn't* been in the *now* just now. I had been busying my brain with the problem.

"Aunt Felicity's going to kill you," I said. "You've destroyed her umbrella. It was by William Morris: a family heirloom."

"I only sawed off the handle," Undine said. "I needed it for my carapace. You can't make a Bornean river turtle without a carapace, can you? What would contain the guts? Besides, the birds would peck it to death. Did you know that the Greek playwright Aeschylus was killed by an eagle dropping a tortoise on his bald head to break the shell? Ibu said a soothsayer told him he'd be killed by a falling object, and he was living out-of-doors to make sure that it didn't happen. Ibu said that's a perfect example of poetic justice."

"Listen," I said. "Can we talk about this later? I haven't had breakfast and I'm famished."

"Breakfast can wait," Undine said with surprising authority in her voice. "I was actually coming to see you. We need to talk, you and I."

"About what?"

"Come back into your bedroom," Undine said. "It's hardly a matter for public discussion."

Not that we were in the booking hall of St. Pancras Station: This was the remote and half-abandoned east wing of a minor country house on the outskirts of nowhere. There were no spies in the woodwork—and besides, no one gave a kangaroo's kadiddle what we talked about anyway.

Undine had a forefinger to her lips.

And suddenly I understood. She had come to me with information about the Missioners. She had been in their rooms. Miss Stonebrook's corrective corsetry was proof enough of that.

I held open the door and Undine dragged in the wicker monstrosity which, after its rough usage as a Bornean river turtle, now looked like the wreckage of a primitive airplane: the kind of thing in which boys like Dieter used to launch themselves from the tiled rooftops, with sometimes tragic results.

"Sit here," Undine ordered, pulling a straight-backed chair to the middle of the room.

"Why?"

"Don't ask questions," she told me. "Just do as I say. Sit."

To my consternation, I obeyed her.

Undine began to pace the room, hands clenched behind her back at first, then wrung before her, as if in grief.

She cleared her throat dramatically. "What," she asked, "is my place in this household, as you see it?"

She had caught me off guard.

"I . . . I . . . you're part of the family," I said.

"Besides that," Undine demanded, fixing me with a piercing glare.

"Well . . . you're one of us. You're blood. We love you."

"Is that all?"

"Well . . . yes. No. I don't see what you're getting at."

Undine let out an exasperated snort. "Do you ever stop to consider my feelings?" she asked in an icy voice.

Feelings?

What was there to feel? The little girl had been brought to Buckshaw by her late mother, Cousin Lena, of the Cornwall de Luces, who had more than likely been personally responsible for my mother's death.

When Lena herself had come to no good end ("May she baste in 'ell," Mrs. Mullet had once blurted in an unguarded moment), the little girl had been taken in, as you would take in a baby rabbit found in the field ahead of the mowers.

Why do these images of rescuing small creatures keep coming into my mind? Could they be glandular mirages?

Although I had recently been reading Professor Marshall's great work on biological and clinical chemistry, I could not for the life of me remember what he had to say upon that particular topic.

"I consider everybody's feelings," I said. But was it true?

"I am going to tell you my feelings," Undine said. "You are going to sit there and listen to them. And then you are going to tell me what you think about what I've told you."

My head was spinning.

"All right," I said. "Fire away. Tell me how you feel."

"Fraught," Undine said.

"I beg your pardon?"

"Fraught," she repeated. "Don't you know what that means?"

"Of course I do," I told her, even though I didn't.

"It means freighted," she said. "Loaded down. Laden with some burden, usually something unpleasant, like anxiety. F-r-a-u-g-h-t. That's how it's spelled, and that's how I feel. Fraught."

"Why?" I asked.

"I didn't ask to be brought here." She resumed her pacing. "I had no choice. I feel that I am an intruder. That I am unwanted. And that is why I feel fraught.

"Now, then," she said, dusting her hands, "you must tell me what you think."

"It makes me sad," I said.

Undine stared at me for a long moment, then shook herself vigorously, like a retriever coming out of the water.

"Thank you for listening, Flavia," she said. "I'm glad we had this talk. Now let's go down to breakfast. My belly thinks my throat's been slit."

I sat staring across the kippers at this strange little girl who suddenly reminded me so much of myself.

"Wherever did you find that contraption?" I asked, lowering my voice and leaning toward her.

"I thought you'd be interested," Undine said. "That's why I pinched it from Miss Stonebrook's room."

"Weren't you afraid of being caught?"

"Caught?" She giggled. "Me? I'm just a little girl. I was going to make a rocket ship from the thing, wasn't I?"

I didn't tell her that I had already seen and inspected the device: That would be cruel.

"Thank you for thinking of me," I said. "What do *you* make of it?"

Undine spread the fingers of her left hand and began to tick them off. "(a) It's a costume. She's an actress. (b) It's part of a disguise. She's a criminal. (c) She has some tropical disease and needs to keep her clothing from touching her bottom."

"Excellent," I said. I hadn't thought of one of those myself.

Undine was grinning at me like a goblin across the table.

"Ah! 'Ere you are," Mrs. Mullet said as she came into the room and fixed her eye on Undine. "And what do *you* fancy for breakfast?"

"Scotch eggs," Undine replied instantly. "And hold the eggs. That's what Ibu used to tell the waiter when we stayed at a posh hotel."

"No doubt she did, dear," Mrs. Mullet said. "An' it must 'ave been very amusin' at the time. Now, then, 'ow many pieces of toast are you 'avin'?"

The Rolls purred as contentedly as a kitten. It seemed happy to be stretching its mechanical muscles on the long run to London and beyond.

"Undine has promise," I said, letting my words fade tentatively into the silence.

"I agree," Dogger said.

Outside, trees, hills, and sky rolled by in an endless panorama of autumn. The last harvesters were at work in the patchwork fields, their machines crawling like clockwork bugs across the landscape.

"She's a very strange person," I said.

Above a distant hill, rain slanted down in ruled lines from the black bottoms of a cloud that billowed up into towers of matchless white in the glorious sunshine above.

"Yes, she is," Dogger agreed. "But when you come to think of it, Miss Flavia, we are all strange persons."

The rest of the journey passed in relative silence.

Gollingford Abbey was much as we had left it. When I remarked upon this fact, Dogger said: "Change is unwelcome in prisons and hospitals. It is only their sameness which makes them tolerable to those kept captive within their walls."

We parked on a small crescent of loose gravel that lay to one side of the entrance.

We were climbing the steps when rather a round man in a white jacket and peaked cap stepped out of the vestibule. He appeared to be a porter of some description.

"Looking for someone in particular, guv?" he asked Dogger.

"Yes. Yes, we are," Dogger told him. "And you are?"

"Courtwright," the man answered, lifting his cap and plopping it back on again with a broad smile. "Gilbert C. Courtwright. You can call me Gil—they all do. Even those that I'm in charge of."

"Thank you, Gilbert," Dogger said. "We shall be much obliged if you will direct us to Dr. Brocken."

"Dr. *Augustus* Brocken?" Gil said, removing his cap again and staring into it as if further instructions were printed in the hatband.

"That's right," Dogger told him. "He is, perhaps, expecting us."

Which was true, I realized. Dogger has a way of making statements that resonate in worlds other than the one in which we live, shimmering between them, seemingly without effort. It is an art which I much admire, and which I hope someday to master.

"Ah! Dr. Brocken," Gil said. "That's a sly one, that is."

"I beg your pardon?" Dogger said, his eyebrows rising.

"It's a joke, guv. We all say that. 'E likes his peace and quiet. No trouble at all. If it's a nice day we put 'im out in the morning sun and bring 'im in at night—with the bed-sheets."

"You have a well-developed sense of humor, Gilbert," Dogger said.

"You 'ave to, guv, in a place like this. Otherwise you'd go lulu."

"Lulu?" Dogger said.

"Round the bend. 'Arpic. You know: monkey wrenches for breakfast."

"Ah," said Dogger, "I see. And where shall we find Dr. Brocken?"

Gil made a broad sweep of the arm toward the grounds. "Third oak on the right, and round the other side."

"Thank you, Gilbert." Dogger extended a hand, which Gil took with, as they say, alacrity. "You've been most helpful."

We strolled off across the lawn, and when we were out of Gil's earshot, I said to Dogger: "It started out as a rainy day last time we were here, didn't it?"

"I was just thinking that myself," Dogger said.

We had no trouble locating the third oak on the right, and on the far side of it, on a wooden bench that ringed its trunk, was sitting Dr. Brocken, as we had been told he would be. In his white suit and broad-brimmed hat he looked like a tropical planter.

"Good afternoon, Dr. Brocken," Dogger said. "I hope you are well?"

The doctor made no reply.

"May we sit?" Dogger asked, gesturing toward the bench.

Again: silence.

We sat down quietly beside him, me on the left and Dogger on his right.

Although I watched the doctor carefully, I could see no flicker of awareness. He might as well have been made of stone.

"I should like to inform you, Dr. Brocken," Dogger said, "that we've been retained by your daughter, Mrs. Prill, to look into certain missing letters—letters which she has reason to believe were stolen from her."

I tried to catch Dogger's eye, but he evaded me. Why was he using the phrase "has reason," as if Mrs. Prill were still alive? Had anyone informed the doctor of her death? And if they had, what was his reaction?

Dogger went on: "We have so far been unable to locate these stolen documents. Acting, then, as her agents, we propose to search your room in the hope of shedding some light on the matter. Do you approve? Do you grant us your permission?"

Dr. Brocken didn't so much as flicker an eyelash.

"Or do you forbid us?" Dogger went on.

A sudden gust of autumn wind rattled the leaves above our heads.

And then the doctor began to choke: a small spasm at first which quickly became a wholesale heaving of his chest.

"Run to Dr. Brocken's room, please," Dogger told me. "Fetch a glass of water."

He began to slap the doctor on his back.

I ran like the wind, across the lawn, up the steps, and

into the foyer of the abbey. At the door I reduced my pace to a stroll: the reluctant stroll of a young person forced into an unwilling visit with some reeking old ancestor. No point in drawing attention to myself.

It didn't matter anyway: There wasn't a soul in sight.

In less than a minute, I had made it to room 37 and locked myself in.

As for the water, I never gave it another thought. Dogger had said "Run to Dr. Brocken's room." And he meant it.

Had he wanted water, he would have told me to run for water, and no more.

I had received his coded instructions and deciphered them correctly. I knew what I was being told to do.

The room was unchanged from our earlier visit. Painted an institutional white, like milk that has had every particle of goodness skimmed from it, the small chamber contained a bed, a chair, a table, and a dresser.

Depressing to think a life has come to this.

I gave the bed, table, mattress, and pillows a good old going-over, and found nothing out of the ordinary. I unscrewed the metal caps on the bedposts and looked inside, upended the chair to inspect the bottom of the seat, searched the dresser inside and out, all with no result.

There was nothing left.

Even though it couldn't have taken me more than ten minutes, the hot, stale air of the room made it seem a lifetime. Dogger would be expecting me back with the water, if for nothing else but show. He was quite capable of dealing with a choking fit without my assistance.

I went to the window to see if I could spot the oak where he and Dr. Brocken were sitting. Perhaps they were already on their way back to the residence.

As I brushed against the curtains, something at my feet went *bump!*

I dropped to my knees and lifted the hem of the draperies, a heavy, cheap kind of red-dyed sacking that could be drawn, if required, to darken the room in the daytime.

Was it a lead weight, perhaps, sewn into the fabric to make it hang straight without bunching up?

Hospitals didn't go in for such luxuries. Function was everything. Even the birds in the cheap print on the wall were meant to calm; meant to provide an illusion of freedom, and of the outdoors.

I groped along the bottom of the curtain.

Aha! There was something in there. Something rectangular.

By manipulating the object with my fingers in a milking-the-cow movement, I was able to slide whatever it was along until it fell out—with a *plop!*—onto the floor.

The seam had been cut open at the end. I had found the doctor's hidey-hole.

I picked up the object and lifted it up into the light.

It was a wallet, and no ordinary one at that—remarkably heavy, with sterling silver corners and stamped with the name of an expensive maker in Bond Street.

I was not interested in the money, although I guessed there were several hundred pounds in banknotes. Tucked in behind them were a number of folded letters, and half a dozen business cards (*Augustus Brocken, "Brocken's Bal-*

samic Electuary," Hoverford House, London WC) engraved in an elaborate and tasteful green and white that fairly screamed of the healthful outdoors. In the little domed pocket meant to contain coins was a railway ticket.

I had the thing in hand when there was a battering at the door.

"Open up!"

I knew the voice. It was Gil.

I shoved the letters and the ticket into my pocket, tucked the wallet back into the hem of the curtain, and scrambled to my feet.

I dashed to the sink, filled the glass with water, and went to the door. Biting my tongue in concentration, I slid back the bolt, slowly and in utter silence.

"Give it your shoulder!" I shouted, and stood back.

The door flew open with a *bang!* and Gil came hurtling into the room, flailing his arms to keep his balance.

"Oh, thank you, Gil," I said, making my hand—and the glass of water in it—tremble noticeably. "The lock must have jammed. I couldn't get out. You're a lifesaver."

He was still moving—slowly but menacingly— toward me.

Steeling myself, I stepped forward and gave him a peck on the cheek.

Well, in truth, not so much a peck as a real wet smacker. It stopped him in his tracks as effectively as if he'd been slapped in the face with a flounder.

He reached up and touched the place where I had kissed, with as much wonder as if I were the princess and he the frog.

And then he began to color: pink at first, but changing rapidly through all the shades to a brilliant ruby red.

I thought he was going to pop a gasket.

And then, as quickly as it came on, the flush began to recede. I could see him getting a grip on himself.

"You oughtn't to be in here, miss," he hissed in a confidential undertone. "Private rooms are strictly off limits in the absence of occupants."

I knew he was quoting from some official decree: some show of force by the Invisible Rule Makers, whose commands are observed mostly in the breaking of them by people like me.

"I'm sorry," I said, because it was the required answer. "But Dr. Brocken was choking and needed a glass of water."

"You should have asked at the desk," Gilbert said. "There's hoses enough on the grounds, when it comes to that."

On and on he prattled: I ought to have done such and such: this, that, and the other.

I have noticed that it's the same with all petty officials: Once they catch you breaking a rule, they lecture you, not just until the cows come home, but until the cows have eaten dinner, hauled on their flannel pajamas, climbed into bed, listened to a bedtime story, put out the lights, and drifted off to sleep to dream of pastures new.

There is only one way to deal with such authority.

"You're absolutely right, Mr. Courtwright," I said. "I ought to have thought of that. I must compliment you on your vigilance. How may I make amends?"

In cases such as this, you can never slather it on too thick. What the tyrant wants is utter and abject remorse. Anything less is a waste of their time.

"A small contribution to the Attendant's Beanfest Fund?" I suggested. "Or a letter of commendation to the superintendent?"

I stopped just short of suggesting a bronze statue of himself in the park, with mouth open in a silent shout and a finger raised in an angry warning to rule-breakers.

Already I could see that he was coming off the boil. Enforcers are reluctant to make actual decisions.

"Just don't do it again," he muttered.

Had the emergency been a real one, Dr. Brocken might have choked to death by now.

"Have you the time, Mr. Courtwright?" I asked. "We mustn't miss our train."

Courtwright pulled back his sleeve and glanced quickly at his watch, a rather superior thing with various dials more for show than practicality.

"Half two," he said, rather grudgingly.

"I'll be getting along, then," I said, preparing to make my exit. "I shall remember to say a prayer tonight for all those in authority over us, and so rule their hearts and strengthen their hands, that they may punish wickedness and vice."

And I escaped before he could hit me with a brickbat.

Dogger was sitting silently on the bench beside Dr. Brocken.

"Thank you," he said as I handed him the glass of water. He took a sip.

"Ah," he said. "Most refreshing. Dry work, this."

"Is he all right?" I pointed to the silent doctor.

"Fit as a fiddle," Dogger answered as he got to his feet.

"Thank you, Dr. Brocken," he said. "You have been most cooperative."

And I thought I knew what he meant.

·SEVENTEEN·

As Dogger turned the long, shining bonnet of the
Rolls toward London and home, I could barely contain
myself.

"I found his wallet!" I said. "It was hidden in the hem
of the curtain."

"It was bound to be somewhere like that. It wasn't in
his pockets."

I glanced at him in amazement.

"Thumping the back of a choking victim provides an
admirable opportunity to do a bit of pocket-angling."

"Dogger!" I said. "I'm surprised at you."

And we both laughed. Somewhere in his hazy past,
Dogger had had to become an accomplished picker of
pockets, as well as several other of the shady arts.

"These ought to be interesting," I said as I hauled out
the folded letters and the railway ticket.

Dogger glanced away from the road for an instant. "If you'd be so good as to read them aloud to me," he said.

I flattened out the letters and cleared my throat.

"'Dear Agustus,'" I began. "And they've misspelled 'Augustus,' Dogger," I pointed out before going on. "'The game is up. The cat is among the pigeons. Saints preserve us! Put your money where your mouth is. Do you take my meaning? Don't let the grass grow under your feet. Yours faithfully, Hahnemann.'"

"Hmmm," Dogger said. "Next, please."

"'Farewell, farewell. The fox is among the hens.
Is there no balm in Gilead? Fly away home. Your
house is on fire and your children are gone,
'All except one,
'And her name is Ann,
'And she hid under the baking pan.'"

"Is that all?" Dogger asked. "No signature?"

"No," I said. "Only the first letter is signed."

"Excellent!" Dogger said. You could actually hear the pop of the exclamation mark.

"Excellent? It sounds like a lot of mumbo jumbo to me."

"Have you read Plato?"

"No," I said. "At least, not yet."

"You ought to," Dogger said with a smile. "You will find him remarkably enlightening."

Even though he didn't show it, I could tell that Dogger was itching to share a bombshell with me.

"For instance?" I prodded.

"For instance, Plato observed that the mask which the actor wears is apt to become his face."

I thought about this for several long moments before I replied. "I can see that," I said. "It makes sense."

And it did. How often had Mrs. Mullet told me, when I was pouting in winter, that my face might freeze and I'd look like that for the rest of my life?

"Plato also pointed out," Dogger went on, "that the man who has no self-respect will imitate anybody and anything."

"Mmmm," I said, nodding sagely. "Interesting. But it doesn't tell us much about these letters, does it?"

"On the contrary," Dogger said. "It tells us everything."

Although I tried to control it, my eyebrows must have shot up in a pair of inverted Vs. I could feel my forehead stretching.

"Really?" I said. I couldn't hide my astonishment. I stuck my forefingers behind my ears and pushed them forward so that they stuck out like Dumbo's.

I didn't need to say "I'm all ears." Dogger knew what I meant.

"Let us first deal with the minor points of the first letter," Dogger told me. "It is the work of a mind that, while clever, is not half so clever as it thinks it is. Writing entirely in clichés is calculated to thwart any attempt to trace the writer by analysis of the grammar or linguistic usage. The internal references, such 'the game is up' and 'cat is among the pigeons,' suggest that the recipient of the letters has been found out. 'Put your money where your mouth is' might well be a reference to blackmail, while 'Don't let the grass grow under your feet' could possibly be construed as a death threat. The name Hahnemann refers, of course, to Samuel Hahnemann, the founder of the system of medicine called homeopathy."

"*Like cures like!*" I said. "Dr. Darby mentioned it."

"Precisely," Dogger said. "Indicating, perhaps, that the dark doings of Dr. Brocken, whatever they may have been, had to do with that art."

"The infusions of balsam," I said. "Brocken's Balsamic Electuary."

"Perhaps not in the beginning." Dogger steered out and around a muddy gray Fergie that was driving at a crawl in front of us. "Perhaps more toward the end."

"'Saints preserve us'!" I exclaimed. "It's in the letter! It refers to the ribboned bone and the dust I found in Miss Truelove's potting shed! Someone is on to them!"

"Possibly," Dogger said, "but not necessarily."

My puzzlement must have been written across my face.

"But just for the moment, if you please, let us consider the second letter."

I held it up in front of me for reference as he spoke.

"This one is much more simple," Dogger said. "There is no salutation. 'Farewell, farewell' suggests that a blackmail attempt has failed, and that the incriminating evidence is about to be handed over to the authorities."

"Or has *already* been handed over," I said.

"No. There would be no point in writing the letter if it had been. A final demand, if you like. A direct threat."

My mind was racing like a runaway tram.

"The use of the phrase 'no balm in Gilead,'" Dogger

said, "refers directly to Dr. Brocken's electuary. So that there cannot be the slightest doubt who it is that is being addressed. The rest of the message is the crucial part."

"'Ladybird, ladybird, fly away home,'" I said, quoting not from the letter but from the nursery rhyme. "'Your house is on fire and your children are gone. All except one, and her name is Ann . . .'"

"Anastasia," Dogger said, and my blood ran cold. Anastasia Prill.

Who was already dead.

Hiding under the baking pan had apparently not been good enough.

"We found her dead in the *kitchen*," I whispered.

I almost dropped the letter from my fingers, which had gone suddenly numb.

"It was just as she told us," I said. "The letters were a threat against her father's business. She *didn't* tell us that the threats were against her—against her life."

"No," Dogger agreed. "She didn't."

A bell was clanging loudly in my hippocampus. "Hold on," I said. "I just remembered. You said you didn't believe the letters existed."

"I believe I suggested that they almost certainly existed, Miss Flavia, but that Mrs. Prill herself had stolen them."

"And?"

"And I have seen or heard nothing to make me change more than the latter part of that perhaps hasty opinion."

Dogger seldom loses me, but he had lost me now. Things simply didn't add up.

"All right," I said. "I give up. You've stumped me."

"Excellent," Dogger said, tapping his forefingers on the steering wheel. "Being stumped often offers a whole new beginning. It sometimes generates just enough anger to solve the case."

"I'm not angry," I pointed out. "Simply stumped."

I wasn't going to let him get the upper hand.

"Just so," Dogger said. "Then let us return to the first letter."

I rested the letter on my lap.

"'Dear Agustus,'" Dogger quoted from memory.

"Yes," I said. "The blackmailer misspelled Dr. Brocken's first name."

"Intentionally," Dogger said. "As I have already observed, these letters were written by a mind that is not half so clever as it thinks it is. It is meant to throw us off the scent. Who would suspect a person that misspells his own name?"

Dogger left the question hanging in the air, where it hovered for what seemed like an eternity.

"Good God!" I exclaimed. "Pardon me, Dogger, but good God! Are you suggesting that—?"

"Indeed I am, Miss Flavia. I now believe that Dr. Brocken wrote these letters himself."

"Him*self*?"

I felt like Lady Bracknell, in Oscar Wilde's play *The Importance of Being Earnest*, when she says "Haaannndd-baaaaaag?," stretching the word to such a ridiculous length that it was in danger of collapsing under its own weight.

"It seems not only possible, but very likely," Dogger

said, glancing over several times at the letters in my hands. "The handwriting, you will have observed, is very masculine—very determined. Heavy pressure on the pen. Powerful downstrokes but hasty terminators: the mark of an impatient man. The wavering of the loops indicates that he was writing more slowly than normal in an attempt to disguise his handwriting. You can sometimes camouflage the hand, but you cannot camouflage the man behind it."

I had, in fact, noticed the masculinity of the handwriting, but I hadn't put it into words. The eye must see and understand before the mouth can speak.

Except in the case of Daffy, of course.

"Now, then," Dogger said, "let us proceed to the railway ticket."

"I'll read it to you," I said. "The printing is quite small. It's a monthly return ticket, Southern Railway, First Class, from Brookwood to Waterloo. Ten shillings."

"And not another from Waterloo to Hinley?"

"No, just the one," I said. "There wasn't another in the wallet."

"As I should expect," Dogger said. "He'd have destroyed it. A ticket to London is an alibi, whereas a ticket direct to Hinley, or even to somewhere as nearby as Doddingsley, might well be a ticket to the gallows."

"You mean—"

Dogger smiled at me: the most angelic smile that I had ever seen on a human face.

"But don't breathe a word. All of this is, as yet, mere conjecture."

We rode in silence for a while, and I realized, as the miles went by, that something was troubling me. I raked through the ashes of my mind, searching for the faintest spark.

And then I saw it!

"Dogger!" I said. "Do you remember asking me if I'd brought anything away from Miss Truelove's place? You said that in law, there is a distinct line between trespassing and burglary?"

"Quite true," Dogger said. "You are worried about removing the letters and the ticket from Dr. Brocken's room."

I nodded, already imagining myself in handcuffs and leg shackles.

"There is also a distinct line between burglary and a commission to recover the said letters. We have recovered them."

I noticed that Dogger didn't mention my removing evidence from the scene of a crime. Even though Gollingford Abbey was not, strictly speaking, the scene of Mrs. Prill's murder, it now seemed almost certain that criminal activity of some description had taken place there.

It was all so infernally complicated.

·EIGHTEEN·

WE ARRIVED HOME TO find a police bicycle parked in the forecourt. We leaped out of the Rolls and dashed into the house. At least, I did—and Dogger wasn't far behind.

In the middle of the foyer, Mrs. Mullet stood dabbing at her eyes with the corner of her apron.

"Oh! Oh!" she said when she saw us. "Thank goodness you're 'ome. You got 'ere just in the neck of time, didn't they, Constable?"

Constable Linnet looked up from his notebook, in which he had been scribbling with his pencil, and nodded assent.

"It's Miss Undine," Mrs. Mullet said, and then broke down.

"She's gone missing, I'm afraid," Constable Linnet informed us.

"Last seen?" Dogger asked.

"Not since breakfast," Mrs. Mullet managed, her lips trembling pitifully. "Just after you left. She asked me to make 'er a sandwich, poor dear, and wrap it up in butcher's paper. I ought to 'ave known."

"Did she say where she was going?" I asked. I was trying to put myself in Undine's place. The last words she had spoken to me were about Miss Stonebrook's peculiar harness.

Had she crept back to return it to Miss Stonebrook's bedroom?

"And the ladies?" I asked.

Mrs. Mullet shrugged. "Took 'em up breakfast in bed. Thought it would be nice, like, after that woman Stonebrook's bad breathin'."

Which told me everything I needed to know about Mrs. M's opinion of Ardella Stonebrook. The words *that woman* can convey more emotion than a thousand-page novel.

"If you'll excuse me for a moment—" Dogger said, and vanished in the direction of the kitchen. A minute later he was back.

"Their car is gone," he reported.

As Mrs. Mullet began a low moaning, Dogger put his hand on her shoulder.

"Maybe they've taken the little girl for a ride," Constable Linnet said, and Mrs. Mullet's moaning rose to a banshee wail.

"I wouldn't 'ave called you if I thought they 'ad, Archie Linnet," she replied through her sobs, and the constable blushed. That his given name was Archibald was an open secret among the villagers of Bishop's Lacey.

"She didn't come 'ome for dinner. It isn't like 'er. I went through the 'ole 'ouse callin' 'er name, but she didn't answer. Poor little mite. Somethin's 'appened to 'er. I just know it."

"Did she say anything?" I asked Mrs. M. "When you gave her the sandwich?"

"She just took it and ran off. She 'ad a magnifyin' glass in 'er 'and."

My heart sank.

What a horrid mistake I had made in discussing Miss Stonebrook's appliance with a child. Undine had likely taken it into her head that she was a detective. Even though she knew nothing about it, she was going to solve the case on her own and present it to me, wrapped up in ribbons, when I got home.

Wrapped up in ribbons. The very thought of the words caused me to shudder.

If their car was not in the coach house, where had the Missioners gone? Had they caught Undine snooping through their belongings? Had they flown the coop?

But why would they? I wondered. As far as I knew, they were still scheduled to deliver their lecture on Christian Health at the parish hall.

Could I kill two birds with one stone? Or, maybe even three?

*

Bent over Gladys's handlebars, I whistled along like the wind between the hedgerows.

My mind was made up. I would share some of what I knew with Cynthia Richardson. Being a vicar's wife, she was probably bound by some complicated oath to observe confidences: the Seal of the Kitchen Confessional; the Vow of the Vicarage; something like that.

At least I hoped she was.

Gladys loved lounging in the churchyard grass, and I left her lying there to graze or ruminate as she saw fit.

I banged on the door of the vicarage. There seemed to be a great deal of noise coming from inside: Raised voices rang out, clearly audible from the porch.

Were Cynthia and the vicar having an unholy row?

I banged again and the shouting stopped.

After a moment, the door opened, and I found myself staring up into the face of Colin Collier. I'd forgotten about the Vicar's Vestry, and the lads from Christ Church.

"Hello, Collie," I said. "Remember me?"

"Flavia," Collie said, opening the door wider and waving me in. "Of course I do. How could I forget you?"

There are certain things that a male can say that set female hearts aflutter. Not that it had ever happened to me, personally, of course, but Daffy had read enough Jane Austen aloud that I thought I knew the feeling, if that makes any sense.

"Is Mrs. Richardson at home?" I asked, getting down to business to avoid embarrassment.

"Cynthia? Of course she is. She was just now coaching us in a game of carpet hockey. Care to join us?"

As soon as Cynthia saw me, she blew a shrill blast on her whistle.

"*Time!*" she shouted. "Up scrub brushes. The dirty dishes shall wait no longer. You must earn your keep. Off with you."

With mostly happy grins, the young men swarmed off into the kitchen and the distant clatter of crockery began.

"Now, then," Cynthia said, collapsing into an easy chair and waving me into another. "What's up?"

"It's Undine," I replied. "She's gone missing. I thought she might be here?"

Cynthia smiled a rueful smile. "Here?" she said. "I should hardly expect to find her here. She thinks the church a confounded chamber of horrors. Those were her own words: 'A confounded chamber of horrors.'"

I wanted to say "No wonder!" but I did not. Considering what had befallen her mother at St. Tancred's, it came as no surprise that Undine would take rather a dim view of the place.

"Well," I said, "Mrs. Mullet's reported it to the police, so I suppose it's in their hands now. It just seemed odd that she should disappear at the same time as—"

Watch it, Flavia! Loose lips sink ships. My natural urge to gossip with Cynthia had almost betrayed me.

"As whom?" Cynthia asked.

"It's nothing," I said, trying vainly to backpedal. "Just that Miss Pursemaker and Miss Stonebrook haven't been seen since this morning, either."

Cynthia threw back her head and laughed, a loud, braying laugh that didn't really become her. "In that case," she said, gasping for breath, "you've come to the right place. The ladies in question are sitting, at this very moment, at my kitchen table consuming the remnants of the pudding. Carpet hockey puts one in want of a hearty tea."

"What?" I gasped. The image of Miss Stonebrook and Miss Pursemaker engaging in a game of floor hockey with the lads of Christ Church was too ludicrous for even my highly developed imagination.

"Come along." Cynthia rose from her chair. "If we're quick about it there might be a crumb left for each of us."

"No, thank you," I said. "I'd better be getting along. I'm rather worried about Undine, and I won't be able to rest until she's found."

"I understand," Cynthia said. "But I shouldn't worry if I were you. Undine is a very resourceful person for her age. I shall tell the ladies you were asking about them."

"Yes . . . yes, do that," I said, relieved at not having to confront the Missioners. I still wasn't sure how they fitted into the grand scheme of things, and it wouldn't do to make another misstep.

"Oh, by the way," I asked, "when are they giving their lecture on Christian Health? I wouldn't want to miss it for the world."

"Tomorrow evening," Cynthia answered. "Seven sharp. Doors at six-thirty. Come early and avoid the stampede."

Was she being facetious? With Cynthia, one never knew. She was sometimes, as Winston Churchill said of Russia, a riddle, wrapped in a mystery, inside an enigma.

But perhaps as the wife of a Church of England clergy-man, she needed to be.

Outside, I circled the vicarage and, sure enough, be-hind it was the hired Morgan three-wheeler. The ladies had gone round to use the kitchen door, and parked it at the rear.

Sometimes, when Fate deals you into a game you weren't expecting, you can only play your cards to the best of your ability.

Here was a fresh opportunity to search the car more thoroughly in a place where the ladies would be least ex-pecting it. After all, the church and its land were hal-lowed ground: No one would think for an instant of their vehicle being rifled.

And who knows, I thought. *They may well have hidden any number of incriminating articles in the Morgan since the last time I looked.*

The ladies themselves, I reasoned, couldn't see me from the kitchen windows. Cynthia had said they were sitting at the table: Their heads were surely not high enough to see over the sills. A bit of practical trigonom-etry, worked out in my head, convinced me that this was the case. A mental green pilot light went on.

All clear.

But what about the Christ Church lads? They were scattered about the kitchen, at the sink and elsewhere. But what did it matter? They had all seen me in the churchyard. I was no stranger to their eyes. They wouldn't pay the least attention to me taking a stroll in the vicar-age garden.

After all, I was only a girl.

And so, it was with supreme confidence that I approached the car.

The canvas top was down, folded into the boot. Without a glance over my shoulder—I didn't want to look suspicious—I strolled up and struck an admiring pose in front of the Morgan, as if I were a gawker at the Earl's Court Motor Show.

I balled up a bit of my sleeve in my fist and brushed away an imaginary fleck of dust from the gleaming radiator, then stepped back to admire my handiwork.

I counted to twenty, but no one came swarming out of the vicarage.

I was as safe as houses.

There is a method for searching cars, and I followed it to a T.

First, I walked round the vehicle and stopped behind it, admiring as I went. Then I squatted, out of sight—twice—once to look as if I were picking up something I had dropped, and the second time to do the dirty work.

I was now on my knees, searching the glove box and looking under the seats.

Nothing aside from a road map—which I examined, in vain, for pencil markings—a box of paper facial tissues (with nothing hidden in or under them), and a small brass compass.

Standing up, I stretched, as if I were becoming bored, and stared off into the distance for a few moments. Then, turning again to the Morgan, I leaned over and shoved my hand under the folded top and into the boot.

My fingers came into contact at once with a slightly sticky packet: oilcloth, by the feel of it, and quite heavy.

I hauled it out and turned my back to the house. With trembling fingers I opened the flaps.

Curses! It was a motorist's tool roll: everything needed, from spanners for removing wheels to a lever for removing tires and a Dunlop kit for repairing punctures, which included rubber cement, dusting chalk, and a wicked looking awl, whose use was not immediately evident—at least, to me.

For a couple of ladies traveling alone, it was probably a wise weapon kept comfortably concealed.

I wondered what else might be tucked away in the boot. I shoved the repair kit back to where I judged it to have been, stretching my arm to its limit—reaching into the far corner of the luggage space.

Something seized my wrist like an iron vise.

A guttural voice snarled, "What the devil do you think you're playing at?"

One reads occasionally of persons whose kidneys have almost fallen out from shock, and I can now vouch for the truth of what I had, up until now, taken to be old wives' tales.

My guts went numb. There's no better way to describe it.

My wrist was firmly clamped beneath the folded canvas car top, and something was shaking it like a dog shakes a rat. No matter how hard I pulled, I couldn't break free.

I was about to commit the one unforgivable offense for

a de Luce, which was to burst into tears, when there came from the car boot an unmistakable giggle.

A giggle that was all too familiar.

"Did I frighten you, Flavia?"

My wrist was suddenly set free, and my first impulse was to brain the child.

And yet, at the same time, I was so overjoyed to see Undine's idiotic face grinning out at me from the depths of the Morgan that my impulses were instantly neutralized: like mixing an acid with an alkali. What could I say? What could I do?

"No, you didn't frighten me," I replied. "I knew you were in there all along. Now, come with me. Everyone is simply livid with you, including me. Mrs. Mullet's called the police. Whatever were you thinking?"

Undine began unfolding herself and clambered from the boot, clutching in one hand the magnifying glass she had taken from Buckshaw.

"That's mine!" I protested, when I saw the powerful lens. "You stole it from my laboratory! I thought you'd taken the one from the library."

The little rotter had found the laboratory key I had hidden so cleverly in the hollow doorknob.

"Oh, piffle," Undine said. "The one in the library is a joke. Not nearly powerful enough for a professional. I needed something with sufficient magnification for fingerprints and fibers."

Fingerprints and fibers! I almost laughed aloud.

"And did you find any?" I asked.

"No," Undine said with a jerk of her thumb, "but there's a dead rat in the boot."

"One of yours?" I asked, even though sarcasm was probably lost on this pudding-headed mooncalf.

"No. It was there all along."

"All along?" I asked. "What do you mean, all along? How long have you been in there?"

"All day," Undine answered. "I'm a very patient person."

"Listen," I told her, "I've got to get you home. We shall call in at the police station on the way and tell Constable Linnet you're safe. Then we'll decide what we're going to do with you."

"Meaning punishment?" Undine asked. "Am I to be forced to walk the plank?"

"It depends," I said, which was all I could come up with on the spot without wracking my brains to ribbons.

·NINETEEN·

AS IT HAPPENED, WE didn't need to make a stop at the police station. I had no sooner set Gladys's wheels beyond the churchyard wall, with Undine clinging happily on behind, than Constable Linnet himself appeared.

The constable had chosen to take the shortcut across the fields from Buckshaw, rather than using the slightly longer lane, and as a result, looked red, shaken, and peevish.

He flagged us down and hauled out his notebook.

"Is this the child who was reported lost?" he asked. He knew perfectly well it was, but he apparently needed to go through the official rigmarole as if he were a clockwork copper.

Well, two can play at that game, I decided.

"Constable Linnet, this is Undine de Luce. *Miss* de

Luce. Undine, this is police constable number thirty-seven, Linnet."

I wasn't quite sure if this was the way in which such an introduction was formally to be made, but I didn't give a fig if it was or not.

"How-do-you-*do*, sir," Undine said, offering her hand. "I'm very happy to make your acquaintance."

I was ridiculously proud of her. Whatever else she may be, Undine had been properly brought up.

The constable shook two of her fingers as a gesture of goodwill and returned to his notebook, where he made a squiggle.

"And where did you locate her?"

"At the vicarage," I told him.

"And your name?"

At least six hilarious replies came to mind, but I settled for rolling my eyes up toward heaven.

"Flavia Sabina de Luce."

He duly wrote it down. "And she is unharmed?"

What did he mean, "unharmed"? What could possibly befall Undine at the vicarage?

"She's perfectly fine, Constable," I said.

He snapped closed his notebook and placed the pencil in his breast pocket. "I'll complete my paperwork at the station. You'd better take the little girl straight home. They'll be worried about her."

"No need for any paperwork," I said. "She's safe and sound."

I didn't want my doings part of a police report.

"Nonetheless," said Constable Linnet, and pushed off on his bicycle.

Undine watched his departure through the magnifying glass. I was grateful she hadn't flourished it in his face.

"How went the investigation?" I asked.

"Mostly a slosh." Undine frowned. "No fingerprints, no footprints, no clues. Other than this."

She reached into her pocket and produced a paper bag, which she reached round and waved under my nose. The remains of her sandwich, I supposed.

"What's in it?" I asked.

"A *rat!*" she shrieked in my ear. "I told you I found a rat. Did you forget?"

"No," I said, "but you needn't wave it in my face. It might be carrying the bubonic plague."

"I hope so," Undine said, enthusiastically, and we rode home in silence.

Having delivered Undine up to Mrs. Mullet for a stern lecture on responsibility and the necessity of always reporting one's whereabouts in a world filled with kidnappers, I carried the paper bag upstairs and knocked at Dogger's door.

"Undine has been found," I told him at once, to ease his mind. "She was at the vicarage. The Missioners were there, too, so I was able to kill two birds with one stone. Speaking of killing, Undine was hiding in their Morgan. She found a rat in the boot: very appropriate, don't you think, since she was a stowaway?"

Dogger's eyes lit up. "Excellent," he said. "But what has killing to do with a rat?"

"If you don't mind coming along to the lab," I replied, "I shall be happy to demonstrate."

Two minutes later, to avoid interruptions, we had locked ourselves into the laboratory. Undine had left the key in the lock.

"If you'd be so good," I said, hauling out and handing to Dogger one of a pair of wartime gas masks which I kept on hand in case of chemical mishaps.

Dogger nodded approval, even though he hadn't yet seen the bag's contents.

We strapped on the masks, the transparent eyepieces causing our eyes to bug like giant insects, and our voices, when we spoke, came as hollow, mocking echoes from behind the stifling rubber.

"I presume you know already what's inside?" Dogger said.

"Yes," I admitted. "I took a quick peek. But only with one eye."

I placed the bag on a metal dish and, choosing a surgical scalpel from a drawer under the microscope, made a long incision in the paper and peeled back the edges.

"Hmmm," Dogger said, unflappable as always, leaning in for a closer look. "*Mus rattus rattus*, the black rat. Not native to this country. Smaller than its relative, *rattus decumanus*, the brown or Norway rat, which, by the way, the Jacobites liked to pretend came over with George the First, and called the Hanoverian rat. The Tories called it the Whig rat.

"These little fellows, the blacks, are thought to have originated somewhere in Asia, and being great globe-trotters, had, by about 1800, hidden themselves aboard ships and sailed as far as Africa and the South Pacific."

"I wonder where this one came from?" I said. "Was it hiding in the ladies' luggage or is it a local rat? It might have been born in a pile of rags at Bert Archer's garage. Or in the stuffing of the Morgan's seats."

"I should think the former," Dogger answered. "The black rat is thought to be near extinction in this country, except in the larger seaports. They have been the victims of their larger and more fierce cousins, the browns.

"I suggest that we put on surgical gloves before we proceed. Now, then, notice the wedge-shaped upper fore-teeth, and the three lower grinders on each side of the jaws. A hungry rat will eat anything from furniture to paper, although they prefer seeds, nuts, and grains."

I could think of other things that rats ate, but in order to maintain a certain decorum—if not scientific detachment—I decided not to mention them.

I let my eyes stray from the stained brown teeth to the glassy eyes.

"Look, Dogger!" I hadn't noticed it before. "Look how dilated the pupils are!"

"And the slight emesis," Dogger said. *Emesis*, I remembered, meant "throwing up," and it was true: On what had been the bottom of the bag was a partially dried dark blot of what I took to be rat puke.

"We must pursue this to the farthest end of the last

thread," Dogger said, and I knew, almost instinctively, what he meant. I handed him the scalpel.

With one long and decisive incision, Dogger had laid open the rat from snout to scuppers.

"How do you know what to look for?" I asked.

"It's a matter of experience," he replied, and I knew better than to ask any more questions. Dogger, as I have said before, has been through hell.

"Those objects that look like what our American friends call cocktail sausages," he said, pointing, "are the small intestine, and beneath them, the large. This little sac is the caecum, which joins the two. We should expect to find what we're seeking in the cocktail sausages."

Dogger was making light of a grim job, I knew, to protect my sensitivities, but he needn't have bothered. I don't know if you've ever dissected a rat, but to me, there was only one word for it: exhilarating.

There, before my very eyes, were all the wonders of the animal kingdom, laid out in a glistening panorama, like some rich and detailed altarpiece from the Middle Ages: the lungs, the liver, and the ileum, whose function, Dogger told me, is to absorb certain nutrients, such as vitamin B, and, of course, the saucy little sausages of the small intestine which, at a sudden stroke, now fell open, revealing a dark, damp mass of barely digested matter.

In our ghastly masks with their enormous eye sockets and their dangling rubber breathing hoses, we must have looked like a couple of aliens from a flying saucer dissecting a small earth creature in the name of some ghoulish intergalactic expedition.

"Dragendorff's solution," I said, and Dogger nodded agreement.

Because I had so recently made it before, it was the work of only a few minutes to make ready a fresh supply: the bismuth subnitrate, the glacial acetic acid, the potassium iodide, all prepared to perfection with precisely the proper amounts of water.

"Will you do the honors?" I asked, handing Dogger the A solution and the B solution.

Gravely, Dogger took the glass containers, and with deft hands made ready a flame-dried residue of the rat's last meal.

We both of us watched, rapt, as the Dragendorff's solution went pink with the presence of physostigmine.

"It died in the bag!" I said, excited beyond all reason.

"So it would seem," Dogger said, reaching for a pair of tweezers.

He plucked from a crease in the bottom of the bag a hard, dark kernel. I reached for the magnifier.

Dogger took the glass and peered through it. "A Calabar bean," he said. "Beyond question."

Our eyes met, staring at each other through the goggled glasses of the gas masks.

There was so much to say, and yet so little.

"Shall we incinerate the remains?" I asked, pointing to the small carcass. "We could do it in the garden. Undine will have forgotten about it by morning."

"I'm afraid not," Dogger said. "The remains will be required by the police as evidence. We must hand it over at once."

My heart skipped a beat. "Inspector Hewitt will be thrilled with what we've found."

If the truth be told, I could hardly wait to see Inspector Hewitt again, if for no other reason than to be in touch—however remotely—with his wife, Antigone.

Dogger shook his head. "On the contrary. The inspector will not be pleased. They will, of course, carry out their own tests, but it may well be argued by some future defense that we have tainted the evidence."

"But we didn't *know* it was evidence," I protested. "We were merely conducting an experiment on a dead rat."

"I think the inspector knows us better than that." Dogger smiled grimly. "*Much* better than that."

As Dogger removed the rat's carcass to a biologically safe container (a salvaged vacuum-sealed preserves jar), I swabbed down the instruments and work surfaces with a powerful disinfectant. One could only hope that Undine had not handled the furry corpse, but then I recalled that her earlier life had given her experience of vermin far greater than my own.

At the sink, with rolled-up sleeves, as Dogger and I washed our hands and arms with carbolic soap, scrubbing again and again, companionably, like fellow surgeons at St. Bart's, I realized that this was one of the happiest moments of my life to date.

God's in His heaven, I thought, *all's right with the world.*

But for all the tea in China, I could not have told you why.

My thoughts were interrupted by a thunderous knocking at the door.

"Flavia! Open up. It's urgent."

"All right," I called out. "I'm coming. Keep your shirt on."

I caught Dogger's eye and he gave me an affirmative nod. All traces of our recent experiment had been safely cleared away.

I unlocked and opened the door and Undine came hurtling into the room like a human cannonball. She stopped just short of treading on my toes.

"What's on your mind?" I asked, pleasantly.

"Where's my rat?" she demanded, head cocked, hands on hips, and one foot placed ahead of her at a menacing angle.

"It's gone to heaven," I said, trying to put a lighthearted face upon what we had done to the creature. "It is, at this very moment, being awarded its little rat wings and its little rat halo."

Undine's eyes widened. "Do poisoned rats go to heaven?" she demanded, and my heart misfired.

"What do you mean, poisoned?" I asked.

She drew herself up to her full height—which wasn't very much—and focused her pale blue eyes upon me. Magnified by the round black frames of her spectacles, it was a most unnerving sight.

"The rat puked in the bag," she said. "I saw it with my own eyes. In Singa*pore*"—as always, she pronounced it with the accent on the last syllable—"it is common knowledge that poisoned rats puke before they kick the bucket. Isn't that right, Dogger?"

"It is, indeed, Miss Undine," Dogger said.

"In Sing*a*pore," Undine went on, "the poisoned rats are buried in deep trenches, so that the dogs and cats and owls won't eat them, isn't that so, Dogger?"

"It is, indeed, Miss Undine," Dogger said.

"So, there!" Undine said, stepping back. "Are you going to bury mine in a deep trench?"

"In due time, Miss Undine," Dogger told her. "Meanwhile, we shall hand it over to the proper authorities."

"Good job," Undine said. "I was going to do that anyway. Saves me the trouble."

"Did you enjoy your outing with Miss Stonebrook and Miss Pursemaker?" I asked, trying to distract her from a topic I didn't want to discuss.

"It wasn't an outing," Undine scoffed. "I hid myself in the car boot in the coach house. I thought you knew that."

"I probably did," I said, "but I forgot."

"They scared me skinny," Undine said, making her eyes go wide in a goggle-eyed stare. "I thought the bottom was going to fall out of the thing and scatter my parts all over the road. You have no idea!"

"Very brave of you," I told her. "But why?"

"I remembered what you said. That Miss Stonebrook might be a criminal. I wanted to find out what she was up to."

"I said no such thing," I said. "It was *you* who said she

might be a criminal—or an actress, or that she might have some disease—"

"Of the *bottom*!" Undine crowed.

"And what did you discover? Hold on—wait a minute. I'm not so sure I really want to know."

"It wasn't all that interesting, actually," Undine said. "It wasn't easy hearing them, what with all the noise and the dust. And when I *could* hear them, it was boring. *Boring.*

"They were going to the vicarage to meet Mrs. Richardson—to plan their talk. They wondered what she would serve them for tea. Miss Pursemaker said she never looked forward with any great happiness to the meager bill of fare likely to be encountered at a country vicarage."

My ears perked up as I realized that I was listening to a virtual dictating machine that had been hidden in the boot of the Missioners' hired car.

"You've remembered her words very accurately, Undine," I said.

"Of course I have. Ibu was teaching me to develop my eidetic memory. Most people nowadays call it 'photographic memory,' but its proper name is 'eidetic memory.' That's what *I* have. Ibu said people think it's rum, queer, or unusual, but it isn't. Balzac and W. H. Hudson, the naturalist, had it, and so did Jan Christian Smuts and the historian Thomas Babington Macaulay, and so do I."

"Go on," I said.

"Some authorities believe that eidetic memory is no more than a primitive form of—"

"Hold on," I said. "I meant go on with what you overheard in the boot of the car."

"Ha! I thought you might." Undine grinned with a devilish glint in her eye. "Miss Stonebrook said that any grub they might be offered at the vicarage would undoubtedly be better than the swill that was forced upon them by that Prill woman."

Undine looked at me expectantly.

"Interesting," I said.

She slipped into an unnervingly accurate mimicking of Miss Stonebrook's voice.

"'Fancy having to feed ourselves at midnight, like half-starved burglars at The Ritz. And after all the trouble we went to with those—'

"I'm not allowed to say the next word," Undine said, looking from Dogger to me and back again, searching our faces.

"I shall give you permission, Miss Undine," Dogger said. "Mind you, just this once, since it may well be a matter of life and death."

I was struck by how wonderfully Dogger dealt with the child. His was a kind of gentleness which, I think, cannot be learned and cannot be taught.

"'Bloody beans'!" Undine exploded. "'After all the trouble we went to with those bloody beans.' That's what she said. Those were her exact words."

"Thank you, Undine," I said.

"I'm sorry I said it twice," Undine said. "I sometimes suffer from an excess of zeal."

Dogger and I both smiled. We couldn't help ourselves. We could barely resist laughing aloud—at least, I couldn't.

"An excess of zeal is no great fault, Miss Undine," Dogger assured her. "I have sometimes suffered it myself. Perhaps we shall learn together, you and I, to curb our tongues upon occasion, and to keep our most secret treasures for our own private enjoyment."

"Roger, wilco," Undine said. "Message received and understood. Over and out."

·TWENTY·

ALONE IN MY ROOM, I pondered the evidence.

How I loved the sound of those words, "pondered the evidence." They captured the very essence of the investigator's life: the threads of the lives of others, grasped and woven into a string . . . a cord . . . a rope, a noose, perhaps, which might end up round a killer's neck. And yet, in spite of it all, the lonely solitude which, I was coming to realize, was bound to be forever at the very heart of Arthur W. Dogger & Associates.

Alone in my room, I pondered the evidence. A perfect phrase. I would jot it down for future use.

Like it or not, there are times when you need to be alone; times when you need to be lonely; times when you need to need other people.

Why had I never thought of this before? It was remarkable that I had overlooked such an obvious fact.

Because it seemed the right thing to do, I sat for ten minutes staring out the window and across the Visto, where early autumn was sweeping the land with its broom of many colors, and the trees were washed in all the glory of an early sunset.

Time was passing. I didn't need to be reminded of that.

I took a notebook and, at the top of a fresh page, wrote down the date and the time. Below that, I wrote:

QUESTIONS

(1) Will Dr. Brocken be able to go on pretending he's gaga? Dogger thinks he is malingering. Can invisibility be bought by the very wealthy? What can we deduce from the railway ticket?

(2) Why—and when—did the Missioners choose to leave Mrs. Prill's house? Why were they there in the first place? How did the Calabar beans come to be in their hired car?

(3) What is the real reason for Miss Stonebrook's wicker contraption?

(4) How does Miss Truelove fit into the scheme of things?

(5) Could I possibly be wrong about Mme. Castelnuo-vo's finger?

I could see at once that none of these questions was likely to have a simple answer. They were each as complex as the case itself, which was one of the most bizarre I had ever encountered.

What I needed was a jolly good chin-wag, no holds barred, with Cynthia Richardson and then with Dogger. Only by chewing over the evidence, reducing it to ribbons, and then reassembling it, would the truth come out.

There was always the possibility, of course, of confronting the Missioners face-to-face and asking them what the dickens they were up to.

Providing, naturally, that they were not murderers. If they were, any undue notice on my part would only serve to alert them, or worse, put my own life at risk.

No, in the case of those two globe-trotting ladies, I needed to play my cards carefully. It wouldn't do to spoil everything at the last minute by—as Undine would say—an excess of zeal.

Tomorrow evening was their lantern lecture on Christian Health at the parish hall.

I intended to be there, front and center, and the first to lead off the inevitable question period.

I had a couple of real corkers in mind.

No matter how hard I tried, sleep would not come. I tossed and turned, counted sheep, tried to work out, in my head, the cube root of the present year, 1952 (which I think was twelve-point-something), recited what I could remember of *The Charge of the Light Brigade*, which wasn't much, and tried to recall the name of that annoying girl who sang "The Teddy Bears' Picnic."

It was none of it any use. At the end I lay awake staring at the shadows on the ceiling, trying to move them, in my mind, into a semblance of the Mona Lisa.

Finally, I thought of something interesting: I would spell out the chemical name *octamethylcyclotetrasiloxane*.

Backward!

E . . . N . . . A . . . X . . . O

What a lovely name, I thought, for a laxative. Enaxo: the perfect purgative for putrid people.

Confound it. I would have to start over.

E . . . N . . . A . . . X . . . O . . . L . . .

In my dreams, I was riding in a first-class carriage of the London Necropolis Railway, built on a rail bed of rattling bones. Across from me, in plush comfort, sat two ladies in full mourning costume: everything from shoes to gloves to veils in somber black, with not so much as a smidgen of shine.

They were dead, of course. I knew this by the blueish tinge of their chalk-white faces, seen faintly through their veils as through a glass darkly, and their deep, sunken eyes.

Although they seemed to be staring straight ahead, their full veils made it hard to tell.

"Lovely day," I remarked. It is hard to know what to say to a corpse. Even the oldest and fattest of the printed manuals on manners—Mrs. Whatsername's, for instance—give no advice on how to address the dead.

Especially those to whom you haven't been introduced. Familiarity would seem to be out of the question.

"Lovely day for a funeral" might be a most dreadful faux pas, and "I'm sorry you're dead" could well be etiquettical suicide.

The solution was, as it is in so many other instances of British life, to press my lips together and give a microscopic nod and turn to looking out the window.

I see you. I grieve for you. Now fizz off.

Meanwhile, these two defunct dames sat perfectly still, apart from the rocking of the train, staring apparently straight through me at the pattern on the carriage's upholstery behind my back.

As if *I* were the invisible one.

This somehow hurt me deeply. It offended a sense I never knew I had before. Something needed to be done about it. Such a slight demands a response.

"Going far?" I asked.

That ought to give them something to think about.

I was chortling an inward chortle when one of the two specters leaned forward and, in a perfectly cultured voice, replied, quite pleasantly, "To the end of the line."

I couldn't believe my ears! I had been put in my place by a stiff.

While I was fishing for a comeback—which I was quite certain was beyond my limited experience in chatting up corpses—I noticed something odd about the second dead woman. Her hands were folded daintily in her lap, but in spite of her black silk mourning gloves, it was obvious that one of the fingers was limp and empty.

I couldn't take my eyes off it.

My breath seemed to have rushed out of my chest: I was as winded as if I had run full tilt to the top of some legendary mountain.

My mouth was dry. I swallowed.

And then I found my voice.

"Mme. Castelnuovo?" I asked.

The alarm clock scared the soup out of me. *Perhaps*, I remember thinking foggily, *that's why it's called an* alarm *clock*.

Nevertheless, my hand was shaking as I reached out to quiet the stupid thing.

Breakfast at Buckshaw was the one thing that hadn't changed a whit in living memory. But now, with Feely gone, it seemed a different occasion altogether, and hardly a festival.

While Daffy still sat hunched in silence over a book at her end of the table, and Undine, seated across from me, kept up her usual running chatter, something was different. It was as if the table itself had suffered some grievous loss. None of us glanced—not even for an instant—at the empty place formerly occupied by Feely.

Even when Mrs. Mullet came scurrying in with our eggs, the mood didn't much improve.

"Is this one boiled medium hard?" Daffy asked, eyeing the egg suspiciously.

"'Course it is, dear," Mrs. Mullet said. "Just as you like 'em."

"How can I be sure of that?" she asked.

Break it open and find out! I wanted to scream.

It was going to be one of those days. I just knew it.

"Because," Mrs. Mullet replied, "I boiled it while I sang 'All Things Bright and Beautiful.' All seven verses of it, with the remainders sung after every last one of 'em, plus one extra at the end. Six minutes on the button. Just the way you likes 'em."

And she began to sing:

"All things bright and beautiful,
All creatures great and small,
All things wise and wonderful,
The Lord God made them all."

Daffy rolled her eyes.

"Each little flower that opens,
Each little bird that sings,
'E made their glowing colors,
'E made their tiny wings."

Daffy let out an exasperated sigh.

"The rich man in 'is castle,
The poor man at 'is gate,
God made them 'igh and lowly,
And ordered their estate.

"Now eat your egg, dear, before it gets cold and I 'ave to take it 'ome and chop it up for the chickens."

Daffy decapitated the egg neatly with her egg spoon, and, diving into it without another glance, returned to her book—one which Carl Pendracka had lent to her at Feely's wedding—something by a person called Capote, who looked by his photo on the dust jacket like a fairy-tale princess who has just been kissed awake by the wrong prince. I knew the book must have its merits because Daffy kept covering her mouth to keep bits of the egg from falling out.

When Mrs. Mullet had retired to the kitchen, Undine leaned across the table and said to me in a loud, confidential tone: "I slipped that wicker thing back into Miss Stonebrook's room. I'll bet she didn't even notice it was gone."

"Hmmm," I said. It was best to be noncommittal about questionable deeds.

And then I made a sudden decision: rash, perhaps, but great decisions often are.

"Daffy," I asked, "what do you know about wicker costume?"

Daffy looked up from her book and there was no fire in her eye. One sure way of capturing her attention was to ask her a question that could be answered with a pyro-technical display of knowledge.

"Wicker," she said, marking her page in Capote with a finger, "was used by the Druids in spring and midsummer bonfire festivals. Caesar said they constructed great effi-gies in which they placed their sacrificial victims, who were then burned to death."

"I was thinking of something smaller," I said. "Something that could be worn, like a corset or a girdle."

"Then why didn't you say so?" Daffy asked. "The willow tree, from whose osiers wicker is made, is thought to contain spirits, and is often used in the quaint costumes of village dances."

"Why?" I asked.

"According to Sir James Frazer, in *The Golden Bough*, it's because of sympathetic magic, the Law of Sympathy, which can be broken down into two branches: the Law of Similarity and the Law of Contact."

Already she was losing me.

"I see," I said.

"The Law of Contact, or contagious magic, assumes that things that once have been in contact will remain so forever. Whatever is done to one will be done to, or felt by, the other. A good example of this is the Tooth Fairy: Your tooth is taken to be preserved forever in the Land of Faery, and so will you be preserved, back here on earth."

"That makes sense," Undine said, poking a finger back among her molars.

"It doesn't make sense," Daffy said. "That's the sense of it."

Seeing both of us baffled, she went on. "The Law of Sympathy, on the other hand, is based on the idea that like effects like, whether the objects have ever been in touch or not. It is also called homeopathic magic. You make a little doll of Miss Truelove because you don't like her. You place inside it a sample of her hair or fingernails, if you can lay hands on them, and stick the doll with pins. Miss Truelove suffers a massive heart attack and dies."

"Voodoo!" Undine shrieked.

My mind suddenly slowed, as if it had turned to jelly.

"Why do you mention Miss Truelove, in particular?" I asked, measuring my words. "Why not someone else?"

"Oh, *pffft!* I just picked her name out of the air because she happens to be the first domineering tyrant who came to mind. I could just as easily have said Flavia de Luce and you'd be trembling for a fortnight."

Undine was slowly wringing her hands, rotating them over the chafing dish.

"It is not wax that I am scorching," she chanted. "It is the liver, heart, and spleen of Felicity de Luce that I scorch.

"Ibu used to say that," she said. "It was a joke."

My blood ran hot. My blood ran cold.

Did this little girl have the faintest idea of what she was saying?

Had her mother been a witch? Had she actually placed a curse on Aunt Felicity? Or others?

Could it possibly be that the late Lena de Luce had been responsible for the downfall of my family? Had all of our fortunes been cast into the flames, years ago, in Singapore?

I had never in my life wanted more to be alone.

My blood had now become like lead.

"And a most amusing joke at that," I heard myself saying. "Now run along and help Mrs. Mullet with the herb garden. She might even bake you your own batch of scones."

Undine needed no more encouragement. She vanished into the kitchen, bearing off on high, as if it were a trophy, her own soiled breakfast plate.

"You were saying?" I said to Daffy.

Daffy glanced up from her book again with that pained, long-suffering look of the interrupted reader.

"What?" she asked.

"Willow," I said. "Wicker costumes."

She rolled her eyes dramatically up toward the ceiling, as if speed-reading through every single page that she had ever read in her life, all the way from "A was once an apple pie" straight through to Mr. Capote, who lay impatiently open on the table.

"Tribal," she said. "Ritual. Rhodesia. Rites of passage."

"Thank you, Daphne," I said.

I had heard enough.

All I needed now was to figure out what it meant.

·TWENTY-ONE·

DOGGER MET ME IN the foyer.

"Inspector Hewitt is here," he said. "He's come for the rat. I've shown him into the drawing room."

Under ordinary circumstances, I should have collapsed with laughter at such an incongruous scene. It was right out of a play by J. B. Priestley: *An Inspector Calls*, perhaps, in which the so-called Inspector Goole turns out to be an angel bent on vengeance, or, more than that, quite possibly God Himself.

"Thank you, Dogger," I replied. "Tell him I shall be with him in a moment."

I needed to freshen up. To slap a little color into my cheeks; to wipe the eggy traces from my lips.

I also needed time to think.

Dogger had told me yesterday that we would need to

hand over the rat at once, but it had slipped my mind. He must have reported it himself, and now here was Inspector Hewitt at the door—well, in the drawing room, actually—with me as unprepared as a head of raw lettuce.

Think, Flavia, think.

And by the time I strolled into the drawing room, my hand extended in greeting, the answer was at my fingertips.

"Inspector Hewitt," I said. "How lovely to see you."

"Flavia," he said, shaking hands.

"I ought to explain, straightaway," I said, "that the rat in question has already been anatomized, and I must take full responsibility for that. My cousin Undine found it in a paper sack in the boot of a hired car, and I was worried sick that it might be a carrier of typhus, or some other filthy disease. I wanted to assure myself that there were no notable abnormalities of the intestines."

"And were there?" the inspector asked, opening his notebook.

"None," I said. "And if you mean did I note any pleural infusion, bubo, or granularity of the liver, the answer is no. Nor were there any fleas in evidence, although I understand that fleas desert a dying rat much as they do a sinking ship."

Fortunately, I had read Gasquet's *The Great Pestilence* (A.D. 1348–9), a signed first edition of which was shelved, alongside Hankin's fascinating little book *On the Epidemiology of Plague* (a second edition, but also signed), in Uncle Tarquin's library in what was now my laboratory.

I could tell that the inspector was slightly taken aback.

He had come here, I guessed, to rap my knuckles, even though I hadn't broken any laws—at least, not knowingly.

"As for what we *did* find," I continued, "I shall let my colleague, Mr. Dogger, explain."

Inspector Hewitt smiled.

Why? I wondered. *Does he not take me seriously? Is he smirking at our partnership?*

"Thank you, Miss Flavia," Dogger said. "We have notified you, Inspector, because our findings indicate the cause of the creature's death was ingestion of physostigmine, a poisonous alkaloid found in the Calabar bean, *Physostigma venenosum*, of which we found an untouched sample in close proximity. That, and other findings—such as the presence of the same toxin in the partially digested contents of the animal's intestines, for which we performed the accepted chemical testing—suggested forcibly that you ought to be involved without delay."

Bravo! I wanted to shout.

But I didn't. Rather, I opened my own notebook and scribbled a couple of lines in a make-believe shorthand which I invented on the spot.

Two could play at this game.

"Ah," said Inspector Hewitt, with another possibly self-satisfied look on his face. "And what made you think that, Mr. Dogger?"

Dogger's reply was like the crack of a whip. "We thought that, Inspector Hewitt" (I was so happy to hear him use the word "we" that I almost hugged myself) "because of the way in which the rat's poisoning mirrored, almost precisely and most uncannily, that of the late Mrs. Prill."

There was the longest silence I have ever heard in my life. I sat, not daring to move a muscle.

After several eternities, Inspector Hewitt rubbed his nose and said: "I'm afraid I couldn't conceivably comment on that, Mr. Dogger."

But he wrote in his notebook, nonetheless.

"Nor would we expect you to, Inspector." Dogger smiled, as smooth as glass. Smoother, actually. Dogger made glass seem as prickly as a cat's tongue.

"However," said Inspector Hewitt, "now that Mrs. Prill's name has been brought up, would it be out of order to ask why you were at Balsam Cottage?"

"Not at all, Inspector," Dogger said, before I could open my mouth. "Mrs. Prill had invited us for tea."

I fought back a gasp. Had the inspector noticed?

And yet it was true enough: Mrs. Prill *had* invited us for tea.

"And was it a strictly social call, Mr. Dogger? Or otherwise?"

"The lady was dead when we arrived, Inspector," Dogger reminded him.

"Ah, yes," Inspector Hewitt said. "So she was."

I went suddenly numb. Cold sweat began to form at the nape of my neck. Was the inspector implying that Dogger and I were official suspects? That *we* had murdered Mrs. Prill before coldheartedly calling the police?

I did the only thing I could think of: I kept my mouth shut.

Silence is sometimes the only answer.

Standing up, Inspector Hewitt closed his notebook and turned as if to go, but stopped abruptly before he was halfway to the door—as if he had suddenly remembered something.

"I believe I have heard mentioned the name Arthur W. Dogger & Associates," he said. It was hard to gauge his tone.

He stood staring at us from the middle of the Axminster.

My heart sank. This was the moment I had been dreading: the confrontation with the official police. Were we to be hauled off to the dungeons and interrogated? Hung up in chains and scourged within an inch of our lives?

And then Dogger did something that I will never forget until my dying day—if I live that long.

He brought his heels smartly together with an almost audible *click* and, bending at the waist, gave the inspector a most courtly bow.

You could have cut the air with a carving knife.

"Yes, well then," the inspector said at last, "if you'd be good enough to let me have the rat . . ."

"What do you think that was all about?" I demanded when the inspector was gone.

"Apart from the rat," Dogger said, "I suggest he was searching for the missing link."

"Between Mrs. Prill's murder and the Missioners, you mean?"

"I believe so," Dogger said.

"Do you think he's questioned them?"

"Sure to have," Dogger said. "It's no secret they were guests at Balsam Cottage, or that they hired their car from Bert Archer. But only time will tell. The Lord moves the police in mysterious ways, His wonders to perform."

"What about Mme. Castelnuovo?" I asked.

"A case of which, I believe, the police remain quite unaware. For the moment, at least, we have her entirely to ourselves."

"Would you like a cup of tea?" I asked. "We've scarcely had time to talk."

"A most timely suggestion," Dogger said. "I shall ask Mrs. Mullet to fetch us a cup."

"And leave the pot!" I said, enthusiastically.

"And leave the pot," Dogger agreed.

A quarter of an hour later, settled in over tea and biscuits, I reached into my pocket and placed the railway ticket on the table.

"A ticket to the gallows," I said, reminding Dogger of his words.

"Quite possibly," he said.

"But for whom?"

"Ah!" Dogger smiled. "That is the question. And a very great question it is."

I could see that he was eager to lay out his theory in order to pull together his thoughts. The work of detection is very like the piecing of a patchwork quilt, where countless bits of fabric are laid out in limitless combinations of position and color until suddenly, the one true outcome—which has been there unrecognized from the beginning—leaps out at one with startling clarity.

Dogger was unconsciously squeezing the fingertips of his left hand with his right fist, which told me that he was engaged in intense thought.

I poured us each another cup of tea, securing the lid of the pot with my left forefinger, as Mrs. Mullet did, to keep it from spoiling the occasion by toppling onto the table, half sticking my little finger out at a broken angle in comic pretension.

If he noticed, Dogger didn't let on.

"The ticket," he said at last, "was unpunched."

I nodded, as if I had noticed, even though I hadn't.

"Which means?" I asked. "That it was unused?"

"Not necessarily," Dogger replied. "Not all travelers turn in their tickets at the end of their journey. The railway system is not so fussy as it once was."

I waited for him to continue.

"A passenger from Brookwood to Doddingsley or Hinley would necessarily require two tickets: one from their point of origin to Waterloo Station, and a second from Waterloo to their destination."

"Go on," I urged.

"If that traveler wanted an alibi, it would be necessary to produce only the first ticket as proof that they had been in London at the time in question."

"Unless someone else were able to prove otherwise," I observed.

"Exactly," Dogger said. "It might also occur to a criminal mind to punch or otherwise cancel the ticket oneself as circumstances required, or not, as the case may be.

"Furthermore, it would be necessary to destroy the second ticket showing that his or her journey had continued beyond London."

"His or her?" I asked.

"There is much yet to be discovered," Dogger said. "Because the ticket has not been punched, it remains unclear if the purchaser traveled at all. If not, it is of interest only as an indicator of intent. Perhaps they intended to make a journey but were unable. Still, unpunched does not necessarily mean unused.

"Railway tickets, as we know," he went on, "may be canceled in any one of several ways: by mechanical punch, by tearing in half, by marking in ink or crayon. It sometimes depends upon the class of ticket, and upon whether it is required for a return journey. In this case, we have a first-class monthly return which remains unsullied."

"But only as far as Waterloo," I said. "It's getting to sound like one of those railway mystery novels you see at W. H. Smith, isn't it?"

"We may assume one of three things," Dogger said, ignoring my question. "Either the ticket was retained by Dr. Brocken as proof of a supposed trip to London—"

"In spite of his being gaggers," I interrupted.

"Yes, which is only a further tangle in our tale." Dogger smiled.

I could see that he was enjoying this.

266 · ALAN BRADLEY

"Or he was intending to travel to London—and perhaps beyond—but did not, in fact, do so."

"The ticket is good for a month," I said. "It's still valid."

"Indeed," Dogger said. "There is also the slight possibility that it was purchased by some other party and planted in Dr. Brocken's wallet, although it seems improbable."

"Why?" I asked.

"You found it in a wallet concealed in the hem of a drape in the doctor's own room. Unlikely to be known to anyone but the doctor himself."

"Or one of his keepers," I suggested.

"Yes. That possibility *had* occurred to me. Did you happen to notice Mr. Courtwright's wristwatch?"

I *had* noticed it.

"Yes," I said proudly. "A rather elaborate affair with dials for sun, moon, and tides, for all I know, and a ring for setting the time in various parts of the world."

Until now, I had overlooked its significance.

"Such as Singapore," I added excitedly. "Or French West Africa."

Whole new avenues were opening in my mind.

"Well observed," Dogger said. "We mustn't read too much into it, but it *did* seem rather a fine watch for a man in Mr. Courtwright's position."

There was a light knock at the door and Mrs. Mullet peered in.

"I've come to clear away the tea things," she said. "I 'ope you're finished. Alf will be expectin' me 'ome. We 'as to get 'im spic an' span for the lantern slides tonight. 'E's volunteered to take tickets at the door, Alf 'as. 'E says I mustn't look at some o' them pitchers from Africa. They're not decent, 'e says.

"''Oo knows? I might *learn* something, mightn't I?"

And with a flourish of her apron, she was gone.

The evening, when it came, was warm for September. Outside, the churchyard was wreathed in low floating fog, with wisps of faint smoke from local bonfires drifting among the leaning tombstones.

Indoors, the air was stifling. In spite of Cynthia's fears, every single soul from Bishop's Lacey and beyond seemed to have crammed themselves into the parish hall for an evening of instructive entertainment. Perhaps because the crops were well in hand, many of those in attendance were farmers and their families, free of the fields and enjoying their first night out since springtime. Consequently, there was in the air a noticeable earthy scent with overtones of horse manure.

"Fresh, like," Mrs. Mullet whispered confidentially into my ear. She was sitting directly behind me and leaning forward to deliver this observation. "Their boots, most likely."

I rewarded her with a grin.

In the very center of the front row, separated from the commoners of the parish by an almost tangible odor of sanctity, sat Miss Truelove, hemmed in by several of her Altar Guild henchmen—or, in this case, henchwomen.

"This seat taken?" someone asked. I looked up, baffled for a moment.

"If so, I shall toddle off and perch elsewhere."

"Mr. Mould!" I exclaimed. "What are you doing here?"

It was Dieter's best man, Reggie Mould.

"Reggie, if you don't mind. Thought I'd stay over for the excitement. Took digs at the Thirteen Drakes. Been rattling around taking a squint at the countryside. Thought it would be a treat to see what it looks like from the ground, if you know what I mean."

His horribly burnt skin was grotesque in the lighting of the parish hall, as if he were some made-up creature for a village pantomime.

I tried not to stare.

"I'll bet you miss your sister," he said. "And Dieter, too. Wizard couple."

"Terribly," I replied, although to tell the truth, I had scarcely given them a minute's thought.

Reggie settled himself painfully into the wooden chair, then rubbed his hands together and looked round the hall in apparent pleasure.

"Looking forward to this all week," he said. "Christian Health. Meat and potatoes to a chap like me. Can't have one without the other. And lantern slides! Penny plain and tuppence colored. Scenes of darkest Africa. It will be a treat to see it again."

"You've been there before, Mr. Mould? Reggie, I mean?"

"Did my flight training there," Reggie answered. "RATG. 'Rat G' we used to call it: Rhodesian Air Training Group. Part of the EATS, the Empire Air Training Scheme. Far too many acronyms, don't you think? But that's the military for you: O-A-T-S. Oats. Means 'obfuscation and torrents of'—well, I mustn't say, must I? Are you enjoying yourself?"

"I'm looking forward to hearing Miss Pursemaker and Miss Stonebrook speak," I answered. "I've always had a great interest in Christian Missions and Christian Health."

"I'll *bet* you have." Reggie gave me a light elbow in the ribs. "I'll bet you *have*."

I turned round and craned my neck, surveying the packed house. Alf Mullet, standing behind a card table at the door, caught my eye and gave me an animated thumbs-up. "The Kitty," as he referred to it, was obviously overflowing.

As I discreetly returned Alf's signal, Inspector Hewitt appeared at the door, dug into his trouser pocket, and placed a banknote in the wicker basket. Behind him was his wife, Antigone.

I couldn't help myself. I leaped to my feet and edged my way between legs and rows of chairs until I was at the door.

"Antigone!" I said, wiping an eye that had suddenly become disgustingly damp.

We hugged each other. Twice.

Antigone stepped back, keeping her hands on my shoulders.

"Let me look at you," she said. "You've grown. I shouldn't have recognized you."

"And the baby?" I asked. "How old is the baby? She was born in January, wasn't she?"

"She's eight months," Antigone replied. "Soon to be nine, and already developing her own little personality. Yesterday, as he was feeding her, she growled at her father. Thank you, by the way, for the lovely hamper."

"What's her name?" I asked, barely hearing, my heart in my mouth. For a time I had been convinced that the Hewitts named her Flavia.

"We named her Phoebe, after my mother."

"Oh," I said. "That's a nice name."

"We thought so," Antigone said. "Phoebe, in Greek, means bright and shining. Actually, it much has the same overall meaning as your name: Flavia de Luce."

In spite of it being evening, in spite of our being indoors, the sun came suddenly and unexpectedly rushing out in all his glory. I had to shield my eyes from its radiance with the back of my hand.

I touched Antigone's arm and turned upon the inspector my most dazzling smile.

"I'd better get back to my seat," I managed to say. "I think the excitement is about to begin."

·TWENTY-TWO·

THE BUZZ AND CHATTER from the audience faded and turned quickly to applause as the vicar appeared on the stage, smiling broadly, followed closely by Miss Pursemaker and Miss Stonebrook.

He handed them gallantly into the waiting chairs and began ruffling through a sheaf of papers.

Behind them, in the shadows of the wings, George Carew, the village carpenter, was paying out a rope which lowered a large, square cinema screen—actually a patched and neatly mended bedsheet from the vicarage stretched upon a wooden frame—into position. When he got it where he wanted it, and had knotted the rope, George, too, was rewarded with a round of hearty applause and mild laughter.

The vicar searched an endless-seeming number of pockets before locating his spectacles—to much giggling from the younger members of the audience—after which he put them on upside down, before noticing and switching them round, with embarrassed glances to the sidelines.

It was an act, I realized: a way of making people relax; of making them feel welcome, of promising an evening of light entertainment, and all of it done without uttering a single word.

"Ladies and gentlemen," he began, "parishioners of St. Tancred's, all of you from Bishop's Lacey and environs, and those who have come from afar to be with us tonight, welcome, welcome, welcome.

"We are greatly privileged to have with us two dedicated ladies who have donned their seven-league boots, spanned oceans, and, in fact, girdled the globe to be with us tonight.

"Miss Pursemaker and Miss Stonebrook have come, as they say, from darkest Africa to share with us some of their most remarkable experiences in the field of Christian Health, and I, for one, can scarcely wait to hear their story. And so without further ado, I give you—courtesy of the diocese, I might add; I promised the bishop I wouldn't forget to mention that. He is, after all, not only great friends with these remarkable ladies, but he's also paying for their journey (*scattered laughter*)—Miss Doris Pursemaker and Miss Ardella Stonebrook: *Missioners extraordinaires!*"

As he stepped back applauding his guests, I could see that the vicar was proud of having worked in the word "extraordinaire," which he pronounced in the French manner with all the correct intonations of palate, nose, and sinuses.

At the mention of their names, Miss Pursemaker leaped to her feet, while Miss Stonebrook, halfway out of her chair, peered round as if to see if there were another Ardella Stonebrook in the hall and she herself was an imposter caught in the act.

They took up their positions behind the small lectern that had been placed at the left side of the stage.

Miss Pursemaker was the first to speak. "Thank you for your warm reception," she said. "It makes us feel almost as if we were back in Africa."

She paused for the expected laugh, and after a long moment, it came.

She held up a hand to stop the scattered chuckles. This was a woman accustomed to public speaking.

She waited for silence before she spoke. "We are all of us dying," she said at last in a tragic voice. "I am dying, Miss Stonebrook here is dying, and you are dying: each and every one of you."

She paused, waiting for her words to take effect, looking from face to face of the audience in turn. There had never been, in the history of the world, such total stillness.

Miss Pursemaker let it lengthen . . . and go on lengthening into what seemed likely to become an eternal hush: a trial of wills, until, at last, in total desperation, someone at the back of the hall coughed.

"Some of us are dying," she went on, "because our bodies lack nourishment. Others, because their souls are starved."

Again, she paused to let this sink in.

"But in one way or the other, we are all of us hungry—some more than others."

A couple more coughs went up.

"Which brings us to Africa," she said suddenly, snapping her fingers.

Instantly, as the room lights were switched off and an image appeared upon the lantern slide screen behind her, I knew that Mr. Mitchell, the village photographer, was at his command post in the balcony, drafted in as usual to operate the grotesque black lantern slide projector without mixing up the glass slides or presenting them upside down.

On the screen now was a hand-colored map of Africa, each country shown in varying shades of red, pink, and green. On the west coast, tucked in under the chin of the continent between Cameroun and the Belgian Congo, was French Equatorial Africa. An inky black arrow pointed to it on the map.

"The village of Lambaréné, in French Equatorial Africa, lies upstream about one hundred and fifty miles from the coast, and just seventy-five miles south of the equator. Here, in this tropical climate, when winter comes in July, the mercury can plunge to as low as seventy degrees."

Someone at the back of the hall gave off a whistle of astonishment. I suspected it might be Carl Pendracka, but in the near-darkness I couldn't really tell.

Miss Pursemaker plowed on. "With an annual rainfall of about eighty inches, which is about four times what you receive here in Bishop's Lacey—your good vicar has been kind enough to supply me with the latter figure— you can easily imagine that unspeakable diseases flourish in such a tropical climate."

She clicked a little wooden clicker—it was called a cricket, Mr. Mitchell once told me—and the map of Africa vanished to be replaced with a black-and-white photograph of the two ladies seated in what appeared to be a dugout canoe equipped with a miniature outboard motor.

"Here we are on the Ogooué River in our little craft loaded to the gunwales with medicines and Bibles. Perhaps you'd like to say a word, Miss Stonebrook?"

The slide changed to what appeared to be a clearing in the jungle. A woman wrapped—I wanted to say "swaddled"—in a white nurse's uniform was working a patch of rough-looking soil with a hoe.

"Thank you, Miss Pursemaker," Miss Stonebrook said. In the reflected light of the screen, her skin looked more mottled than ever: as if she were a black-and-white photo illustrating tropical diseases in a Victorian medical manual. Whatever she had, I hoped it wasn't contagious. All we needed now at Buckshaw was blackwater fever.

"Here I am cultivating my herbal garden," Miss Stonebrook continued. "The low shrubs you see are actually peanuts, or ground nuts, as they are known—*nkatie*, they are called in the Akra or Gã language—which constitute the main agricultural product of the country. The oil extracted from these nuts has many medicinal uses, not the least of which is the treatment of a number of tragic tropical skin diseases."

She said this without batting an eye.

How very, very curious, I thought.

I touched Dogger's wrist gently, bent over, and whispered as light as a feather into his ear. "Odd that she doesn't use it herself."

Scarcely moving his head, Dogger whispered back, "Pellagra."

Even in the semidarkness he saw me raise my eyebrows.

"The three Ds: diarrhea, dermatitis, and dementia. Possibly fatal if left untreated."

I turned my attention back to Miss Stonebrook, who was now saying: ". . . which shortage of funds forced us to develop rather a complex barter system with the outside world. Medicine for medicine, so to speak."

What did she mean by that? I wondered. Were they trading raw materials for commercially prepared pharmaceuticals? Swapping peanuts for the recently discovered antibiotics? Sap for serum?

A thought went through me like a lightning bolt, but there was no time to dwell upon it. I needed to pay close attention to the words of these Missioners.

But it was all beginning to add up.

". . . money in the boxes which Miss Truelove and her Altar Guild are now passing round," Miss Stonebrook continued. "Dig deep! Dig deep!" she urged, pointing to the oversize image of herself and her hoe and peanut crop on the screen. "Every penny goes straight into the pocket of God."

There was a stir among the audience, and I saw that small, colorful cardboard boxes were being passed along the rows from hand to hand, and the quiet of the lecture hall was broken now by the clink of coins, as well as the occasional rustle of a paper banknote.

Even at the best of times, simoleons and sanctity have always made strange bedfellows, and never more so than now. The Missioners had not even waited until the end of their pitch—and, yes, I have to admit that I had already begun to think of their presentation as a pitch—before passing round the plate.

I glanced at the vicar, who still sat center stage, but he was engaged in one of his usual distant mental wrestling matches, probably financial. This whole thing, after all, wasn't of his own doing. He had told us at the outset that the Missioners were traveling at the expense of the bishop and the diocese.

The only consolation I could think of at the moment was a brilliant remark Sir Arthur Shipley had once made during a chemical lecture, to the effect that: "Even the Archbishop of Canterbury comprises fifty percent water."

Miss Pursemaker clicked her cricket again and the scene on the screen showed a cluster of low, white buildings.

"Here you see Dr. Schweitzer's famous hospital at Lambaréné, and the doctor himself seated in a chair in the front row. If you look carefully, you can just see Miss

Stonebrook's white cap behind the tall gentleman at the extreme left. It is good to reflect, I think, and particularly you boys and girls in the audience, that you are looking at a remarkable scene, a very great rarity: *a gathering of martyrs.*"

I glanced quickly at Dogger, but he didn't give a flicker.

"Martyrs, you must remember, are not just those dry-as-dust names in crumbling books in the vicarage library, but real people. *Living* people. People just like you, who live, eat, breathe, and bleed solely for the sake of others.

"Now, then . . ."—*click*—"the next slide . . ."

And so it went till the bitter end. The money boxes, as Miss Stonebrook had mentioned, were collected by Miss Truelove and her cohorts from the Altar Guild, who shook them shamelessly, as if to show up, by their relative emptiness, how stingy were our contributions.

"Well, what did you think?" I asked, turning to Reggie Mould as the lights went up and people headed for the door.

"Wizard," he said. "Absolutely wizard. I haven't seen tactics like that since the Battle of Britain."

So it wasn't just me.

I wigwagged my arms at Undine, who had struck up a conversation with Cynthia Richardson near the door, telling her that it was time to go.

"Pellagra," I said to Dogger. "Is there a connection be-tween pellagra and asthmatic attacks?"

"There is, indeed," Dogger replied, "although one that is indirect and not yet fully understood. The disease is caused by a deficiency of niacin, or vitamin B$_3$, as they call it nowadays."

"Nicotinic acid," I said. I knew it well: good old C$_6$H$_5$NO$_2$.

"Correct." Dogger nodded. "Among the many symptoms of such a deficiency are a tendency to peevishness or anger, a tendency to emotional or psychological disturbances, and, in extreme cases, even physical violence."

On the stage, Miss Stonebrook was fussing busily with her notes, chatting with someone who had come up to ask her questions.

I remembered that I had prepared several questions myself, but there had been no opportunity to ask them, and it may well have been that it was now too late. She had already answered several of them without my prompting.

"What a great pity, isn't it?" I observed to Dogger as we made for the exit.

"What's a great pity?"

"That poor Miss Stonebrook might have led an entirely different life if only she'd spread some Marmite on her toast."

In the churchyard, the last stragglers were dispersing when a shadowy figure emerged from the porch.

"Pssst! Flavia, over here."

For a moment I didn't recognize him in the gloom.

"Colin!" I said. "Collie! Collie Collier!"

"I just wanted to thank you," he said, as he came shyly toward me in the churchyard dusk.

"Thank me? For what?"

"For setting me straight."

"Huh?" I said. There are times when I'm not as eloquent as others.

"Our little chat. It set me straight. I've decided I'm simply not cut out for the Church. I've decided to cashier myself as soon as we get back."

"Does Cynthia know?" I asked.

"Of course she does." He grinned. "Cynthia knows everything. In fact she helped me come to my decision. I told her I admired your independent nature, and she said that everyone does. I told her I wished I were more like you."

I could feel the tears welling up in my eyes. No one had ever said such a thing to me. I was unaccustomed to handling praise.

"But what will you do?" I asked him.

"I shall manufacture cricket bats," he said. "It's something I've dreamed of doing since I was a boy. I have a modest inheritance from my mother which will allow me to buy a superb small farm in the Essex marshes, where I shall nurture that most British of all trees, *salix alba*, the cricket bat willow."

His voice was fairly glowing.

"So much for the oak," I said, twitting him.

"So much for the oak." He grinned.

For several long moments, we stood there in the twilight of the churchyard, scuffling our feet and turning up our frail collars against the autumn's evening chill.

"Thank you, Flea," Collie said, touching my hand. And then he was gone.

·TWENTY·THREE·

I FOUND DOGGER, AS I hoped I would, at work in the greenhouse.

"Good morning," I said. "Tending to the tomatoes, are you?"

"September is the month of funguses," Dogger told me. "Or fungi. We must be ever vigilant."

He was removing the finished plants and the debris of a season's growing, tossing the unwanted bits into a bucket for burning in the garden.

"How's your list progressing?" he asked. "Satisfactorily, I hope?"

"My list?"

"Of those who attended Miss Ophelia's wedding."

Curses! I had completely forgotten about it. I had shoved the pages Miss Truelove gave me into my pocket and hidden them later at home under my mattress. Not very inventive, to be sure, but there had been so much to think about: Undine lost, the rat found, our chemical experiments—a never-ending parade of distractions.

"Sorry, Dogger," I said. I didn't want to be a whiner. "I'll go fetch it now."

"No need for apologies, Miss Flavia. I have forgotten more things than you will ever know."

And it was true. The things that Dogger had forgotten would send a soul screaming to the flames of hell for relief. It was insensitive of me to worry about some stupid list.

Minutes later, I was back with the sheets of paper. I spread them out on the potting bench and we leaned over them together.

"These are the seating plans for the reception," I said.

"Much as I remember them," Dogger said. "I suggest we can eliminate the vicar and his wife?"

I laughed, and it felt so wonderful that I laughed again.

"I can't imagine either of the Richardsons shoving a severed finger into a wedding cake," I said. "Not even as a joke."

"Nor the bride and groom," Dogger said. "I think we can safely remove their names as suspects. And we have already agreed, I believe, that the finger must have been shoved into the cake at the reception.

"Or . . ." he added reflectively.

"Or?" I asked. I remembered his saying that idea was but the most likely possibility.

"Or," Dogger continued, "that it was placed there while the rest of us were at the church."

"Of course!" I said. "It was unguarded while we were at St. Tancred's?"

"Correct," Dogger replied. "Although I had asked the ladies of the Altar Guild to keep a particular eye on the cake in our absence."

"But why?" I asked. "Were you expecting . . . ah . . . an incident?"

"You will recall that there was a theory afoot," Dogger went on, gauging his words carefully, "that an assault might be made upon the confection by certain—ah—young purloiners."

"Purloiners" sounded ominous in the plural.

"Me?" I asked. "I'm scandalized that anyone could think such a thing."

And then reason took hold.

"Oh! Of course. You were referring to Undine, weren't you?"

"It was no more than a theory, Miss Flavia."

Was he teasing? Somehow I doubted it.

But now, something was niggling at my mind, like a woodworm that has lost its taste for timber and developed instead a sweet tooth for brain matter.

What was it Mrs. Mullet had said? I placed a forefinger on my temple and tried to hear her voice in my mind.

You'll 'ave to jot down the ones as brought the chairs from the parish 'all, them as brought the flowers, the one as came to fix the telephone, the one as came six times with telegrams, the milk float man, the butcher, the baker—

And the candlestick maker, I had joked.

"Bless you, Mrs. Mullet!" I said aloud. Why hadn't I

listened to her? Wasn't it always the most unlikely suspect who turned out to be the guilty party?

"Hold on!" I told Dogger. "Was either Miss Pursemaker or Miss Stonebrook at the wedding or the reception? I hadn't met them at that time and wouldn't have recognized them. Well, Miss Stonebrook, perhaps, but certainly not Miss Pursemaker."

"They were not," Dogger said. "The same thought had occurred to me."

"Arthur W. Dogger leaves Associate in the dust." I laughed.

Although I felt somewhat uneasy at using Dogger's Christian name—or his "patronymic" as he had once referred to it—I thought that our partnership might allow a one-time breach of protocol.

"Arthur W. Dogger has been left in the dust himself on more than one occasion," he replied.

By referring to himself in the third person, Dogger had somehow managed to distance himself from my possible insult. Had I misjudged? Had the damage been done? Had I breached an invisible barrier which could never be mended?

"I'm sorry, Dogger," I blurted. "It was thoughtless of me. I shall never do it again."

"You would be unable, then, ever to refer to the joint enterprise upon which we have so recently embarked," he replied, dropping a few dead tomato stalks into the bucket.

I, being slow on the uptake, allowed my jaw to go slack.

"*Arthur W. Dogger & Associates*," he said. "*Discreet Investigations*. It does have a nice ring, doesn't it?"

O, how I wanted to hug him! O, how I wanted to pour out my affection!

But there are times, I was learning, when one must not, on any account, give in to impulse. It was, I suppose, what they mean by the whole idea of "being British": holding oneself in check for the greater good; substituting the encouraging word for the crushing embrace.

"Pip-pip," I said, giving Dogger a thumbs-up, and beginning to dislike myself with a newfound feeling that was frankly terrifying.

Like someone who has dropped a bag of marbles on the floor, I scrambled frantically to collect my thoughts.

The list, Flavia. Think about the list.

Actually, there had been two lists: the one Miss Truelove had given me, and the one that Cynthia Richardson might or might not have, but in any case had failed to give to me. Could she be holding out on me for some reason?

I needed to return to the vicarage—and quickly.

I found Cynthia seated on a tombstone in the churchyard.

"Enjoying the autumn weather?" I said in a jovial voice.

"Oh! Flavia! You almost scared me out of my skin."

"Sorry! I ought to have shouted ahead. Gladys is learning to glide as silently as an owl."

"I was just sitting here reflecting," Cynthia said. "It's so beastly quiet since the Christ Church lads have gone. It's never the same without them."

"You? Lonely? That's hard to believe. You'd make a bumblebee look lazy."

"So many things I ought to be doing," Cynthia said. "You asked for that list, for instance. I just haven't had a chance—"

"It's all right," I interrupted. "Miss Truelove has already given me much of what I wanted."

This was going to be a tricky conversation. I couldn't possibly tell Cynthia about the finger in the wedding cake. Aside from Feely and Dieter, I wasn't sure who knew about it. We had rushed Feely off on her honeymoon with scarcely a backward glance, and Dr. Darby would certainly have maintained a professional silence.

The last thing on earth I wanted was for Collie Collier to discover that his mother's body had been desecrated. Although mutilation of a corpse was a complex crime in itself, it was one that I hoped never to have to report.

With Cynthia, I needed to tread carefully.

"I understand you had a chat with Collie Collier," I said.

Cynthia bit her lip and nodded. "He's such a lovely lad," she said. "Denwyn was devastated. He'd pinned his hopes on Collie. Both of us had, actually."

"He'll be all right," I assured her. "He'll be in cricket bat heaven, whacking balls out over the Essex marshes."

"I hope so," Cynthia said. "Perhaps he's better off . . ."

"Than winding up curate in some godforsaken village," I said. "I'm sorry, Cynthia. I didn't mean—"

But it was too late. She was already in tears. I pulled

out a clean white handkerchief which, perhaps for the first time in recent memory, I had tucked into my pocket.

Cynthia blew, long and hard. "It's all so complicated," she said softly. "So infernally complicated."

"Anything I can help with?" I asked.

"No, dear. But I love that you'd think to offer."

"Is it about the Altar Guild?"

Cynthia was not adept at hiding her feelings. She looked for an instant as if she had been poleaxed between the eyes, and then, slowly, she shook her head.

And then she was crying again.

I sat down beside her on the weathered tombstone and put my arm around her shoulders.

"It's all so complicated," she said again. "All so infernally complicated."

"It's about money, isn't it?" I asked.

This was no great leap of deduction. All great problems, when whittled down to their root, were about money. No matter how tangled they seemed on the surface, the bottom was always banknotes.

This was actually something that Mrs. Mullet had told me when I borrowed a pound from Feely's piggy bank and lost it while vaulting on the Visto.

Cynthia grabbed my hand, interlinking her fingers with mine, and it all came spilling out. "It *is* about money," she admitted. "And it *is* about the Altar Guild. I don't know how you do it, Flavia."

"Someone's pilfering the funds," I said. That *had* to be it. "Someone's tinkering with the treasury."

I thought a touch of lightheartedness would cheer Cynthia up, as well as encourage her to tell me more. It is hard to be tight-lipped when laughing.

"No." She shook her head. "No one is pilfering the funds. Nothing is missing. It would be easier if it were."

I squeezed her fingers and waited patiently.

"In fact," she continued, "it's quite the contrary. Some-one is *adding* to the funds. And adding substantially."

"That doesn't make sense," I said.

"It *doesn't* make sense," she agreed. "That's the prob-lem. Denwyn hasn't slept for weeks. He's been poring over the accounts with the churchwardens until his eyes bleed. The auditors for the diocese are due next week. They're coming down from London, and Denwyn fears they'll think he's been—"

"Jiggering the books!" I said.

Cynthia let out a little moan.

"How serious is it?" I asked. "Probably not so bad as you think."

"Eleven months ago," Cynthia said, "we had a deficit of twenty-seven pounds, six shillings, and sixpence. As of two weeks ago, we have a surplus of twenty-seven thou-sand pounds, nine shillings, and sixpence."

"At least the sixpences cancel out." It was a joke as old as Dickens, and I could see by Cynthia's strained look that I ought to have kept it to myself.

"Maybe someone put the decimal point in the wrong place," I suggested.

"We thought of that," Cynthia told me. "But the funds

are in the bank. You can't conjure up money out of nothing."

"And what does Miss Truelove have to say? She is, after all, the President of the Altar Guild."

"Yes," Cynthia said. "She is also the Chairman of the Committee on Altar Work, the Chairman of the Committee on Flowers and Candles, the Chairman of the Committee on Altar Linen, and the Chairman of the Committee on Embroidery, as well as being Secretary Treasurer. She is also the Chairman of the Visitation Committee. The sick seem drawn to her like bees to honey."

"Good lord!" I said.

"Exactly," said Cynthia. "Do you see the fix we're in?"

"But what about Miss Tomlinson? Miss Crawford? Mrs. Charmbury?"

"Those three are merely her minions," Cynthia said with disgust. "Her acolytes. When Clary Truelove snaps her fingers, they jump through their appointed hoops. Clary's Acrobats, Denwyn calls them. I'm sorry. I oughtn't to have said that."

"But how could something like that have happened?" I asked.

"Even in the Church," Cynthia said bitterly, "we have our little treasons."

And although I had no idea what she meant, I knew better than to ask. Some things are beyond human understanding.

"Twenty-seven-some-odd-thousand pounds must have

come from somewhere," I remarked. "Perhaps it was an anonymous donation?"

"Not so far as we can tell. It seems to have inflated from what one would find in the collection plate to its present value somewhere on the way to the bank."

"Did Miss Truelove always make the deposits?"

"No." Cynthia sighed. "That's part of the problem. As Secretary Treasurer, she hands them over to Delia Carfax—you know poor Delia: Fred Carfax the glazier's widow. And always in the green baize bag the offering is put into after the wardens have counted it."

"Could Delia have slipped something extra into the bag? Anonymously? Perhaps an insurance policy paid out on her husband?"

"Out of the question," Cynthia said. "Delia was left virtually penniless. As I told you, it's so infernally complicated. We must take such great care to tread lightly."

"Perhaps someone should be appointed to keep an eye on Miss Truelove. Discreetly, I mean."

I must admit that I was thinking of Arthur W. Dogger & Associates—Discreet Investigations.

"We've thought of that," Cynthia said. "Denwyn and I have been quietly—oh, I'm ashamed to say this—keeping an eye on her."

"And?" I asked.

"Nothing we can put a finger on. Denwyn saw her talking to a stranger in the churchyard just after the wedding, and—"

"Feely's wedding?" I asked.

Cynthia nodded glumly. "A man in a trench coat and

a broad-brimmed hat. Right out of a Graham Greene novel, Denwyn said. No one he had ever seen before. He thought the chap's van had London number plates, although he couldn't be sure. Wouldn't have thought much of it, he said, if we hadn't already been on the alert about Clary. That and the fact that we see so few strangers in Bishop's Lacey."

"Very observant of him," I said.

"Yes. He tried to approach the two of them, perhaps manage an introduction—but the man saw him coming and made off at once. Very furtively, Denwyn thought. Clary claimed she'd never seen the chap before. Just stopped him to inquire the time, she said."

"Clary Truelove wanting to know the time?" I asked. "Clary Truelove who manages the Altar Guild like a military operation? *'Ladies, synchronize your watches!'* "

"Yes, Denwyn thought it odd also," Cynthia said. "He gave her a lift to the reception at Buckshaw, but she seemed reluctant. Unusually jumpy. Couldn't get a word out of her all the way there. She looked him up later to apologize. Told him she thought she was coming down with some nasty bug. Wasn't feeling up to par."

"*After* she'd had time to think of an excuse," I said.

It wasn't a charitable thought, but that's the way my mind works.

"Yes," Cynthia said. "That's what we thought, too."

I needed time to digest this information and to think it through. Cynthia had established, at least, that Clary Truelove had been at the reception at Buckshaw.

I could not tell Cynthia, of course, that the vicar had

likely witnessed the transfer of Mme. Castelnuovo's finger from some unknown undertaker in London into the
hands of Dr. Brocken's patent medicine machine. Miss
Truelove mustn't have been expecting its arrival, and had
jammed the finger into her pocket to hide it from the
vicar. Her unusual nervousness would suggest such a se-
quence of events. Then, at the reception, faced with
being grilled further by the vicar, she had, in desperation,
shoved the thing into Feely's wedding cake, planning to
retrieve it before the cake was cut.

Had Miss Truelove been a willing participant, or herself a victim of Dr. Brocken's filthy scheme? Perhaps we
would never know. Dogger and I hadn't the resources to
track down and bring to justice such a far-flung empire of
crime. Gathering in the loose ends would be up to the
police.

Whatever the case, our duty, clearly, was to bring justice to Mme. Castelnuovo.

Our greatest service would be our silence.

I let my thoughts return to Cynthia and the vicar.

"Going back to the surplus bank account," I said.
"Could it be that someone sent Feely and Dieter a purse
of money as a wedding gift, and that it somehow became
mixed up with the money from the collection plate?"

This, it seemed to me, was at least a possibility. The
ladies of the Altar Guild had managed much of Feely's
wedding, from the ceremony itself to the final wave-off
after the reception: from candles and consecration to
confetti.

"Sounds to me like a conjuror's trick," I said. "Green

baize bag has twenty-seven pounds counted into it by the churchwardens which, when opened at the bank, has increased miraculously to twenty-seven thousand. Presto! Change-o! And Alakazam!"

Cynthia turned her head slowly toward me, her eyes widening.

Even though each of us was thinking her own thoughts, our smiles of recognition came at precisely the same instant.

"Flavia de Luce," Cynthia said, "you are a genius."

She bent over, pecked me on the cheek, then flew like the wind, off among the tombstones, toward the vicarage.

·TWENTY-FOUR·

I NEEDED TO TALK to him at once, but Dogger was nowhere to be found. I had searched the house in vain from
top to bottom; from attics to cellars, from outbuildings to
beyond the hedges which line the Visto.

I had asked Daffy and Mrs. Mullet—even Undine—if
they knew where he was, but they were of no assistance.
Dogger had last been seen in the greenhouse where I had
left him.

The Rolls was in the coach house, indicating that he
had not gone on a household errand, nor was it likely that
he had gone up to London without letting someone know.

It was not like Dogger to disappear.

In desperation, I went to the telephone cupboard, that
tight, airless little cubicle tucked away behind the stairs
in the foyer.

Switching on the dim little light, I sat down and tried

to gather my thoughts, but try as I might, I could make no sense of his absence.

Whom should I call? The vicar? Dr. Darby? The police?

I didn't want to raise the alarm unnecessarily, but with someone like Dogger, who had, in the past, been subject to horrific medical episodes, one could never be too cautious.

I had to admit it to myself: I was rapidly becoming sick with worry.

What if he had taken one of his "turns" in the open air? What if he were lying unconscious—or worse, conscious but helpless—somewhere beneath a hedge? Or in a river?

The very thought of it twisted at my stomach.

Not knowing whom to call, I nevertheless needed to talk to someone; to make an effort, no matter how futile.

I picked up the telephone handset.

"Hello, Miss Runciman? This is Flavia de Luce speaking."

Filtered by the telephone wires, her voice came rasping like an automaton into the earpiece.

"To whom do you wish to speak?" she said.

One had to choose one's words carefully. The Runciman sisters, Flora and Nettie, who operated the telephone exchange at Bishop's Lacey, were not known for being able to keep their lips zipped. The slightest tidbit of overheard gossip might as well be printed in bold headlines on the front page of the *News of the World*.

"To *whom* do you wish to be connected?" Flora demanded impatiently.

At that very instant, a discreet but firm cough interrupted the silence of the cubicle, a cough too close at hand to be a coincidence.

"I'm sorry, Miss Runciman," I said. "I was just checking the line to see if we're still connected. We've been experiencing difficulties recently, and—"

"Obviously you're connected, else I wouldn't be speaking to you, would I?" she said, in not altogether good humor.

With an ominous *click* she was gone.

I replaced the handset and opened the cubicle door. Dogger was seated in the little cupboard across the narrow hall, newspaper in hand.

God bless the man! He had heard me call the exchange and wanted to let me know I was being overheard. Hence the warning cough.

"Oh, there you are, Dogger," I said. "Believe it or not, I was just thinking of you."

Butter wouldn't melt in my mouth—even though it would be no more than a drizzling mess in my overheated brain.

The under-stair cupboard was a storehouse of old magazines and newspapers, dating back, as far as I knew, to Adam and Eve, and perhaps even further.

"You might find this interesting, Miss Flavia," Dogger said, handing me the newspaper and pointing with his finger.

It was an issue of *The Hinley Chronicle*, dated two weeks ago.

Police Seek Confidence Tricksters

The Hinley Constabulary is investigating a recent swindle in which local residents have been promised so-called "miracle cures" in return for substantial sums of money. Preying mostly upon the ill and the elderly, a ring of confidence men, thought to be based in London, have convinced vulnerable pensioners to hand over their life savings in exchange for promises of improved health or remarkably enhanced physical or mental capabilities. "They promised me I'd be able to climb trees again," said Thomas Austin, "just as I did when I was a lad." Mr. Austin, 78, of Hinley-on-Croylands has been confined to a wheelchair for the past fifteen years. "It's cruel hard," he told our reporter, "to think that they got away with my life savings for tuppence-worth of tap water." Police are encouraging any person who may have information which might assist in the apprehension of these heartless swindlers to come forward.

"Tap water," I said. "That's what you're thinking, isn't it, Dogger?"

"Tap water is indeed what I was thinking, Miss Flavia. I was thinking also of Brocken's Balsamic Electuary."

"And so was I!" I said, hopping uncontrollably from foot to foot.

And I was thinking of the chemical manufactory in Miss Truelove's potting shed.

In my excitement, although I did my best, I could hardly explain my train of thought to Dogger.

"Do you suppose I could invent a logical excuse for the two of us to visit The Old Smithy?"

"I'm sure you'll think of something," Dogger answered.

Less than an hour later, we were knocking politely on Miss Truelove's front door, which opened almost immediately—as if she had been expecting us.

"Oh, Miss Truelove," I gushed. "I'm so happy to catch you at home."

Did she flinch slightly when I said "catch"?

Since I already have a reputation in Bishop's Lacey as something of a chatterbox, we had agreed in the car that I would do most of the talking. Dogger is not nearly so adept at untruth as I am—at least I *hope* he isn't.

I drew awkwardly from my pocket a horrid pair of round, black-rimmed eyeglasses issued by the National Health Services, which I wore only when needed for effect.

I stuck the ghastly things onto my nose and peered hard at Miss Truelove, who so far hadn't said a word. The lenses, I knew, would make my eyes seem like an enormous and unpalatable pair of fried eggs that had gone badly off-color.

"Well?" she said, her foot in the door.

"I'm so awfully sorry to trouble you," I told her (you can never overdo adverbs and adjectives when you're apologizing), "but I have a confession to make. May we come in?"

What human being can refuse to hear a confession? Go ahead—name one person—I dare you.

Miss Truelove looked closely from me to Dogger and from Dogger back to me.

It was not as if we were complete strangers. She had known both of us for years.

The door swung reluctantly open and she waved us into her front hall, but no farther.

"Well?" she said again.

"Well . . ." I began.

Although I had sketched an elaborate lie in my head, one must always play these things by ear, tuning and adjusting one's story to the reaction of the person being lied to: the *lyee*, I suppose they would be called.

"I'm ashamed to say," I went on (that's what is called the narrative hook, as Daffy had once explained to me). "I'm ashamed to say that when I was here a couple of days ago, I lost a piece of my mother's valuable jewelry."

Miss Truelove, of course, had been personally acquainted with Harriet almost from childhood. If it took hold, my hook would dig deep.

"I'm sorry to hear that, Flavia," she said. "I'm afraid you must have lost it somewhere else. If I'd come across it, I should have rung you at once."

I took a deep shuddering breath and launched into the body of my tale. It was all or nothing.

"It was very small," I improvised. "A diamond, but one of great historical value."

Miss Truelove was looking at me skeptically.

"I had taken to carrying it with me as a talisman," I persisted. "It was a diamond believed to bring good luck to all who possessed it. Even though—"

I broke off abruptly. Miss Truelove knew as well as anyone what Harriet's fate had been. There was no need to press the point.

"I remember pulling my handkerchief out of my pocket in your kitchen. I'm so ashamed, blubbering like that. You were so remarkably kind and understanding."

Careful, Flavia!

"I think it must have fallen out and rolled under your kitchen table. It's so small neither of us would have heard it. Oh, please, Miss Truelove. I've brought Dogger along to help search. His eyesight is ever so much keener than mine. I'm sure it's here."

I took another noisy breath and bit my lip hopefully.

"Very well," she said at last. "But you'll have to be quick about it. I have a meeting of the Altar Guild in a few minutes. I haven't missed one in more than forty years and I don't intend to begin now."

She waved us into the kitchen and I dropped at once to my knees, crawling to every corner of the slate floor like a demented scullery maid who's mislaid her mop.

"The flowers are lovely, Miss Truelove," Dogger said, admiring a vase of flowers in the windowsill. "They have kept very well."

Miss Truelove blushed. "Well, yes," she said. "I've done my best with them."

"The early narcissi are quite remarkable," Dogger went

on, as if she hadn't spoken. "The show pinks . . . the daffodils . . . and the snapdragons are seldom seen in these latitudes at this time of year."

I knew instantly what he was getting at. These were the very flowers Bunny Spirling had ordered from the Scilly Isles especially for Feely's wedding.

"It's such a shame to discard them after the nuptials," Miss Truelove said. "We can only use certain varieties on the altar, of course. As for the rest, they would only be left to die. As are we poor . . ."

She let her words trail away into nothingness. Almost as if she had lost the ability to speak; as if her soul had turned suddenly to stone.

As I got up from my hands and knees, I accidentally caught her eye, and it was the half-moon eye of a cow headed for the butcher's knife.

"If you'll excuse me now," she said, "I really must go. As I've said already, your diamond is not here, Flavia. You must look elsewhere."

She walked to the hallway expecting us to follow.

Dogger stood motionless in the middle of the kitchen. He inserted a forefinger beneath his collar and ran it round his neck in a cutthroat manner, then collapsed into a kitchen chair, his head hitting the table with an audible bang.

"Quick," I said. "A glass of water! Hurry! He's having one of his episodes."

"No!" Dogger was shouting. "No! *Get away!*"

His specters were back.

I flew to his side and stroked his hands, which writhed

on the table and then in his lap like a pair of warring snakes.

"Water," I said. "Quickly! For God's sake!"

Miss Truelove went to the sink and brought back a glass of water.

Dogger's sudden turns of terror were no secret in Bishop's Lacey. The war demons which haunted him had earned him great respect in the village, rather than ridicule, and he was not the subject of idle gossip.

"Drink this," I said, raising it gently to Dogger's lips, but it was already too late. His tongue was lashing at the corner of his mouth, his teeth grinding horribly.

"I'll ring Dr. Darby," Miss Truelove said, reaching for the telephone.

"No!" I said instinctively. I knew how to handle these episodes of Dogger's better than anyone. He needed quiet, he needed a comforting voice, he needed reassuring, he needed normality.

I guided his twisting head to the tabletop, letting him rest the side of his face upon his arms.

As long as his airway was clear, he would begin eventually to come out of it.

I sat down beside him and whispered in his ear. "It's all right, Dogger," I said. "You're quite safe. They're gone. I've chased them off."

My own heart was racing. *Well*, I remember thinking, *isn't that what hearts are for?*

Miss Truelove was taking down a bottle from the cupboard. Through the clear glass of its sides I could see the shape of coffee beans.

"No, thank you," I whispered, shaking my head. "He mustn't be given any stimulants."

But she wasn't listening to me. She was unscrewing the lid, digging her hand into the beans, and jamming them with the heel of her palm into her mouth.

It took a moment for me to realize what was happening.

"No!" I shouted as I leaped to my feet. I darted across the room and snatched the bottle from her hands. But it was too late: Her jaws were grinding the beans between her teeth and there was a look of triumph in her eyes.

She said nothing, but stood at the sink masticating and swallowing as if she were the victor in some great battle.

I knew now that what I had glimpsed in her eye was madness. She had both surrendered and won, all in one grand gesture.

I made a vain attempt to force her to spit out the beans: Seizing her round the waist from behind, I clasped my hands and pulled violently. She gagged as she fought me off, but it was like wrestling a wildcat. I am not physically a large person, and nor, when it came to that, was Miss Truelove. But her strength was the frenzied strength of a madwoman. I didn't dare risk sticking my fingers into her mouth.

All of this, save for the rustling of our clothes, took place in eerie silence. It was a struggle to the death in the silent cinema.

She collapsed onto the floor and lay there swallowing, pulling her twitching legs up to her chest.

Were the Calabar beans already having their effect? Was Miss Truelove's diminutive size exaggerating the power of their poison?

I'm sorry to report I stood there for a moment gaping, trying to get my rational mind to engage.

Suddenly, a hand gripped my elbow, and a voice spoke calmly into my ear:

"Atropine," it said. I whirled round.

"Dogger!"

"Atropine will do the trick. I wonder if there's any about?"

I'm afraid I gaped.

"There's deadly nightshade and stramonium in the potting shed," I said.

"If you would be good enough to fetch the berries," Dogger told me. "Use those gardener's gloves beside the sink.

"Sorry if I alarmed you," he added. "There seemed no other way."

Half blubbering with joy, and grabbing the key from a hook, I shot out the back door like the bolt from a crossbow, pulling on the gloves as I went.

In the potting shed I stripped all of the blood-red berries from the four deadly nightshade plants before racing back to the kitchen, bearing them like trophies in my open palms.

Dogger took the poisonous little orbs and without a word—and in a most professional manner—pried open Miss Truelove's mouth with one hand and shoved in the berries. It was obviously a skill that he had mastered in some dim past. He worked her sputtering jaws with his strong hands. I could almost feel the sour crunch of the berries between my own teeth.

"Watch you don't get bitten," I cautioned him.

"The trick of it is," he said, glancing up at me as if he were a beloved instructor and I the beloved pupil looking over his shoulder, "to get precisely, or as near as possible, three and a half times the amount of atropine as the physostigmine she ingested. Otherwise the antidote reverts to a poison.

"As you know," he added, smiling up at me.

I did know, indeed, as would any keen student of the poisoner's art. The balance between physostigmine and atropine is a razor's edge. One either got it right or—

Well, there was no "either." Death was death.

Physostigmine paralyzed the nervous system as if it were a nerve gas, paralyzing the respiratory muscles. As little as three grains for a woman of Miss Truelove's tiny stature would be fatal.

Dogger had wisely chosen the berries of the deadly nightshade, of course, because the alkaloid was already in a more available form than that contained in the datura plants, which would have required extraction by infusion or distillation.

There had been no time for that. It was the berries or nothing.

"If you'd be so good as to boil a kettle," Dogger said, "and look for a hot-water bottle. I, meanwhile, shall continue to rub her extremities."

Inspector Hewitt had once outraged me by ordering

me to put on the teakettle, but with Dogger, I didn't mind. Saving a life is not servile, no matter how it looks.

I found the rubber bottle in a drawer beneath the sink, and before you could say "acetylsalicylic acid," I had filled it with boiling water.

Dogger was now applying a form of artificial respiration, operating Miss Truelove's arms in wigwag fashion and pausing now and then to gauge her respiration.

With a convulsive heave, the woman pitched to one side and vomited a surprisingly copious amount of darkish liquid.

"Well done," Dogger remarked, and went on with his work.

"Best call Dr. Darby now," he told me. "Miss Truelove will require observation in hospital."

As I reached for the phone, Dogger added, "You might also want to give your friend the inspector a ring. We shall expect equal parts of gratitude and fury."

·TWENTY-FIVE·

DOGGER HAD JUDGED INSPECTOR Hewitt's reaction to a T (which stood for a tittle, as I remembered from one of Daffy's lectures on etymology, a tittle being the name of the tiny dot above the Greek letter iota, which was the smallest possible piece of printing. I almost wished she were here to enjoy the inspector's verbal pyrotechnics).

We were seated across from Inspector Hewitt at his desk in the Hinley Constabulary. He had closed the door, resumed his seat, swiveled his chair, and fiddled with his Biro, during which Dogger and I sat expectantly, saying nothing.

"Let me begin," the inspector began, "by extending to you the thanks and appreciation of the chief constable. Certain of the information you have provided us is of real value."

He paused, as if to change gear. "However, you must

realize that none of your assistance can or will be acknowledged publicly, and I must now ask you to give me your word, respectively, that you will maintain absolute secrecy."

"Our motto, Inspector," Dogger responded, "is contained in the name of our consulting firm: Arthur W. Dogger & Associates—Discreet Investigations."

He smiled maddeningly at Inspector Hewitt.

"A motto is scarcely enough, Mr. Dogger," the inspector retorted with an ironic smile. "I shall require more than that."

Dogger smiled back. "I cannot offer you more than my word, Inspector. Beyond that, I have nothing more to give.

"And I am confident that Miss de Luce would say the same," he added.

"Miss de Luce *would* say the same," I piped up, emboldened by Dogger's presence. I could hardly better his words.

For a moment I thought Inspector Hewitt was going to snap his Biro in two: Both of his thumbs were going white.

He suddenly noticed what he was doing, put down the Biro, and leaned forward over the desk.

"Look here," he said. "I'll tell you what. Let's take this discussion entirely off the record. Let's call it . . . a chat among friends. An attempt to understand one another better. Not a word to escape these four walls. Make of it what we will, each of us will draw our own conclusions. Strictly on the QT. No names, no pack drill, eh, Mr. Dogger?"

It was a cryptic reference to Dogger's military service: a phrase I had often heard Alf Mullet use. It meant "anonymity guaranteed," zipped lips, a denial that white was white and black was black, upon pain of death.

"I believe we can work out some mutually agreeable arrangement, Inspector." Dogger nodded and settled back into his chair. I did the same.

"Let us begin, then, at the beginning," Inspector Hewitt said.

"And go on till we come to the end: then stop," I blurted, quoting the King of Hearts in *Alice*. Inspector Hewitt shot me what began as a glare, but which he managed to twist at the last possible instant into a wry, scowling smile. I almost felt sorry for him.

"You have not yet satisfactorily explained how you happened to be at Balsam Cottage when you discovered Mrs. Prill's, um, *remains*."

"I believe we have, Inspector," Dogger said. "She invited us for tea."

"Why?" Inspector Hewitt demanded.

"We may never know," Dogger replied. "As I have stated already, the lady was dead when we arrived."

"Is it your belief that she wished to consult you— *professionally?*"

He pronounced this last word with the slightest bit of distaste: the slightest trace of lemon on his lips.

"That *is* my belief, Inspector," Dogger said, "but the lady was dead when we arrived. Beyond that I cannot speculate."

"I see," the inspector said, shuffling papers. "Then how

did it come to pass that you became involved with Dr. Brocken, the father of the deceased?"

Without a word, Dogger tossed the conversation into my lap. It was absolutely marvelous. We had perfected psychic communication.

"That's quite simple, Inspector," I said. "When Cynthia—the vicar's wife, I mean—asked if she could billet the two Missioners, Miss Pursemaker and Miss Stonebrook, at Buckshaw, we heard that they had spent the few days previous with Mrs. Prill at Balsam Cottage. So when Mrs. Prill turned up dead, with what looked to us suspiciously like alkaloid poisoning—"

"The connections seemed obvious," Dogger broke in. "The ladies in question have arrived recently from French West Africa where the Calabar bean is native."

Inspector Hewitt scribbled a few lines in his notebook. "The *Calabar* bean," he said with great interest, as if he had never heard the term before.

"*Physostigma venenosum*," Dogger explained patiently. "The ordeal bean, or *esere*, as the natives call it, contains the poison principle *eserine* or *physostigma*. It is interesting to note, incidentally, that the concentration of that alkaloid reaches its peak at this time of year, hence the speed with which it acted in the cases of both Mrs. Prill and Miss Truelove, suggesting, perhaps, that the beans were freshly arrived from their point of origin.

"But you already know that, Inspector," he concluded. "Your chemical analyst will already—or soon will—have handed you a complete report."

"Indeed," Inspector Hewitt said.

He sat back in his chair as if to gather his thoughts. He glanced at the calendar on the wall and made another note.

"And how does Dr. Brocken come into your story?"

"Dr. Brocken is famous, if not notorious—perhaps internationally—for his patent medicines, notably Brocken's Balsamic Electuary," Dogger answered. "He is what was once charmingly referred to as 'a quack': one who sells worthless nostrums to a gullible public. That he also happens to be the parent of the late Mrs. Prill, who met her death through administration of an herbal alkaloid, is nothing if not suggestive."

I wanted to applaud. I wanted to leap up out of my chair and wrap my arms around Dogger and hug him until the jam ran out. But I would have to wait until later.

"And it is *he*, you are suggesting, who is the ringleader of these so-called confidence men—these swindlers—"

"Those are the words of *The Hinley Chronicle*," Dogger corrected. "Not mine. I should not be half so charitable."

The room fell silent as each of us was lost, for a few moments, in our own thoughts.

"But what perfect cover!" I said. I couldn't help myself. Until now, I hadn't admitted my outrage, but now it came suddenly gushing out, unbidden.

"A madman, gaga in a private hospital, sitting at the center of his web, pulling strings that reach to the far corners of the Empire," I said.

"Yes. Sounds like something out of Sherlock Holmes, doesn't it?" Inspector Hewitt said, and with those words, I realized suddenly that he was on our side. In spite of the niceties of the dance, the carefully prescribed steps in which each of us must be careful not to tread upon the other's toes, we were, when all was said and done, conspirators for justice.

I couldn't hold back a smile. I shot him one of my beamers which had in it a trace of gratitude.

It was at that point that Dogger took up our account. "When we began to realize," he said, "that these charlatans were extracting an essence from human body parts—"

Had my eyes deceived me? Had Inspector Hewitt recoiled physically? Had he not known about the bones and powder?

"—in order to impart the supposed gifts of genius, or superhuman ability," Dogger continued, choosing his words carefully, "we knew that these shocking conclusions could never be made public; that they could be shared only with you, Inspector Hewitt; that they must never be made known outside this necessarily confidential conversation which, I must assume, is still entirely off the record."

Inspector Hewitt pushed back his chair and got up from his desk. He walked to the window and stood staring out into the stony street.

Dogger shot me a glance, but it was only fleeting.

"It looks like rain," Inspector Hewitt said at last, turning reluctantly away from the panes of grimy glass.

What did he mean? I wondered. Was the coming rain a good thing or a bad? I suppose it depended upon who was being rained upon. From somewhere in the lumber

room of my mind came trotting out the words "He ma-
keth his sun to rise on the evil and on the good, and sen-
deth rain on the just and on the unjust," or something
like that. It was in the Bible, wasn't it?

It *was* certainly going to rain on old Dr. Brocken, as
well as all of those who had aided him in his nefarious
schemes.

"What about Miss Pursemaker and Miss Stonebrook?"
I asked. "What will become of them?"

Inspector Hewitt sat down at his desk and pulled out a
pipe from one of the bottom drawers.

"With your permission?" he asked.

I waved my hand, and he began to stuff the bowl with
a rich tobacco. I could smell the stuff even from where I
sat.

"The ladies in question," he said, lighting a match and
letting it hover in midair, "have been taken into custody."

And he left it at that, turning his attention to setting
fire to the tobacco in his pipe, sending up curling gray
clouds that reminded me of the smoke signals in a cinema
western.

If only I could read them!

"Look here," the inspector said. "I'm still not completely clear on the operation of this confidence scheme.
Why, for instance, would Brocken and his crew go to all
the trouble of distilling the stolen bones and remains to
the umpty-umpth degree? If I understand the lab boffins
correctly, the distillations reduced any such matter to
fractions of millionths? Why not sell plain water?"

Dogger smiled. "It is my experience, Inspector, that

there is an honor among thieves that cannot be understood by the likes of you and me. Call it justification. Rationalization. Call it a ticket to heaven. Even the most foul of us likes to believe we have a saving grace."

"I suppose we do, Mr. Dogger," Inspector Hewitt agreed. "I suppose we do, at that."

"It is the hallmark of the beast in us," Dogger continued, "which requires a modicum of truth in our transgressions, no matter how finely distilled; no matter how thinly diluted."

"You, sir, ought really to have been a police officer." Inspector Hewitt smiled.

"I think not." Dogger smiled. "If I were, I should know who killed Mrs. Prill and how, precisely, it was done: whether Brocken himself came by train to Hinley and Balsam Cottage, or whether he sent one of his confederates. I should know, also, the role of our ladies from Africa, and in particular, their part in obtaining and transporting toxic substances from the tropics, and human remains from parish to parish here in England, wherever their speaking tours have taken them, including Bishop's Lacey."

As I have noted before, Dogger was becoming positively garrulous in the presence of strangers. The establishment of our humble little consulting firm was causing him to blossom in the most surprising and unexpected ways.

"You believe, then," said Inspector Hewitt, "that one or both of these ladies from Gabon administered the fatal beans to Mrs. Prill. Or that they provided said beans to the gullible Miss Truelove, for her to do the actual deed."

"We have not made that particular connection," Dogger answered. "Although such may well be the case. As for what I *believe*, that makes little difference, Inspector. If I *knew*, I ought, as you say, to be a police officer."

It was a bold reply.

"A falling-out among thieves, is that what you are saying?" Inspector Hewitt asked.

"Something like that, Inspector," Dogger said, lowering his eyelids.

It was the prearranged signal.

"Oh!" I said, reaching into my pocket. "I almost forgot. We found these letters and this railway ticket in Dr. Brocken's room at Gollingford Abbey. We knew that they would probably be crucial to your case, and that they ought to be put into your hands immediately, before someone else could destroy them."

I shoved the evidence across the desk. "Sorry about the fingerprints and so forth."

O, how I wish I could have conducted a chemical analysis on the look Inspector Hewitt gave me! It was composed of equal parts skepticism, outrage, acceptance, gratitude, resentment, relief, and surrender. I had never seen anything quite like it.

"You will note, of course," Dogger added, "that these letters implying blackmail, sent to his daughter, were most likely written in his own hand."

"Trying to convince her that the jig was up," Inspector Hewitt said.

He was a quick study.

"As you say." Dogger smiled. "And quite possibly retrieved from the scene of the crime by his own hand. Or perhaps previously written but not yet sent. I'm sure you will have no trouble in tying up the loose ends."

Inspector Hewitt put his pipe in the ashtray and stood up, grating the legs of his chair on the floor.

"I mustn't take up any more of your time," he said, shaking hands with each of us. "I'm sure you have many, more pressing, cases awaiting you."

Dogger pulled himself up to his full height, which was rather substantial when he wished it to be.

"Ah, Inspector Hewitt," he said, "you ought to know better than to ask us that."

"I didn't think you were going to get away with it," I said. "I thought the inspector would go up like a Roman candle."

We were purring our way home to Buckshaw in the Rolls, and the day was drawing in. A light mist lay across the fields and smoke hung in the lanes.

"My remark was not meant to be impertinent," Dogger said, "but rather the recognition of respect among equals."

"Meaning you didn't want us to come away with our tails between our legs." I laughed, delighted at the thought.

"Just so," Dogger agreed. "It is best always to have an understanding with authority, even if it *is* written in invisible ink."

I clapped my hands together.

"Still," I said, "he was *livid*."

"No," Dogger said. "He was not livid. He was merely playing the game."

Playing the game made me think of Collie Collier, swishing his willow cricket bats on a pitch somewhere in the Essex marshes.

"I'm glad we were able to keep that horrible business of Mme. Castelnuovo's finger to ourselves," I said. "It would have been unbearable for her son if *that* had come out."

"Yes," said Dogger, "*that* is our true reward. And those, if I am not mistaken, are the lights of Buckshaw across the fields."

· T W E N T Y ‑ S I X ·

TWO SMALL FIGURES ARE moving in a vast, darkening landscape. One of them is Dogger, and the other one is me.

I wonder, as we walk, if we are being observed; and if we are, what the observer thinks we are doing and what we are talking about.

But here in the vastness of the great cemetery, it seems unlikely that we would be overseen or overheard by anyone except the dead, all five hundred acres of them.

We are in no hurry, as suits the occasion. We stroll slowly along the rows of graves as is proper to a pair of discreet investigators who had just brought to a mostly successful close their first official case.

"There are still several points that trouble me," I tell Dogger. "I wonder if we ought to set aside time for a discussion at the end of each inquiry? A verbal postmortem?"

"An excellent idea, Miss Flavia," Dogger said. "What, in particular, is on your mind?"

"Well, Miss Truelove, for one," I replied. "How can someone who has given her life to the Altar Guild have been, all those years, extracting useless solutions from plants and the bones of the dead, and money from the wealthy?"

"The best answers," Dogger said, "are often found in contraries. Great good presupposes great evil. In fact, one cannot be present, relatively speaking, without the other. It is uncommon to find both polarities embodied in one person, but it is not entirely unknown."

"Cynthia Richardson told me that the sick were drawn to Clary Truelove like bees to honey."

"Yes, they would be," Dogger agreed. "Particularly those with bank accounts."

"I wonder why we never heard of it? Bishop's Lacey is such a small place."

"The victims of confidence schemes most often remain silent," Dogger said. "They live in fear of their gullibility becoming the subject of gossip. Shame can be greater than the need for justice.

"Or even vengeance," he added.

"Do you suppose the grip the gang had over her was a religious one? That they were taking advantage of her natural inclinations to charity?"

"Much more serious than that, I'm afraid," Dogger

said. "By what Cynthia Richardson told you, she was using the church's own bank accounts to store the proceeds of crime."

"Of course she was! That's what Cynthia meant about my being a genius for suggesting sleight of hand. But how could Miss Truelove get away with it for so long?"

"The ways of the Church and the merchant bankers are deep and murky waters, indeed," Dogger said, "particularly when they overlap. I don't suppose we shall ever really know. I don't envy Inspector Hewitt having to sort it all out."

"But she must have been receiving *something* for the little manufacturing plant in her potting shed, as well as her financial jiggery-pokery," I said.

"I expect she was," Dogger said.

"But why? Why risk everything?"

"Self-esteem," Dogger said. "Temptation . . . power . . . excitement . . . danger. The list goes on and on. But one expects that, at bottom, the proper answer is pride."

His words rang true. How many of the old proverbs are about pride and its effects? The Bible is bursting with them.

"Yes," I said. "That was what struck me also about Miss Pursemaker and Miss Stonebrook: their utter lack of humility."

Dogger nodded. "Humility is a most excellent barometer," he said, "and ought to be looked for in all those we are made to look up to."

"That wooden contraption of hers—Miss Stonebrook's, I mean—is still a puzzle. Do you suppose she was using it to smuggle contraband past His Majesty's Customs inspectors?"

"She may well have been, but there is more to it than that."

I could see that he was not going to tell me. We walked in silence for a hundred yards.

"All right," I said at last. "I promise to stop whistling the theme from *High Noon* in the car."

Dogger laughed aloud, and his laugh was as the sound of tinkling bells.

And then he became suddenly serious. "Miss Stonebrook's wicker frame is a sacred tribal costume which was used in religious ceremonies in Northern Rhodesia. To have taken it from its makers is in itself sacrilege. There is a similar item in the British Museum, whose acquisition several years ago has generated considerable controversy."

"Which ought to have told us all we needed to know about Miss Stonebrook," I said. "Do you suppose she was the one who administered the fatal beans to Dr. Brocken's daughter?"

"It is my experience," Dogger replied, "that one who would despoil an altar is capable of anything."

"Even murder?" I asked.

"*Especially* murder," Dogger said.

We were now approaching the chapel, and the darkness was deepening. We had timed our visit for an hour when we were least likely to be observed.

"Plot 124 should be over there," I said, pointing. "I think I recognize the twisted tree."

"So it is," Dogger said.

Moments later, we were standing at the grave of Mme. Castelnuovo. A night wind had sprung up, and dry leaves scraped like scuttling crabs across the marble slabs.

We stood in silence for a few minutes, as if suddenly somehow reluctant to do the task that we had come to do.

At last Dogger took from his pocket the garden trowel we had brought from the greenhouse, and getting down onto one knee, he made a clean incision in the grass, then opened and deepened it to the dark soil beneath.

Time seemed suspended, and I knew that I would never forget this moment until the end of my days.

"If you are ready," Dogger said, and I stepped forward and knelt.

From my pocket, I took the small cylindrical object which I had wrapped tenderly in one of Feely's silken Liberty scarves, one that I had purloined from her dresser: a flame-colored reminder of the fiery plains and the mountains and the cobalt skies of the Spanish plateau; the colors of earth, and air, and fire.

"Ready," I said.

And as Dogger spoke the words we had agreed upon, I pressed Mme. Castelnuovo's shrouded finger into its final resting place.

"Amen," we said together.

As we stepped forth side by side into the darkness, toward the waiting car, I thought of what a strange world it was, where life was lived pressed so tightly cheek to cheek with death: with so little space between, that they might well be one and the same thing.

But in the end, when you stop to think about it, we are, after all, no more than mere particles of dust, drifting along together through eternity, and so it is pleasant to think that we have—in this way or that, for better or for worse—reached out and touched one another.

That, in the end, is what chemistry is all about, isn't it?

ACKNOWLEDGMENTS

ONE OF THE GREATEST pleasures of completing a book is reaching the point where you can at last say thank you.

So thank you, to all those kindred hearts who have seen in Flavia something of themselves, and who have taken the time to write and share their experiences. A writer is nothing without readers, and I have been particularly blessed.

Special thanks to Denise Bukowski and Stacy Small of the Bukowski Agency, who have looked after things while I've been away, these many hours, days, and weeks, at Buckshaw. Thanks also to my editors and publishers Kate Miciak at Delacorte Press in New York, Kristin Cochrane at Doubleday Canada in Toronto, and Francesca Pathak at Orion Books in London.

I am reminded of the famous *New Yorker* cartoon by Rowland B. Wilson, in which a slave, dressed in rags and bound in chains, is about to board a galley. "What a magnificent ship!" he is saying to his jailer. "What makes it go?"

Every book makes its way out into the world powered by hundreds of souls who slave quietly away unseen, like those who row the stately triremes, and I would be guilty of theft and neglect if I didn't single out Loren Noveck, Sharon Propson, Susan Corcoran, Maggie Oberrender, Sharon Klein, Zoe Maslow, Martha Leonard, and Quinne Rogers, who have labored so powerfully at the thankless oars.

At Random House Audio, I thank Jayne Entwistle, Cathi Thorburn, and Orli Moscowitz, who, with their special talents, have opened up whole new worlds for Flavia and her listeners.

My thanks, also, to the many editors and translators who have worked so diligently to bring Flavia to a worldwide audience (thirty-nine territories and approximately three dozen languages at last count!). My bookshelves runneth over. Literally.

Words cannot express my gratitude to my dear and lamented late friend, Dr. John Harland, who, over the years, offered so much of his time, his knowledge, and his friendship. Without him, the Flavia books would have been . . . well, I hate even to think about it. Fair winds and safe seas, John. And thank you.

And finally, to my wife, Shirley, whom Saint Paul, having foreseen the lot of an author's wife, described so perfectly in the glorious words of the 1599 Geneva Bible:

Love suffereth long: it is bountiful: love envieth not: love doth not boast itself: it is not puffed up:

It doth no uncomely thing: it seeketh not her own thing: it is not provoked to anger: it thinketh no evil:

It rejoiceth not in iniquity, but rejoiceth in the truth:

It suffereth all things: it believeth all things: it hopeth all things: it endureth all things.

Love doth never fall away, though that prophesyings be abolished, or the tongues cease, or knowledge vanish away.

Isle of Man, 28th April, 2018

PHOTO: © JEFF BASSETT

ALAN BRADLEY is the internationally best-selling author of many stories, children's stories, newspaper columns, and the memoir *The Shoebox Bible*. His first Flavia de Luce novel, *The Sweetness at the Bottom of the Pie*, received the Crime Writers' Association Debut Dagger Award, the Dilys Award, the Arthur Ellis Award, the Agatha Award, the Macavity Award, and the Barry Award, and was nominated for the Anthony Award.

Alanbradleyauthor.com
Facebook.com/alanbradleyauthor

ABOUT THE TYPE

THIS BOOK was set in Goudy Old Style, a typeface designed by Frederic William Goudy (1865–1947). Goudy began his career as a bookkeeper, but devoted the rest of his life to the pursuit of "recognized quality" in a printing type.

Goudy Old Style was produced in 1914 and was an instant bestseller for the foundry. It has generous curves and smooth, even color. It is regarded as one of Goudy's finest achievements.